With an ear-blasting ⬛⬛⬛⬛⬛⬛ light, the door to the ⬛⬛⬛⬛⬛

Taziz cried out in shock, but did not loosen his choke hold on his human shield. The barrel of his pistol remained jammed against Private Rivera's temple. A pair of figures slipped into the room, sweeping the room until they focused on Taziz and the American POW.

Taziz screamed, "Stop where you are, Americans! Or Private Rivera dies!"

Rivera growled, "Private Rivera says go to hell, Captain Scumball. It ain't my day to die." He bent his knees slightly, and summoned enough strength to deliver a sharp elbow jab that caught Taziz hard in the solar plexus. Taziz stumbled back as Rivera rolled away.

Taziz whipped his pistol in Rivera's direction, thinking in his panic that he could issue an ultimatum. He opened his mouth to scream something, and the members of TALON Force opened fire on full auto, lighting the room with explosive fire.

Just before passing out, Rivera thought: *Wow. Never seen a man explode like that before. . . .*

TALON FORCE

BLOODTIDE

Cliff Garnett

A SIGNET BOOK

SIGNET
Published by New American Library, a division of
Penguin Putnam Inc., 375 Hudson Street,
New York, New York 10014, U.S.A.
Penguin Books Ltd, 27 Wrights Lane,
London W8 5TZ, England
Penguin Books Australia Ltd, Ringwood,
Victoria, Australia
Penguin Books Canada Ltd, 10 Alcorn Avenue,
Toronto, Ontario, Canada M4V 3B2
Penguin Books (N.Z.) Ltd, 182–190 Wairau Road,
Auckland 10, New Zealand

Penguin Books Ltd, Registered Offices:
Harmondsworth, Middlesex, England

First published by Signet, an imprint of New American Library,
a division of Penguin Putnam Inc.

First Printing, December 2000
10 9 8 7 6 5 4 3 2 1

Special acknowledgment to Stephen Mertz

People sleep peacefully in their beds at night
only because rough men stand ready
to do violence on their behalf.

—George Orwell

Prologue

The constant, high-pitched whistling of the F-16s in flight enveloped Captain Larry Davis. The steady drone did not soothe his senses, but rather honed them to a razor's edge.

He and Jack Jackson, the weapons system officer seated directly behind him, and the pair of F-16s holding formation with them, were angling north over the rugged mountainous terrain of the frontier separating the southern Yugoslavian states of Kosovo and Macedonia, seventy-five miles southwest of Belgrade. Each F-16 was loaded for bear: AGM-65 Maverick missiles, AIM-9 Sidewinders, and a fully loaded M61 20mm six-barrel chain gun.

The sun was a dull copper ball hugging the heavily forested, uninhabited, foreboding wilderness streaking by far below. It was one of the most feral, inhospitable corners of Europe and reminded Davis of the daunting ruggedness of the Canadian Rockies. This would be a hell of a place to die, thought Davis as the formation of F-16s came within sight of nine-thousand-foot, snowcapped Mount Korab, a landmark in the flight path to the target area.

Davis was thirty-three years old, originally from Columbus, Ohio, married, and the father of three. He loved flying, but he loved his family more. He told himself to keep his mind on the mission. That was his best insurance against buying it over this remote part of the world.

There were other factors in favor of his survival, of course. Jack Jackson was not only his best friend, but the dozens of sorties they'd flown together had proven without a doubt to Davis that Jack was the best damn WSO he'd ever had. A fighter pilot's life depends on the man riding behind him. The WSO's responsibilities included keeping an eye on the radar screen, deploying countermeasures when taking fire, and more often than not activating the weapons system while the pilot tries to maneuver through unfriendly skies. Yeah, Jack, the big black dude from St. Louis, was the best.

Their mission was flying cover for a flight of F/A-18 NATO bombers. Their primary target was the heavily entrenched stronghold of a renegade Serbian militia force that was making an unbearable reality even worse for the tattered masses of Albanian Kosovar refugees. The fleeing throng had thought they'd reached safety in Macedonia . . . until heavily armed Serbian thugs came gunning for them. The fragile peace established in this region was in serious jeopardy, with the very real possibility of a rapid escalation of mass violence and destruction directed from the Serbian staging area.

This "secret" stronghold, situated in the border frontier between Kosovo and Macedonia, had so far proved impenetrable and was well fortified with short-range tactical surface-to-air missiles and antiaircraft artillery. During the preceding day and night, wave after wave of NATO jets had been forced to break off, barely able to drop a single bomb. Two U.S. planes had been shot down. Intel was that the Serbian force was covertly preparing yet a new offensive against the refugee communities within Macedonia that were supposedly guaranteed safety by NATO forces.

Davis had heard vague rumors that there was some

ominous new wrinkle to this latest chapter in the age-old inhumanity of "ethnic cleansing." He'd heard speculation in the Officers' Club that the Serbs were about to use new extreme measures against the Kosovar Albanians. They were rumors, though. There had been nothing concerning this during that morning's briefing.

The dozen or so planes constituting today's force package were approaching from different bases at different speeds over the Balkans and would be arriving at the target area, what NATO pilots called "working the kill box," in a precisely timed pattern. A nearby AWACS command plane was acting as traffic cop. Navy and Air Force EF-111s packed with powerful jamming transmitters had already cleared the way, throwing a high-tech shroud over enemy radar and antiaircraft missile systems by transmitting patterns of white noise. It caused radar screens to go blank, forcing the SAM crews to turn on their own battery radar. Then the F4-G Wild Weasels had sailed in with their high-speed antiradiation missiles (HARMs) that locked onto the SAM batteries, disabling the radar antennas with specially designed shrapnel. Next came the fighter planes, the F-16s, to clear a safe corridor that would allow the bombers to use their smart bombs.

Davis glanced at the video image of the upcoming terrain projected onto his Heads-Up Display, mounted over the instrument panel directly in front of his line of sight. The HUD screen presented the pilot with all necessary flight and weapons information, while identical information was simultaneously presented on one of the WSO's CRT displays.

When they were two miles from the target area, Major Humphrey's voice crackled across the radio. "This is Falcon Leader. Falcon One and Two, flare out. I'm going to give these yahoos their wakeup call."

"Roger. Copy," Davis said, and was echoed by the pilot of the third fighter plane.

With the throbbing hum of the F-16 surrounding him, the terrain passing below like a mottled green-and-black blur, Davis acquired visual sighting of the stronghold; a walled, fortified square set down in the flats of the delta adjacent to the Lim River, which wended its way lazily through a mile-wide valley. He banked away in one direction while Falcon 1 flared off in the other, establishing a defense perimeter while Humphrey went in for the first strafing run.

Not that there was much chance of encountering enemy aircraft. Since almost the beginning, the Yugoslav Air Force had remained largely hidden in camouflaged, bomb-proof shelters. But even if the Serbs did manage to scramble a handful of fighter planes, the jammers would have already cut them off from their ground-based command and control centers, which is why they were staying hidden, and flying blind.

Antiaircraft artillery flashed like strobe lights as Falcon Leader made his run, dropping a one thousand–pound bomb that mushroomed into a red fireball, blistering the sky brighter than the rising sun. Humphrey's plane banked away like a silver bullet.

"Take it, Falcon Two." The major's stern voice crackled across the radio. "Good luck, boys. It's hot down there."

"Copy that, Major. Going in."

Davis swooped around for the approach and started a steep descent, diving sharply at one thousand knots. He hit the afterburners and hurtled straight toward the target. A sudden tone from the radar system indicated that a missile had been launched at them. Davis maintained his course and speed, and cursed under his breath. The HUD indicated the missile type as infrared-guided. It was less than a quarter mile away.

"Got it?" he snapped.

"Got it," Jackson replied.

Davis executed a sharp evasive maneuver. He could

feel his facial muscles fluttering under gravitational pull.

At the same instant, Jackson activated a flare, its blossoming burst of heat designed to draw the heat-seeking surface-to-air missile off target. The concussion of the flare detonating came at the same time that the missile disappeared off the HUD screen. The flare had done its job.

Davis looped around for another approach. Flak was hammering the sky all around the F-16.

The briefing had been damn thorough. The missile launcher site they were after on this run was located at the southeast corner of the base. This was always the trickiest part of a strafing run. Once a plane was directly over the site, it was relatively safe since the SAM launchers couldn't shoot straight up. The principle threat was the heavy antiaircraft fire they were being exposed to. In the next few heartbeats it could go by the numbers . . . or turn to shit. Wrapped in the keening sensation of high-speed aerial combat, Davis retained a complete professional cool.

"Fire when you've got a lock on them, Jack. This is one hell of a high-threat area," he told his WSO.

"Target acquisition," Jackson replied. "Lock on."

The WSO targeted the item on the CRT image by placing the cursor on it, and the info instantly processed and downloaded into the weapons system. With a *whoosh,* one of the Mavericks punched out, sizzling like a fiery finger, trailing smoke toward the source of the artillery flashes a half mile away. The missile was a fire-and-forget variety and as soon as it was launched, Davis maneuvered the F-16 into another break turn and resumed his holding pattern on the perimeter for Falcon 3 to make its run.

That's when it happened. They were climbing, flak exploding in angry flashes all around, when the plane was jolted mightily. Immediately the power of the climb slackened. The HUD started beeping and blinking: *Caution . . . Turbine failure . . . caution . . . turbine failure . . .*

Jackson cursed.

"Leader, this is Falcon Two. I'm hit. I'm dropping fuel fast," Davis snapped.

Humphrey's voice responded instantly. "Get the hell out of here now, Captain. *Move it!*"

"Affirmative," Davis replied. The F-16 was losing altitude, bucking wildly. "Heading out. Okay, Jack. Let's nurse this wounded bird home."

Jackson was already setting the cursor on his CRT for the return flight across the Adriatic to Brindisi, the NATO air base located on the heel of Italy's boot.

Davis hit the burner for a fast escape. The F-16 was a hell of lot harder to handle at high speed when damaged, but all he had on his mind now was getting the plane back to Brindisi and hauling his own ass back to the United States so he could see Mary and the kids and Columbus, Ohio. He hit the burners . . . and nothing happened. The plane began to wobble precariously, then the nose dipped. The hit they'd taken was obviously worse than he'd first thought.

At this low altitude, chances were that they would go into an uncontrollable dive. When that happened, they would impact in seconds. Even now the F-16 was hurtling well off course, beyond the target areas, heading deeper into Kosovo.

"We're not going to make it, Jack."

"I hear that," Jackson responded calmly. "Bail?"

"Bail," Davis confirmed.

Simultaneously, they activated their ejection seats.

Davis's body was violently expelled from the cockpit into the air. His body arced away from the F-16 that was already streaking groundward. He seemed to hang suspended there so high above the ground, the world a topsy-turvy panoramic swirl of endless, tumbling sky and earth. Then there was only the sensation of falling falling falling . . . until the chute finally opened with a loud popping *snap!* Davis's body jarred as his descent was checked. As he drifted downward, he spotted Jackson riding down not more than a dozen yards off to his right.

Then the F-16 hit the ground. Davis saw the flash and a moment later heard the explosion from two miles or more downrange. They descended, the air so quiet that he could hear his own labored breathing.

Jackson's eyes locked on the burning wreckage of the F-16 in the distance. "Well, there goes twenty million of the taxpayer's dollars," he called over to Davis.

As the endless panorama of the earth came up to meet them, something caught Davis's attention: the cluster of a small village of modest wood and stone dwellings. From that direction, along a road running close to where they would be touching down, an open four wheel drive vehicle with three them aboard was speeding in their direction.

"Forget the plane," Davis called over to Jackson. "We've got company!" He worked his risers, attempting to steer himself away from the road.

The vehicle left the road, bouncing across a flat, open field, continuing toward them.

Jackson saw it, too. "Those bastards aren't going to take me alive, Captain." Across the distance and the muted sigh of air, Davis clearly heard the gravelly voice of his WSO conveying resolve.

Davis called back, "Jack, don't do anything nuts. They could be locals just coming to see the excitement." The optimism sounded hollow even to his own ears. His guy was cramping with apprehension as the four wheel drive vehicle on the ground continued to rapidly close the distance. The vehicle was rocking and bumping along at a high rate of speed. Davis scanned the vicinity. Everywhere else were towering pines and rugged cliffs. There was no other place to land.

There was no more time to converse. They each hit the ground with a bone-jarring impact. Rolling once,

Davis came up running, instantly popping the quick release box and shrugging off his parachute harness. Looking around, instinctively pawing for the .45 automatic he wore in a shoulder holster over his flight suit, he saw his buddy hustling toward him from some twenty yards away.

But Jackson drew up short when the vehicle swerved to a rocking halt between them.

As dust swirled about the vehicle, the men aboard leaped to the ground. They wore typical Serbian civilian attire—American jeans and jackets—and each of them was holding an assault rifle. Two of them faced Davis while the third aimed his rifle at Jackson.

One of them screamed in badly broken English, "Americans, put down your weapons! Do it now or die!"

Snarling something that Davis didn't hear, Jackson began to yank out his pistol.

All Davis heard was the short, stuttering burst of the rifle.

The bullets blew Jackson off his feet, stitching his chest, expelling his guts out of his back, blood spraying from gaping exit wounds. Jackson hit the ground with an audible deadweight *thump!* and did not move. Then all three rifles were aimed at Davis.

"American, throw down your gun or die!" the Serb shouted.

The butt of Davis's pistol was slippery in his fist despite the chilly mountain air. He looked into the muzzles of those rifles pointed at him. He thought of his wife and his daughters. He thought about wanting to see them again.

He threw down his pistol and raised his hands. "Don't shoot," he said as calmly as he could. "I'm your prisoner."

Chapter 1

A tight combat formation of three Apache AH-64 helicopters thundered through the predawn darkness at 190 knots, skimming across the flat desert floor at two hundred feet, hugging the terrain to stay out of radar view. At two miles and closing fast on the primary target, the pilot of the lead chopper, Hunter Blake, spoke across the radio. "Assume attack position."

The other pilots broke away into the darkness.

Hunter's gunner, Travis Barrett, was positioned in the lower front seat of the Apache. "All systems locked and loaded." His Texas accent across the intercom held no emotion, purely professional.

"Well, all right," said Hunter coolly. "Time to rock and roll. Let's find something to blow up." Like his weapons man, Hunter was outfitted in a flight suit without rank or designation and wore a shoulder-holstered .45 automatic. He throttled down the Apache as the outlines of low brick buildings began materializing in the Forward Looking Infrared System.

The Apache AH-64 helicopter is the most heavily armed, fastest armored aircraft in the world. Hunter and Travis's chopper, like the other two helos in this formation, was fully armed with 100-pound "tank killer" missiles, a fully loaded 30mm chain-gun cannon and 70mm rockets. The choppers were part of the

325th Attack Helicopter Company, stationed at a secret air base well inside Saudi Arabia. Its mission in
the years since the end of Desert Storm had been to
patrol the Iraqi border; a boring, routine mission.

But there was nothing routine about this particular mission.

Today's deep insertion into Iraqi air space was
tasked with the rescue of seven American military personnel listed as missing in action from the Gulf War.

Forty-five American soldiers were currently listed
as MIA from that war. While many of these are cross-
referenced as killed in action/body not recovered, the
strained relations between America and Iraq in the
years since the war have resulted in muddled, uncertain, unreliable channels of communication that have
resolved nothing regarding this issue.

The installation looming ahead in the greenish glow
of the FLIR was a prison camp that supposedly held,
along with a couple dozen Iraqi prisoners, at least
seven Americans who were not cross-referenced as
KIA/BNR. This reported group of MIA/POWs was
the first to be located since Desert Storm. These
American POWs had been convicted in provincial
Iraqi civilian courts for "crimes against the people"
and sentenced to slave labor with no record of their
capture or internment acknowledged by Baghdad. It
was mean-spirited vengeance and nothing more. They
were nuts, Hunter reflected, thinking they could get
away with it. But then, Iraq's leaders had proven that
they were nuts from the beginning. And now they
were about to get a taste of American payback.

Hunter positioned his Apache in a five hundred–
foot hover. "Big Bird, this is Apache Leader," he said
over the radio. "Are you with us?"

"In position and on your ass, sir."

The response from the Blackhawk's female naviga-
tor, Jenny Olsen, was, as always, calm and in control,
self-assured as hell. The large gunship was a half mile

back, maintaining a holding position, waiting to ferry in the rest of TALON Force—Stan Powczuk, Jack Du-Bois, and Sarah Greene—to undertake the dangerous job of locating and extracting the MIAs.

At the TALON Force base for this mission in Ri-yadh, Saudi Arabia, Sam Wong, TALON Force's in-formation management specialist, was sitting at his computer terminal, monitoring and assisting via the TALON Force's Unmanned Aerial Vehicles, which he was controlling from afar.

A Predator 5, a pilotless aircraft-type UAV with wings and propeller, approximately the size of a mo-torcycle, was racing along above the Apache forma-tion, facilitating the communications relay, allowing Sam to assist by providing him with thermal and video imaging of the combat zone, along with laser designat-ing for targets. Even more valuable was the intelli-gence Sam had passed along moments earlier from the UAV launched from the Blackhawk. A Hummingbird, a helicopterlike UAV, had bulleted on ahead of the formation to provide a thermal view of the target area, identifying buildings, antiaircraft artillery, troops, and vehicles. There was full audio and video linkage be-tween Sam and the team, allowing Travis and the oth-ers to view this data in real time via their BSDs.

Hunter focused on being one with the flying, state-of-the-art hardware at his fingertips. Sitting behind the stick, he felt as if the helo was an extension of himself, controlled by his instincts, capabilities, reflexes. Hunter Blake was the consummate pilot. If it had wings, he could fly it.

"There it is," Hunter growled to Sam over the intercom.

They wore helmets with a Target Acquisition and Designation Sight/Pilots Night Vision Sensor device attached. In the shimmering "illumination" of his de-vice, Hunter clearly saw the target site: a square of several acres, with barbed wire and gun placements forming the perimeter. Inside the perimeter was a cluster of barracklike buildings and a watch tower at each corner. The site was at the base of a gentle rise of hills, but nothing else was gentle about the surrounding landscape. The terrain was harsh, desolate, barren plateaus and an endless expanse of unpopulated desert in every direction. Hunter saw surface-to-air launchers positioned at each corner of the perimeter and the ZPU-4 four-barreled antiaircraft artillery.

"Sam, your toys are working nicely," Hunter reported over his comm net. "The real thing is just like those UAV relays you've been sending us."

"Would my children lie?" Sam asked with mock indignation.

"They hear us coming," said Travis into his comm net.

Lights were already flicking on all over the prison camp, like fireflies coming to life in the darkness.

"Let's hope this was worth the trip," replied Travis. "I'd fly around the world to bring our boys home from a hellhole like this."

Hunter held the Apache in a steady approach. "We *did* fly halfway around the world to get here," he reminded Travis in a mildly chiding tone. Then his tone shifted into complete combat cool as he linked into the tac net. "All right, gentlemen," he said over the air. "Let's deliver these punks a wakeup call that they won't forget."

In front of him, Travis zeroed in on a row of SAM launchers. Everywhere he looked, he directed the FLIR beam that automatically allowed him to sight in on any target. It was not necessary for the Apache's WSO to actually eyeball a target once the infrared beam picked it out. Travis sighted, read off the numbers from the instrument panel on the side of the sighting device, and triggered a laser-designated Hellfire missile. The missile tracked unerringly along the laser beam sighting. The SAM launcher disintegrated into a violent red fireball that bathed the surrounding terrain momentarily in the redness of a false dawn. Travis and Hunter instinctively closed their eyes to avoid being momentarily blinded by the bright flash of the FLIR.

All around them now, the early morning sky was exploding into a fireworks display. The night took on a silvery strobelike brightness as munitions dumps erupted in secondary explosions. Other Apache gunships opened fire, spewing death down upon the poorly disciplined defense force.

On the ground, Iraqi soldiers were fumbling to respond. When the Iraqi artillery finally did commence returning fire at the gunships bearing down upon them, small-arms fire also lanced upward at the attackers. Saffron muzzle flashes winked at the Apaches from the towers and the ground placements.

Hunter throttled the chopper into a fast combat approach. But right now, the chiseled features of this former surfer boy from California were smoothed impassively as he piloted the Apache into the blazing barrage, holding station while his gunner acquired a good picture of one of the guard towers.

Sparkling green tracers whizzed around the gunship from almost every point along the perimeter, eerily outlining the prison camp. More soldiers could be seen scrambling about in various stages of disarray at this early hour. They were armed with rifles, firing at the gunships without aiming while racing madly to reinforce the defensive positions.

Travis sent a sustained burst from the chain gun, pulverizing the tower and the men in it, the rounds filling the air with blown-apart debris and body parts.

Another SAM missile was fired. Travis activated the helicopter's "Black Hole" infrared suppressor system.

Blake pulled hard to starboard in a reflexive evasive maneuver. His stomach jolted as the Apache veered wildly aside with the adept agility that had made this gunship such a marvel of success against the Iraqis in the Gulf War.

The missile detonated somewhere behind them, the concussion jiggling the Apache violently.

Suddenly they could hear the *plang!plang!plang!* of small-arms fire hitting their helicopter. Hunter nosed the Apache around in the direction of the ground fire. Travis unleashed a pair of rockets at a machine gun placement, followed by an extended burst of 30mm fire that sent hot leader death into the nearly obliterated bunker.

Blake scanned the perimeter in the glow of the TADS/PNVS. The other choppers had done their work. Each tower was a burning torch, while each of the rocket launchers and antiaircraft emplacements were now massive, scorched holes in the earth.

Hunter keyed the radio to Jenny in the Blackhawk. "All right, Big Bird. It's a hot LZ down there but if we want out of here before Baghdad knows what's going on, it's now or never."

"It's now," Jenny replied. "We're coming in."

Hunter and Travis continued scanning for targets, along with the crewmen of the other Apaches that hovered over the trailing clouds of smoke gathering above the prison compound.

Hunter heard gunfire that scored a direct engine hit. He felt the cyclic control stick begin shimmying wildly in his grip. Then silence replaced the racket of the Apache's transmission. On the flight control instrument panel, every gauge dropped to zero.

The engine was dead.

Hunter had mere heartbeats to react. He rammed down the collective pitch-control lever, flattening the helo's blades. The Apache went into a fast, dangerous, descending glide.

With his peripheral senses, Hunter heard the other Apaches zero their concentrated firepower into the source of the gunfire that had struck his Apache, rendering that remaining bunker into a vaporized pit. Hunter was hoping like hell for autorotation of the blades; that air from the chopper's downward speed coursing up through the blades would keep the blades spinning. He shot a glance at the tachometer. Though the blades were registering a slight climb in rpms, the gunship was still angling downward at close to seventy knots.

With the collective pitch-control lever and the cyclic-control stick shuddering in each hand, Hunter kept his attention on the mounting rpms of his blades. Still plummeting at gut-wrenching speed, he yanked back on the cyclic lever when the Apache was a mere fifty feet from the ground. The Apache pulled abruptly upward until it was practically standing on its tail, the rate of its descent halted as if an invisible leash had been yanked.

This was the moment of truth, Hunter knew . . . the most critical point of a dead-engine landing.

He shoved the cyclic stick forward again at the exact moment the Apache air-braked. Hanging there, only fifteen or twenty feet off the desert floor, with the rotors still going, the helo's nose abruptly dropped into a level position. Hunter eased in on the collective once more, very gently.

The ground came racing inexorably up toward the Apache. The chopper hit with a grinding, screeching, crunching impact, then it skidded, screeching across rock-ribbed ground before plowing to a halt with its undernose buried in a sand dune.

0640 hours
Inside the Blackhawk gunship

The Blackhawk arrived on the scene moments after the Apache's crash landing. Everyone aboard the

Blackhawk overheard Travis and Hunter's conversation across the comm net.

After only seconds of silence, Sam's grim voice replaced theirs. "I saw the whole thing through Predator 5, and it passed on the crash site coordinates. Here they are."

Olsen said, "Save your breath, Sam. We have visual contact."

Lieutenant Jennifer Olsen was officially assigned to the top echelon of the Office of Naval Intelligence. She was a buxom blonde bombshell, a tigress in fatigues.

She allowed her attention to be distracted from sighting of the down Apache only long enough to focus her night vision sighting devise on some vehicles she spotted in the flames over by the prison compound. She loosed off a burst from the Blackhawk's chain gun.

A line of parked military Jeeps burst apart in a series of flashing multiple explosions.

Standing behind her in the Blackhawk's cockpit were TALON Force commandos Stan Powczuk and Jack DuBois, who wore their Low Observable Camouflage Ensemble suites.

The suite fit not unlike a cross between a scuba-diving wetsuit and a nighttime commando strike suit. Weighing in at a mere sixteen and a half pounds, the suite provided full-body armor protection, as well as voice, digital, and holographic communications, laser designation, and high-powered optical sensing. It was also equipped with immediate and automatic medical trauma aid in the event that a nonfatal wound was sustained. The ensemble's most science fiction aspect was its Low Observable camouflage capability, a series of woven microcomputers that, when activated, sensed the color and shade of a trooper's background and precisely mirrored that background image, whatever it was. When a trooper "went to stealth," the suit automatically blended in with the backdrop, making the wearer nearly invisible.

Stan and Jack were armed to the teeth. Primary weapon of the hard-punch ensemble was the XM-29 smart rifle, an incredibly high-tech weapon that fired bullets directed by a millimeter wave sensor and aiming device located beneath the barrel. Made of special alloys and remarkably light, weighing a mere nine pounds, the XM-29s carried two hundred 5.56mm rounds and also featured a four-shot 20mm grenade launcher under the barrel. Each man also wore an XM-73 pistol holstered in a fast-drawn underarm shoulder rig, along with three electronic eavesdropping UAV bugs, a wide-bladed knife sheathed at mid-chest, and ammo packs, grenades, and a small pouch attached to a belt.

Jenny tapped the pilot on his shoulder and pointed in the direction of the crash site, clearly visible a half kilometer to the east.

The pilot nodded his understanding and banked the chopper into a glide. He was a towheaded, ruddy-cheeked "top gun" in his late twenties who looked like he would like to be ogling Jenny, had they not been entering a fire zone.

Although each team member aboard could see the disheartening sight of the Apache's wreckage, it was the door gunner, Captain Sarah Greene, manning the M-50 mounted in the open side bay door, who exclaimed the harshest expletives across the intercom, making Jenny wince and chuckle at the same time.

Off duty, Sarah's temperament was that of an idealistic, natural, holistic granola-eating Birkenstock wearer who believed unflinchingly in the goodness of humanity. It never failed to startle Jenny that on missions such as this, Sarah, who drove a Volkswagen Microbus and gave money to Greenpeace, morphed into the most bloodthirsty, accurately deadly killing machine Jenny had ever seen working an M-50.

The pilot landed the Blackhawk fifty yards from the crumpled wreckage.

Jenny found herself hoping like hell that Travis and Hunter had somehow survived. It had obviously been a rough landing, judging from the badly disfigured remains of the Apache. After so many missions in the field, she'd come to think of these guys as family.

Two rumpled figures lurched from the wreckage.

At Jenny's side, Jack grunted a heartfelt, "Well all fucking right." Jack DuBois, twenty-eight, was a Marine/ Force Recon specialist; a six-foot-five solid chunk of muscle. "Let's cover them."

"I'm with you, bro," grunted Stan without a moment's hesitation. He darted after Jack, swinging his rifle around to port arms as they leaped from the chopper.

In the open sliding door of the Blackhawk, Sarah was swinging her big M-50 caliber back and forth, restlessly scanning for targets but finding none way out here in this remote quadrant. They were well-removed from the blitzed rubble of the prison camp, from which could now be heard the crackle of small-arms fire, punctuated only occasionally by larger booms as the other Apaches continued to pulverize the camp's antiaircraft resistance.

It was the smell of fuel vapor stinging his nostrils that had brought Travis Barrett back to consciousness only seconds earlier. Opening his eyes, Travis realized that Hunter had already dragged him from the Apache.

"Come on, Trav!" Hunter's exhortations had further penetrated Travis's reeling senses as he felt himself being guided to his feet.

Travis willed his brain to clear, and like a good soldier, his brain commenced responding to the direct order. He and Hunter scrambled quickly away from the Apache toward the cloud of dust being kicked up from the Blackhawk's mighty backwash as it touched down.

"Keep moving," Travis heard Hunter urge him as they lurched along. "Double time! That Apache is fixing to blow big time, dude."

Even under these circumstances, Travis heard himself grouse, "Jesus H, Hunter. You sound like a goddamn Californian."

Two figures with rifles emerged from the mini dust storm: Jack and Stan. Then Sarah became visible in the glow of the landing lights, where she stood behind the mighty M-50.

The cavalry to the rescue, Travis found himself thinking somewhat giddily. He also found himself realizing for the first time, with some distress, just how banged up he must have gotten in the landing. Travis Barrett had often been called "Mr. By-the-Book" or "Mr. Chain-of-Command" behind his back. But the big six-foot-two Texan had never taken offense because the tags were true. From the meticulously maintained brush cut to his ability to size up any firefight situation, Travis was a spit-and-polish soldier who lived and breathed the U.S. Army. And though his mind was clearing, he felt acutely uncomfortable about his temporary disorientation.

He was moving under his own steam by the time they reached the Blackhawk. He gulped in lungfuls of the cool night air. True, the air was polluted with the smell of burning rubble from the direction of the prison camp and, closer in, the fumes of both the downed chopper and the idling Blackhawk. But Travis felt rejuvenated, fully awake, and combat-ready once again.

When he leaped aboard the relatively spacious chopper, he immediately grunted through his headset mic, "What are you waiting for, pilot? We're supposed to have some POWs to take home with us."

Jenny couldn't help but grin at the team leader's testy tone of command. Travis looked a little shaky when he and Hunter had first stumbled from the Apache, but there was no doubting now who remained in charge.

"Aye aye," she responded sharply, nodding to the pilot who commenced liftoff just as Jack and Stan were managing to scramble aboard. Jack was grinning widely. "Welcome aboard, gentlemen."

Those aboard braced themselves as the Blackhawk rose from the desert floor.

Hunter looked slightly worse for wear himself now that they'd survived the crash landing, but he looked fit enough to fight.

"Pleasure to be here," he assured Jack.

Travis strode straight to the rack of smart rifles and pistols that matched those worn by Jack and Stan. "I believe we should arm up . . . dude," he called to Hunter.

"Right as usual, Boss," Hunter said drolly. "And remind me to be so gracious the next time you save my ass."

He and Travis quickly selected their armament, then donned their black synthetic armor and high-tech Battle Ensembles.

As they performed this brief task, Stan made his way forward with a look of offended incredulity across his bearded features.

He barked at Jenny, "You almost left us back there with our thumbs up our ass, sweetheart. And I thought you loved us."

Jenny managed a smile that quirked the corners of her lush mouth. "I do love you, Stan. I just like to make fellas two-step every once in awhile. A girl's got to have her fun, right?"

Stan didn't know whether to laugh or start cursing. But before he could do either, everyone's attention was drawn to the violent explosion of the Apache from the ground below.

The blistering fireball grew smaller and smaller

along their backtrack as, in the cockpit, Jenny had the pilot pour on the knots, resuming the Blackhawk's high-speed delivery of TALON Force into the target area.

Chapter 2

0645 hours
The Iraqi desert

The Blackhawk tore in on a low run that bisected the prison compound.

The collection of structures was perfectly outlined in a square of burning fire that had once represented the defense perimeter. In this remote, desolate sector of the Iraqi desert, this burning square was the only light visible except for the barest gray pin line of dawn on the eastern horizon. The flight lights of the other Apache gunships buzzed around the devastated perimeter, searching for targets like birds of prey cruising for something to devour.

Travis and Hunter were hunched with Jack and Stan near the doorway, rifles held at the ready, prepared to leap to the ground fighting, to search out and extract the American MIA/POWs reportedly held here.

Antiaircraft fire from a ZPU-4 splattered against the armor of the Blackhawk's side, jarring the big helo.

From her position behind the .50-caliber machine gun mounted in the door, Sarah announced across the intercom, "I see the bastards."

She triggered an extended burst from the M-50 at a position that had been camouflaged with netting. Orange-red flame systematically tracked from the nearby hovering Apache gunships as well, destroying the artillery and those manning that gun in a fiery flash.

"Get ready for touchdown, ladies," Jenny said as the pilot pulled the Blackhawk around for the final run at the compound. "Welcome to beautiful Iraq."

As they rotored in, Sarah commenced "softening" their arrival by laying down a heavy carpet of fire from the .50-caliber.

Travis felt like a tiger ready to be unleashed from a cage. He and Hunter had each traded their old-fashioned, shoulder-holstered .45 automatics for the high-tech XM-73 pistol, backup weapon to the XM-29. The sidearm fired a 15mm shell that launched a half dozen smart bullets, effective at up to an eight hundred meter range. This pistol from hell carried a basic load of seven rounds.

The Blackhawk touched down, creating another dust tornado in the enclosed confines of the prison camp.

Three ramshackle structures comprised the inside of the compound. A pair of structures adjacent to the northern perimeter were separated by a parking area filled with a battered fleet of military vehicles parked there, all of which had been purposefully spared during TALON Force's air assault. Between a parking area and one of the buildings, a Russian-made HIP-17 gunship with Iraqi military markings sat unmanned on a helipad.

Travis knew from prior intel that one of these buildings was a cell block overfilled with Iraqi prisoners; everything from dissidents to intellectuals to those who had dared profane their leader's name or had otherwise not fallen in with Iraq's current oppressive, brutal regime. This was the place where "human examples" were exiled to lifetimes of a fate worse than death: hard labor imprisonment in this hellhole, the end of the road for enemies of the state. The building on the other side of the parking area, the troops' barracks near the unattended gunship, had already sustained considerable damage by rocket and chain-gun fire from the other attack choppers.

It was the third building, the one facing the first two across a broad expanse of ground, that was the main target. It, too, had been spared any damage from air fire. This building was separated by a broad expanse of barren ground where the prisoners were gathered before being marched out for the labor of breaking rocks with a sledgehammer in the scorching desert sun; labor that was meaningless, endless, and ultimately, inevitably fatal.

The instant the pilot skillfully touched the Blackhawk down in the center of the compound, the troopers of TALON Force were pouring from the side door of the helo, spreading outward in combat intervals and advancing at a run on the cell block building where the MIAs were supposedly being held.

Rifle fire opened up on them from several points along the front wall of the building, a withering last-ditch defense against this head-on assault.

"Hit it," Travis ordered. "Stealth mode!"

The TALON Force troopers threw themselves to the ground at the first shot. The initial volley ripped apart the air closely above them.

Activating their Low-Observable Camouflage Suits, Travis and his men became instantly invisible, their suits' stealth camouflage registering the exact color and texture of the desert, making them appear as no more than misty vapor.

"I hope no one's expecting me to kiss the ground of this godforsaken shit hole," Powczuk said across the comm net.

Communications between team members was routed to bio-chips embedded under the skin of every TALON Force trooper. Communications were directed skyward from the Battle Sensor Helmet that was part of the ensemble. In addition to ballistic protection, the BSH provided a communications suite and a computer network station with a straight-up link to the constellation of thirty-six TALON Force satellites, thus enabling unlimited, unjammable communications and data transfer between those on the ground and Sam Wong in Riyadh.

Jack muttered, "Let these Iraqi pricks kiss this." He triggered his XM-29's grenade launcher.

The double-door front entrance of the building was blown open in an eruption of wood, steel, and shrapnel.

Travis, Stan, and Hunter also let loose a grenade each from their rifles. The explosive blitz of firepower blew the entire front wall surrounding the entrance inward. Travis thought he heard screams of agony mingled in beneath the shattering blast, but he could only hope it was the death cries of the defenders of this building, and not of the MIA/POWs themselves. If these structures followed standard Iraqi military design, as they certainly seemed to, then the exploding grenades would only demolish the entrance of the office space behind it, with the defenders trapped in between.

Moments later, scores of stunned Iraqi prisoners stumbled into predawn gloom. Although disorganized, they lost little time in making their bid for freedom.

Travis accessed the tactical display Battle Sensor Devise on his helmet, a monoclelike device that generated a laser pathway that imaged into the eye of the wearer, using the retina to produce the illusion of holographic images. The BSD eyepiece provided a three-dimensional grid in front of the eyes.

Travis's thermal view of the compound, as depicted in his BSD, registered no further military response to the mass escape. The defending gunfire from the other cell block building had tapered away after the grenade assault.

Travis and his men hustled forward without hesitation across the distance toward the remains of the building's entrance, where settling dust impeded the effectiveness of their night vision goggles.

They appeared to be no more than strange, vaguely rippling shimmers in the early morning light.

Along the way, Travis glanced across the parking lot at the HIP-17 gunship. While running, he aimed and activated his HERF Wristband RF Field Generator. The HERF gun was based on the principle that electronic circuits are vulnerable to electromagnetic overload. It was really nothing more than a radio transmitter designed to shoot enough energy at a target to disable it. The mute blast of high-energy radio frequency demolished the electronics system of the HIP, rendering it virtually unflyable.

Reaching the building entrance several paces ahead of Travis, Jack opened a pouch on his belt and extracted a small "Dragonfly," Hand Launched Micro Unmanned Aerial Vehicle. The diminutive Dragonfly could see over the next hill, or—as in this case—fly through hallways and rooms of a building and send back digital date. The "invisible man" activated the Dragonfly and released it into the building with a gentle backhand flip, sending the drone zipping merrily on its way into the interior to beam back signals from its three separate minicameras as it flew through the building, a soundless, airborne, high speed "bug."

As soon as the UAV was set free, Jack stepped back from the exposed line of fire inside the structure. He next withdrew the UAV's receiver unit from the accessory pack worn at his hip. The Dragonfly receiver looked like a pocket computer screen. He activated it with a practiced flick of his thumb. This brought into digitally sharp focus exactly what the Dragonfly was seeing as it buzzed its way through the building, transmitting audio and visual signals.

The Dragonfly was presently flitting down a corridor

to the left, lined with office doors, some ripped off their hinges from the initial assault. But there was no indication of human activity in the vicinity. Then it buzzed down another corridor that angled off to the right, leading to a loading dock where rations could be delivered, or prisoners could be loaded on and off of trucks. Nothing there, either. The building thus far appeared to be deserted. That left a middle corridor.

Jack was deactivating and replacing the receiver when the other invisible troopers joined him.

"Middle corridor," he reported to them over the comm net. "There's a heavy-duty door at the end of it, and nobody else around. Everything else is open, deserted, busted up. If our men are in here, they're behind that door."

"Let's find out," said Travis.

They streamed over the rubble through the settling haze, separating once they were inside the building. They fanned out, their NVDs and rifles probing the gloom. The four-man team split in two, advancing as speedily and quietly as possible through the rubble of the middle corridor.

Travis and Hunter hugged one wall, continuing to maintain combat intervals. Jack and Stan likewise proceeded along the opposite wall, toward the closed metal door.

"Stan, you and I are hitting," Travis said into his comm net. "Okay, guys. We're this far. Deactivate stealth. I want whoever's on the other side of this door to see us."

"Shock value will give us an edge," Jack agreed.

They again became wholly visible.

Travis glanced at Jack and Hunter. "You two supply backup."

Jack's features were somber and determined. "Good luck, guys."

Stan snarled, "Let's hit 'em!"

0650 hours
Inside the Blackhawk

In the center of the compound, Jenny remained in the cockpit, next to the pilot who held the chopper at a high idle.

She watched with mild amusement as the suddenly freed Iraqi prisoners had first started running toward the Blackhawk. No such luck, guys, she thought to herself. She said across the intercom, "Sarah, better let 'em know we don't pick up riders.

"Gotcha," came Sarah's response.

She triggered off a carefully aimed short blast, kicking up geysers of desert sand, and the .50-caliber bullets pounded a visible line in the sand between the Blackhawk and the oncoming Iraqis.

They got the idea fast enough.

There followed a hasty exit from the premises, the prisoners overloading the Iraqi military vehicles and speeding away with men frantically clinging to every inch of every vehicle, others running to catch up. Those dissidents would at least have their freedom, their pride, and a second chance to fight on for what they believed in. That would have to do, Jenny told herself. TALON Force had its own agenda.

The sleek, heavily armed Blackhawk looked utterly out of place amid the smoldering remains of the prison camp. Each of the structures had sustained heavy damage, and the Iraqis had laid down their arms and lay with their heads on their hands in the sand.

Rifle fire suddenly opened up on the Blackhawk from the far end of what remained of the troops' living quarters. Some brave or extremely foolish Iraqi regulars were opening fire from around that corner of the building.

Sarah let out another string of expletives that would make a Marine blush. She swiveled the M-50 and cut

loose with a hammering burst that made her body
shimmy as she rode the mighty recoil without ever
losing control of the ferocious weapon.

The rifle fire ceased.

An Apache zoomed close by overhead and delivered a rocket to that corner of the structure.

And that was that. The roof pancaked in a rising
cloud of debris. The structure collapsed in upon itself.

The Apache pulled up, continuing to hold its position and search for targets.

0650 hours
In a cell block of the main building on the Iraqi base

Behind the steel door at the end of the long central
corridor was a roomful of cells.

Specialist Fifth Class Carlos Rivera, U.S. Army,
stood facing that steel door. He found himself simultaneously praying for and dreading this moment of his
rescue. There was a pistol pointed at his head, held
by a madman insane with fear.

Facing that steel door from within, Rivera knew that
this vicious assault on the camp could be nothing else
but his rescue . . . unless his recent daydreams and
delusions had now completely dominated his mental
state. Remaining in the mental fog that had become
his sanctuary from reality, he'd sat calmly in his cell,
even after the power went off and he was in darkness
except for the illumination of the explosions outside
his barred window, where the sounds of war raged.
His once stocky frame was lanky and worn, the skin
having shriveled on his bones as the spirit had died
within him day by day, subjected to back-breaking
labor and inhumane treatment.

They were coming for him. After all these years,
his country was coming for him.

The man holding the pistol to Rivera's head was Captain Taziz, the commandant of this roughshod Iraqi unit. The wiry little officer was quaking in his boots. His eyes were wide, his forehead beaded with sweat. Yet the gun pressed to Rivera's temple was held steady and firm.

This whole fucking thing could be a dream anyhow, Rivera told himself. The constructs of his logic had been ground away long ago. *Let it end,* was all he seemed able to think.

Taziz had his forearm across Rivera's throat, his knee plunged into the small of the prisoner's back. Taziz was not a big man, even for an Iraqi, and Rivera remembered the days when he could have taken the man easily. But that was before countless months in this hell on earth. Taziz liked to think of himself as a cultured man despite having been exiled to this outpost. He even wore a prim little moustache, usually waxed. But now everything about the base commandant was disheveled, including his wilted facial hair. Taziz had been in the headquarters buildings, sound asleep, when the attack had been launched. He had fallen further and further back from the action howling around him, finding his way to safety as his soldiers died around him and his base was destroyed, until he was now literally down to the last man—his human shield, Specialist Rivera.

Taziz snickered into Rivera's ear. "They have come all of this distance, killed all of my men, only to see you die." Spittle sprayed Rivera's ear and face. Taziz was practically foaming at the mouth.

Rivera discovered that he was taking considerable satisfaction in Taziz's panic. "So kill me," he laughed, looking at the empty cells around them. "I've got six good men waiting for me. I'd rather be in their company than yours, you shit-for-brains hairbag."

They stood facing the single door. Rivera found himself struggling within to break free of the dream-like trance he had been in for so many years. He felt Taziz's gun barrel quiver.

"Do not make me blow your brains out before your friends have the pleasure of seeing you die." Taziz's voice wavered with hatred and fear.

Something was definitely welling up inside him, Rivera realized, telling himself that this was *not* a dream. He *could* do something about it . . .

He snickered back at Taziz. "You haven't got the balls to kill me, cock-breath. Then what would you have to hide behind?"

The area just inside the steel door was a large open cell block divided only the bars of seven cells that had been constructed especially for the American POWs who had been brought here to die a slow death.

Seven cells . . . and a torture chamber at the far end. When a prisoner was tortured by Taziz—sometimes to death, sometimes to within an inch of his life—Taziz had always wanted the other Americans to witness the degradation and suffering of one of their own.

There were seven of them to begin with, but now it was down to only Specialist Rivera, who like his fallen comrades had been in the wrong place at the wrong time years ago during the Gulf War. How many years ago exactly? Rivera wasn't sure anymore. He only knew that, one by one, his fellow Americans had died. And now, more than likely, it was his turn.

The world beyond this cell block, beyond that steel door, suddenly grew ominously silent. Rivera had heard the crackle of some rifle fire and the answering salvo from an M-50 and a rocket blast. But compared to the preceding five minutes of hellfire and brimstone, a cloak of relative peacefulness had fallen upon what minutes earlier had been a flaring battlefield. There were sounds of choppers from somewhere outside and nothing else.

Rivera heard Taziz's sporadic, whispered gasps of

breathing echoing in the strange silence of the cell block.

He felt no sense of panic. He was ready for anything and, after several lifetimes spent in this godawful place, he was afraid of nothing, not even the death that had brought salvation to his fellow POWs. But he *did* feel the returning of a pronounced keenness of his senses that he hadn't experienced in a long time. He sensed more than heard the silent force advancing toward them from the other side of that triple-locked and bolted steel door.

Then, with an ear blasting explosion of flashing white light and smoke, the door was blown inward off its hinges.

Taziz cried out in shock, but did not loosen the choke hold on his human shield. The barrel of his pistol remained jammed against Rivera's temple.

A pair of commandos slipped into the room, separating to either side of the smoking doorway while two more appeared as backup, sweeping the cell block with rifles and NVD goggles.

Despite the fact that Taziz was shell-shocked and terrified, he played his hand. "Stop where you are, Americans!" He meant it as a command, but it came out as a frightened plea of desperation. "Stop, or Specialist Rivera dies!"

The awakening Rivera had felt building now blossomed with an abruptness that startled him with its clarity, and he heard himself saying, "Specialist Rivera says go to hell, Captain Scumball. It ain't my day to die."

He bent his knees slightly. With his wrists shackled in front of him, he managed to summon enough strength to deliver a sharp backward elbow jab that caught Taziz hard in the solar plexus.

Taziz stumbled back a half pace under the punch from surprise, and that was enough for Rivera who dived to the side and rolled away as fast as he could. Taziz whipped his pistol around in Rivera's direction. The terrified Iraqi still thought he could issue an ultimatum. He started to scream something at the intruders, shrieking in a voice that sounded like a squealing rat.

The commandos opened fire on Taziz, their strange, bulky rifles on full automatic. The gloom was splashed with flaring muzzle flashes and the walls seemed to quake in the thunder.

Rivera had never seen a man explode.

The rounds quite simply obliterated the Iraqi, as in *whoosh! bang!* look, there's no more Captain Taziz. First he was standing there, aiming his pistol at Rivera and shouting at the Americans. Then the commandos opened fire and, from his frightened face down to quaking boots, Taziz ruptured into a nightmare of ripped flesh, splintered bone, and shredded clothing. All that remained of the sadistic son of a bitch was a nasty, oozing smear that looked like a Jackson Pollock mural on the wall behind where he'd stood.

One of the commandos broke away from the others and rushed over to assist Rivera to his feet with a strong hand. Another silently swept the cell block.

Rivera's ears vibrated, his senses swirled. As he allowed himself to be assisted to his feet, Rivera realized what that old feeling was. I'm a soldier, dammit! If captured, I will fight and resist to the death, Rivera told himself. He became aware that he was leaning on the commando.

He tried to stand erect under his own power but he wasn't that strong. He got dizzy quickly and would have pitched back to the ground if the commando hadn't checked his fall.

"Take it easy, soldier," the man said in the soothing tone of a fellow warrior. "Let us do the lifting. I'm Major Barrett. We've come to take you home.

"About damn time, Major." Rivera's response sounded like the croak of a frog. "Rivera. Specialist Fifth Class."

"Are there any other Americans being held here, Specialist?"

"No. They weren't able to stick around. They're all dead."

"Damn." Travis spat the word as if cursing himself.

"Take me home," said Rivera. The words came clearly enough . . . as did a new realization. He was losing consciousness from shock and general malnutrition. Surrounding sounds grew faint. Shadows of the cell block deepened. Maybe it is my day to die, was Rivera's final conscious thought.

He collapsed.

Travis effortlessly hefted the unconscious man over his shoulder and held him securely in place, hastening back toward the doorway, unhampered by the dead weight. He placed a thumb against Rivera's jugular, detecting a faint but steady pulse. Good enough, thought Travis. At least we got one.

"Let's go," he said, turning to the others.

He didn't wait for a response. He raced ahead of his men, heading through the remains of the doorway, dashing back along the corridor with his human cargo in the direction of the Blackhawk chopper.

Hunter, Stan, and Jack withdrew with the same degree of speed and caution as they'd entered, functioning like the well-oiled fighting team they were.

Hunter said to Jenny across the comm net, "Hear that, sweetheart? Get ready to take us home."

The Blackhawk's rotors were already increasing in rpms.

Jenny said across the net, "I heard. And knock off the sweetheart shit, Blakey boy. That's sexual harassment on the job."

Stan and Jack picked up their pace. They bypassed Travis and Rivera, reaching the remains of the front of the building moments ahead of them. Simultaneously, Hunter twisted around, assisting in their withdrawal as the team's tail end charlie, covering their six with

his XM-29. When Jack and Stan reached the pile of
rubble that had once been the front entrance, they
crouched to either side and scanned the smoldering
remains of the devastated camp.

"Clear to the right," said Stan.

"Clear to the left," reported Jack.

"You're all clear from out here," Sarah said from
the door of the chopper. "Come on home, guys."

"Coming through," Travis said.

He powered ahead, his legs pumping, the unconscious man across his shoulder remaining safely in
place. Jack, Stan, and Hunter caught up with him at
the chopper.

Around them, nothing moved except for dancing,
crackling flames. The line of dawn along the eastern
horizon was turning from silver to pink.

The Blackhawk was quivering as if with anticipa-
tion. The earth shook and the air shuddered to the
whistling of its revving turbines.

Sarah didn't leave her post behind the M-50. Her
NVD goggles swiveled from side to side, as did the
barrel of the enormous machine gun.

Up front, Jenny seemed to know intuitively the precise moment at which Travis leaned backward to set
the unmoving Rivera onto the deck inside the door.
She tapped the pilot's shoulder, and the helo left the
ground like a kicked football, and it was all the commandos could do to heave themselves aboard with
lightning speed or be left behind.

The Blackhawk lifted up and away into a sharply
banked curve, away from the camp at an angle so
severe that everyone had to grab onto something or
risk sliding out through the open door. Each man used
a free hand to steady the inert figure of Rivera.

Stan could only sigh. "Dammit. I can't believe it.
She did it *again*—almost left us behind!"

Jenny spoke across the intercom. "Sorry about that,
gentlemen. AWACS has the Iraqi Air Force trip-wired,

but I still don't want to tangle with any MIGs out of Baghdad."

The helo straightened out of the climb and traveled low and swiftly, hugging the terrain beneath radar range. The shadowy wasteland zoomed beneath like an endless sea of sand.

"You're doing just fine, babe," Hunter assured Jenny across the intercom. "Just get us home in time for breakfast."

Stan couldn't restrain a chuckle. The Navy SEAL was already in wind-down mode from the hot engagement. Every vestige of his ill temper had evaporated.

"Sounds like things could get downright domestic between the two of you," he chided.

Sarah left her station at the M-50 and slammed the side door shut, shutting off the view of the night sky and the Apaches riding in wingman positions. She turned to face the cluster of men, rolling her eyes.

"*Babe*!" she repeated in exasperation, with plenty of sarcastic emphasis. "Jesus Christ, you guys, how many of the enemy do Jenny and I have to blow away before we can be one of you idiot *guys*?"

Travis rose and stepped toward her. He liked his people to be emotionally involved. That was one of the few areas where he had his own theories and chose not to go by the book. Likewise, there was a time for that edge . . . and a time for the sword to be sheathed.

"Cork it, Greene," he said. "You don't want to be a man."

Sarah sighed, relaxing. "You're right about that, Trav." She glanced at the others. "Especially if this collection of cretins is any example."

Stan snorted. "Hell, Sarah, Travis is right. A man gets nothing but the shit work and most of the time he's not even appreciated for that."

Sarah brushed by Travis. "Excuse me, Major. I have work to do."

Sarah Greene's demeanor transformed as she knelt

beside the unconscious Rivera. Dr. Sarah Greene was a board certified surgeon, and it was with the skillful, knowledgeable hands of a surgeon—which moments earlier had been operating that hellacious .50-caliber—that now rested Rivera's head in her lap and unbuttoned his tattered shirt to examine his scrawny chest for wounds or injury.

"Hand me my stethoscope," she commanded of no one in particular, in a tone that brooked no response except immediate compliance.

Before anyone could respond, however, Rivera's eyes blinked a couple of times; his bleary, deep brown Latin eyes began to focus on the beautiful yet concerned features of Sarah. Rivera's mouth smiled weakly, warmly, more in acceptance than desire.

"I have died and gone to heaven." He sighed dreamily.

Sarah sighed too, with a mixture of relief and profound resignation. She grinned at her teammates and said, "I pronounce this man alive and ready for recovery."

Travis allowed himself a good-natured laugh. "Well there you go, Sarah. Now aren't you glad us men are so easy to figure out? Look how much time it saves in making a battlefield diagnosis."

Sam Wong's voice cut across the comm net with an intimacy as if he was physically there with them in the chopper and had experienced the firefight with them. Which he had, in a way, through the audio linkup and the relayed battlefield data that he'd been monitoring from the UAVs.

"Good work, boys and girls," his perky voice chirped from the comm center in Riyadh. "Here are your coordinates for the nearest field hospital inside Saudi."

Chapter 3

"Let me get this straight," said the President of the United States irritably. "When NATO stopped bombing in ninety-nine, the Serbian government in Belgrade allowed NATO ground forces into Kosovo to keep the peace. Part of that deal was that our U.S. Air Force, as part of NATO, would monitor such efforts from the air. Now you're telling me that one of our planes has been shot down over Yugoslav air space, and Belgrade is denying knowledge of it?"

Growing anger and indignation at the report he'd just read coursed through his words. He and his crisis team were in the Situation Room, a wood-paneled, basement bunker beneath the White House.

General George H. Gates, Chairman of the Joint Chiefs of Staff, was a highly decorated veteran of several wars. The burden of command was reflected in the deep lines of his sixty-something features. But his eyes, and his mind, were razor sharp.

"That is exactly the situation, sir. But there are complications beyond that. It's a rugged frontier where those pilots went down. That's why that renegade Serbian force they were after dug in way up there in the first place. There's some question as to whether the plane actually went down into Kosovo or whether they went down on the Macedonian side of

the border. Either way, Belgrade claims they're working on it."

Gates had relayed the report of the downed American pilots to the commander in chief, receiving the
information from the office in Brussels of the supreme
commander of NATO. Within minutes, they had
grouped together for this briefing.

The president made a very unprofessional snort of
derision. "Right. And Belgrade didn't know anything
about those renegade Serb paramilitaries we were
going after, either." The president turned to the third
man in the room, who was seated at the large, bare
table. "Buck, what do you think?"

General Samuel "Buck" Freedman was a commander of the government's Special Operations Command, based out of his office just down the hall from
the Situation Room. Freedman was in his mid-forties
and had plenty of covert operations experience both
in the field and from behind a desk.

Freedman tugged at an ear lobe. "The CIA, the
NSA, and the State Department have all weighed in
with their options, international implications, and the
pitfalls of using standard military tactics. In other
words, Mr. President, they've come up with no workable options as of yet."

The president swung a quizzical glance back to
Gates. "I thought our F-16s had a built-in locator
system."

"They do, sir. Unfortunately, this one malfunctioned
or was damaged when they were hit. We have the
coordinates of their target, of course, so NATO
planes are combing the entire region, as are the satellites and the KLA troops we've allowed to operate
there."

"I don't like the idea of supporting those Kosovo
Liberation Army guerrillas," the president said. "That
could cause real trouble here on the home front. The
KLA is supposed to be demilitarized."

Freedman leaned forward. "We need people like them on the ground, sir, just like we used the Montagnards in Vietnam and the Contras in Latin America."

"I suppose." The president grew quiet, glowering at the can of Pepsi he held. You could almost see his mind working the angles like the politician he was, thought Freedman.

American and NATO warplanes had launched seventy-eight days of air assaults that had been meant to advance a peace that promised Kosovo autonomy within Yugoslavia; an autonomy that the Serbs would only grant under extreme duress.

Freedman knew the historic dynamics of the situation. In his opinion, ignorance of such subtleties had worked to America's disadvantage in foreign military involvement. Thus were sown the seeds of the next generation's wars. It was a cycle Freedman hoped to break and, to him, understanding history was the key.

The ongoing problem with Kosovo was the product of a conflict going back over centuries; the dividing line between the Ottoman and Austrian empires, between Islam and Christianity, and between Serbian and Albanian nationalism. These ethnic groups had historically lived together peacefully only when such coexistence was imposed, such as under the dictatorship of Tito. Recently, the spreading hostilities were temporarily brought to a halt by the NATO bombing campaign, responding to the Serbian government in Belgrade ordering thousands of Kosovars killed and uprooting hundreds of thousands more in a push to rid a province the size of Connecticut of its ethnic majority. There was widespread burning and looting, roundups and reprisals and summary executions. Serbian death squads worked from hit lists, hunting down intellectuals, journalists, doctors, human-rights activists, and community leaders.

To Freedman, the most astonishing reality to be confronted was that the largest NATO military action

in the alliance's fifty-year history had offered only be-
lated relief for that crude savaging of Kosovo. Yes,
the cruise missiles fired from the B-52 bombers and a
U.S. Sixth Fleet battle group in the Adriatic had
slammed into targets in Kosovo and Serbia; bombs
from F-15s, F-16s, Harriers, and F/A-18s hit Yugoslav
air defense systems, fuel and ammunition dumps, and
military barracks. They'd also pulverized Serbia's industrial and military infrastructure. The problem was
that the Albanian Kosovars had for the most part already been "ethnically cleansed," and an alarmingly
large percentage of refugees were still unwilling to return. The memory of neighbors and ethnic groups
committing atrocities against each other would take
generations to fade, if ever.

And now there was K-FOR, the NATO multina-
tional peacekeeping force, managing to maintain a
shaky peace in populated areas of the province, while
renegade Serb paramilitary forces continued to operate in the remote, mountainous, outlying areas of the
province, still burning the occasional village, still killing at random. They were countered by the KLA in
that wooded no-man's-land frontier of Kosovo's borders with Albania and Macedonia. Working with the
KLA also helped balance out the downside of high-
tech surveillance, since many U.S. surveillance systems
require a line-of-sight to work effectively. The craggy,
Balkan terrain hides much of what's going on.

The president finally looked up after having con-
templated his Pepsi for more than a minute. "Jesus.
We've got to figure out how the hell to pull this one
out of the fire. And this has to be an election year.
Damn it all."

He missed the look that passed between Gates and
Freedman; a glance that bespoke of their joint con-
tempt of decisions regarding the lives of fighting men
on foreign soil made for a domestic political reason,
which was usually the case. It's why soldiers invariably

distrusted politicians more than most people do. Freedman knew that the president was hardly unaware of this tension, and the reasons for it in this case.

NATO had undertaken the Kosovo mission with an understanding that Europe, not America, would shoulder the peacekeeping and reconstruction duties. Instead, NATO allies were squabbling and the "international police" in Kosovo that was supposed to bring law and order remained undermanned, underfinanced, and unable to cope.

Freedman cleared his throat. "Uh, sir. I think I have a deep-cover way in which this could be dealt with, possibly without word of it leaking to the media."

Gates harrumphed. "That'll be the day! The media has Kosovo covered like a rug."

Freedman shrugged, dismissing the observation. "In any case, my way would locate the pilots and extract them ASAP, before this can escalate diplomatically or militarily."

Gates eyed Freedman. "You're talking about TALON Force, aren't you? Eagle Team is halfway around the world."

Freedman nodded. "That's why they came to mind. Fact is, TALON Force Eagle Team is just winding up a mission in Iraq, extracting an American POW. The guy's on his way to a field hospital in Saudi, as we speak."

Gates pounded his fist on the table. "I want to go right into Kosovo and pull those pilots out too, Buck. But God knows if we've learned one thing, it's that Kosovo isn't Iraq."

The president paused a moment to take this observation into account, then locked eyes with Freedman across the width of the table.

"Buck, you tell me. Can they handle something like this?"

"TALON Force can handle anything, sir. The very

fact that they pulled off the MIA snatch in Iraq indicates to me that they're perfectly suited to do the same in Kosovo."

Gates nodded in reluctant agreement. "In my opinion, Mr. President, I'd say TALON Force Eagle Team is the only viable option we have."

"All right then." The president spoke decisively, as he always did after his advisors had made a decision for him. "I want TALON Force on this. I want them to locate and extract those pilots, and I *do* mean ASAP."

0730 hours
The desert, forty kilometers inside Saudi Arabia

The nearest field hospital was a mismatched collection of air-conditioned trailers and quonset huts.

By the time the Blackhawk touched down, the eastern sky was streaked broadly with the rosy hues of dawn. During the flight in from Iraq, the shadows of the desert had vanished before the coming onslaught of the heat of day.

The accompanying Apache gunships circled a quick aerial salute before hightailing it off into the wild blue yonder for their return flight to the airfield where they were based.

The Blackhawk set down with a light touch out of consideration for their passenger.

Behind the cockpit, Rivera was stretched out on the emergency cot. Sarah sat beside him, steadying the IV stand that was feeding vital, long-missing nutrients into his system. It would be a lengthy but successful recovery, she knew. Jenny had been able to tell that with one glance in her cockpit mirror at the relief shining on Sarah's face.

Sarah's features—pixieish with green eyes, freckles,

and a pale complexion—were practically unrecognizable from the snarling, murderous fury she emanated while riding the recoil of the enormous M-50. But at this moment, Sarah was in Florence Nightingale/Mother Theresa mode, reflected Jenny Olsen, not unkindly. As far as Jenny was concerned, this troubled old planet needed all the earth mothers it could get, and Sarah certainly qualified for that distinction with honors. In her role as TALON Force's medical specialist, Captain Sarah Greene took seriously—as in deeply felt, commitment-from-the-heart seriously—every human life entrusted to her.

Hospital personnel in medical white, pushing a gurney before them, rushed to the helo from the nearest quonset. They pounced aboard the Blackhawk to assume charge of Rivera, removing him from the aircraft as the pilot throttled down the engine to idle. The blades ceased their churning, but the big bird was ready for another quick takeoff.

The Apaches had promptly departed because that was standard SOP on a covert op like this, especially during daylight hours. TALON Force itself was supposed to be as gone from this field hospital as those Apaches were. But Jenny knew something about each one of her team partners, just as they knew her, and she knew that just like Sarah, Travis Barrett took every mission, every life he was charged with, as a deeply personal responsibility.

She unstrapped herself from the co-pilot seat of the Blackhawk's armor-plated cockpit and strode aft.

Everyone was already performing their post-operative chores with a minimum of conversation. A certain element of fatigue, more mental and spiritual than physical, clung to the atmosphere back here. The wisecracking camaraderie was the glue of a tight unit taking fire together. The natural, relaxed give-and-take of this bunch of highly competent warriors would manifest itself once again after they'd all got their breath back, Jenny knew. And of course there was the muting effect that came with the knowledge that they had *not* been in time to rescue the other POWs who'd been held at that Iraqi facility. They had been far too late for those poor mothers' sons. Nothing TALON Force could have done this day would have saved them, but that hardly eased a palpable, collective ache of disappointment.

Stan, Hunter, and Jack stood at the helo's armory, cleaning and reloading the XM-29s and the smart pistols. Weaponry of this technological sophistication required conscientious maintenance, particularly immediately following heavy use, so as to be equally dependable and smart when next needed.

Sarah was methodically organizing her work area and medical supplies. Sarah had long ago assimilated the necessary mental mechanism that allows the psyche to cut loose the human bonds established during a mission once that mission is finished. For a woman who cared as deeply about the world she lived in as Sarah did, this must have been her greatest discipline, and Jenny admired her for it.

Jenny paused momentarily at the Blackhawk's door to gaze out upon the grounds of this frontline field hospital and the surrounding landscape, which was every bit as bleak and featureless as the prison camp. Within thirty minutes, a med evac chopper would airlift Rivera to where he would receive full-line treatment, she knew. Within a week he'd be on his way to a debriefing and a hero's welcome. This ramshackle collection of structures, with its highly trained personnel and equipment, reminded her of a modern-day version of the MASH unit in the TV show.

As Jenny had expected, Travis was moving briskly alongside the gurney conveying Rivera to the quonset. The medics were expressing considerable irritation at his intrusion onto their turf.

Travis was still in full combat gear. Grime and splatters of other peoples' blood besotted his fatigues and face. Jenny smiled. It was her team leader's job to deliver Rivera into safe medical keeping, and so Travis would not withdraw until the gurney had actually been wheeled into the ER, where he could see with his own eyes that they were going to work on Rivera. Only then did Travis turn away from the building, striding purposefully back toward the Blackhawk. Jenny could not help but experience a wave of affection for the man. And they say us women are the emotional ones, she found herself thinking. So here comes rough-tough-mean-ass-mister-kill-machine Barrett . . . who can't do anything without a heartfelt commitment that always lingers despite his textbook training.

She was distracted from this mental meandering by the urgent crackle of an incoming transmission. She returned to the cockpit and plugged into the comm linkup. Seating herself, she opened her mouth to identify herself for the incoming transmission. Before she could speak, a good-natured voice started chattering into her ear without preamble.

"About time you picked up the phone, toots," said Sam Wong, chirping gamely across the comm net without preamble.

"I was taking a shower. By the way, Sam. Do the elders of the Chinese-American community in Flushing still rear young boys to call women 'toots?' "

Jenny tried real hard not to carry a feminist chip on her shoulder, but found this not always easy to do, dealing with this bunch of sexist knuckleheads.

TALON Force's communications expert was the pup of the group at age twenty-three, a Zen master of computers and electronics to the extent that Sam Wong was actually outfitted with special cybernetic implants that allowed him to access NSA's Top Secret Special Operations computers at Fort Meade, Maryland, from anywhere on the planet.

"Sorry, toots." His habitual, snappy patter didn't skip a beat. "I meant the term with all due respect."

Jenny closed her eyes. "So what's up, info man? We've just dropped off our cargo inside Saudi and I'm about to airlift us the heck back to Brindisi."

"Precisely the reason for pestering you." Sam's voice always sounded crisply clear across the comm net. He could have been speaking from inside one of those hospital buildings right here in the Saudi desert, or from as far away as the North Pole instead of from Riyadh, here inside Saudi. Sam could be irksome at times, thought Jenny, but there was no denying that the workaholic techno-geek was as committed to this special ops unit as any of the rest of them. He was, in fact, the vital link. Modern technological warfare is fueled via information, and that was Sam's job. "We're jumping the gun a little on this one, but something big is breaking. It's going down right now, and it's one hot potato."

"You sound pretty sure of yourself, Sam."

"The general is. He says to instruct you to install yourselves amidst the beautiful environs of the Brindisi air base until we get there. The general wants us in place for something special."

Jenny saw Travis leap aboard the Blackhawk. He gave her a thumbs-up sign. She nodded to the pilot, who revved the big bird into takeoff.

She continued her conversational bantering with Sam, wherever he and the general might be. She knew only that this crystal-clear transmission was being satellite-beamed directly to the Blackhawk via communications channels of Sam's devising, so secure as to be impervious to eavesdropping even by agencies of the U.S. government.

"Can you clue us in at all, Sam? You know how Trav hates surprises."

"Well, let's not get his panties in a knot," said Sam. "Okay, but remember that this is a breaking story as the media likes to say, although even they don't know about this one yet."

"Say, that is hot."

"Kosovo." There was nothing wiseguy in the way Sam pronounced the name of that place. "See you in Brindisi," he added.

Chapter 4

The dreams became nightmares for Captain Larry
Davis, and the nightmares became terrible beasts of
horror that chased him to the edges of his sanity . . .
until the Air Force pilot awoke, soaked in cold sweat.

The stench of fear filled his nostrils and made him
wince. Pain vibrated through him.

They'd placed him in a ten-by-ten foot square room,
empty except for a ratty red plastic lawn chair in one
corner. The walls of the room were white. The ceiling
was white, as was the linoleum floor, with some choco-
late swirls that did little to break the monotony. The
overly bright florescent lighting gave the place the
starkness of an operating room. The door was locked,
of course, and there was no way to turn off the overhead light. A wire mesh was effectively designed to
prevent tampering with the switch. The room could
have been anywhere; near the point where he and
Jackson had parachuted into Kosovo or Macedonia,
or in a subbasement or penthouse level of a ware-
house or an executive suite, from Belgrade to
Moscow.

They'd left him alone in the room for some twenty-
four hours.

He couldn't be sure because they took his wristwatch along with everything but his BVDs. He relied on his inner body clock. Leaving him along for twenty-four hours in an uncomfortable, lighted room in uncertain surroundings. It was standard interrogation procedure.

He tried to catnap, but could not. The nightmares kept waking him up each time he started to slip into a fitful sleep.

This time, he and Carol and the kids were at the beach. In the dream, the Davis family had the flawless expanse of beach to themselves. The day was pristine, the sky a cobalt blue, the ocean like turquoise glass barely stirred by a salty breeze. Gulls were cawing. Waves lapped gently. In the dream, Larry was spreading suntan lotion across his wife's lovely, tanned, freckled shoulders. They were on a blanket by the cooler, keeping an eye on the kids, and everything was perfect. That is, until the sky darkened to coal black although daylight remained. The children only had time to scream, he and Carol only had time to leap to their feet, before the ocean turned blood red and the wave that crested over their startled children left nothing in its wake. . . .

Davis sat up from his prone position on the linoleum floor and leaned his back against the wall, his forehead lowered to a forearm drawn across his knee. He inhaled with slow, steady breaths, replaying in his mind the events that had brought him to this point. He and Jackson in the formation of F-16s. A NATO air strike on a renegade company of Serb paramilitaries who'd been raising hell in the mountains. They'd taken a hit. They'd bailed. And when Davis thought of his buddy dying from that stitching across the chest of AK-47 slugs fired by the Serbs . . . that's when he came fully awake.

The door to the room suddenly slammed inward against the inside wall, opening for the first time since he'd been brought in here. A pair of surly guys in field fatigues stormed in, toting AK-47 rifles.

Without speaking a word, each of them grabbed one of Davis's bare arms, yanking him to his feet and dragging him from the room before he even had a chance to mutter a protest. Even for a guy who prided himself on his buff physical condition, after spending twenty-four hours nearly naked and cold in his skivvies, kept awake partly by the stench of where he'd had no choice but to defecate in the corner of that spotless bare room, the notion of trying now to appear macho or show resistance, even if he could, was ludicrous. He was at the mercy of these thugs, and that was *not* something to comfort the soul.

They left the room and dragged him across what appeared to be the front office of a wholesale business that was no longer operational. There was a receptionist's desk, an expensively carpeted waiting room, and eerily quiet offices of whatever thriving business had resided in these remote mountains. Lumbering or mining, Davis decided.

But right now there was only him, one hapless bastard, being dragged brusquely across the polished marble floor by a couple of Neanderthals. They force-marched him toward the double glass front doorway. They wore their arrogance proudly, like a Klansman wears a hood. These were the scum that burned villages, drove the elderly and infants out into the cold in the dead of winter, machine-gunned untold thousands of civilians before NATO intervention had brought it to an end. They marched him along like automatons, their eyes flat. As with the KLA that warred against these Serbs, only the strong had survived in these holdout units; the baddest of the bad on both sides. As they shouldered aside the tinted glass doors, an image came to Davis of the essence of what this was all about: the barbarians not only *at* but storming *through* the gates of civilization.

They emerged into bright sunshine.

The Serbs practically popped his shoulders from their sockets hauling him across a paved square. The warm sun felt good after the chilly otherworldliness of his confinement, but Davis's feet were killing him. His bare feet had squeaked across the marble floor, scraped bloodily across the pavement, and now they pounded one after the other as the Serbs hauled him roughly down a flight of concrete steps.

The pain coursing through his body was the trigger that brought Davis to full mental clarity. Tendrils of the unspeakable nightmare had released their hold on him.

Davis tried to ignore the desperation within him, instead doing his best to take note of the surroundings he was being navigated through.

They were in the mountains, all right. Snow-capped peaks formed a backdrop to this industrial site, which had been carved out from a remote wilderness. The valley was surrounded by what appeared to be a cordon of impenetrable peaks. Davis recognized none of them from his briefings or maps. As any soldier knows, being "on the ground" gives one a decidedly different point of view of the terrain than as seen from the air.

The Serbs steered him toward a low, long structure. Davis detected engine smells. Gasoline. They were taking him to the garage; the motor pool

He had managed to regain his footing and was trotting along now. The brisk, pine-scented mountain air produced wonders, the fresh oxygen flowing into his lungs, coursing through him. His bare feet hurt like the devil, but he was damned if he was going to allow these cretinous goons to drag him between them as if he were a slave. He would meet his fate on his feet, he told himself. He continued to glance down.

This was a timber business, as he'd suspected. Ordinarily, had the mill been operational, he'd have smelled cut lumber and would have heard the loading of trucks for what must be a lengthy, winding trip down out of these mountains to whatever outpost of civilization was nearby. He saw stacked lumber and a few parked trucks and forklifts here and there, but what was obviously a once-bustling concern was now deserted and unpopulated.

Or at least that's the way it looks from thirty thousand feet up or from higher up in outer space from a spy satellite, Davis thought. Naturally, he viewed everything as an airman, and the closer he and his guards got to the garage structure, the more obvious it became to him that those unattended trucks and forklifts were left out for exactly that reason: to fool surveillance pilots and spy satellites. The office building behind him and most of the other structures, he knew, would be populated with Serb renegade troopers like the two who had him now.

He was hauled into the garage.

It was an industrious place. Men whose ages ranged from their late teens well into their forties were servicing several beat-up American Jeeps and a German deuce-and-a-half. AK-47s were propped against toolboxes and vehicles for quick access as the grease monkeys labored. Except for a few snickers at Davis's apparel, or lack thereof, the mechanics hardly looked up as the rifle-bearing thugs dragged Davis past the bays to a glassed-in-enclosure; what had once been the office of the foreman and the dispatcher, Davis surmised.

Behind a cleared, elegantly inlaid oak desk that must have been the foreman's pride and joy sat a cocky punk in cammo fatigues that matched the others', but were clean and pressed. He was in his late twenties and sat there indolently, his raised legs crossed at the ankles across the desk as he idly inspected the action of a 9mm pistol. He wore the field rank of a major in the Serb army.

Davis reasoned that the file on this hard case must have been erased when NATO moved in to exert pressure on removing Kosovo war criminals from the Serb military. Unfortunately, NATO lacked the resources to apprehend many of these guys.

Initially, this one's first reaction upon Davis being brought before him was to not acknowledge the prisoner's presence until he had first completed inspection of his sidearm. He palmed a magazine into the pistol's handle with a practiced motion and chambered a round, holstering the weapon in a shoulder rig. Only then did he deign to look up at the man standing tall before him. A sneer curled the Serb's lips. They were the lips of a sensuous girl, and there was a youthful pink to this one's cheeks. But there was disdain in his eyes, which were cold as slate.

Davis thought, Oh shit. Everything else, and I've got to deal with a punk renegade Serb CO who thinks he's got something to prove. He decided to try playing this one by the books, which meant biting his tongue, remaining proud, and letting this little creep get in the first word.

The little creep obliged.

"I am Captain Dalma. I am commander of this detachment." Dalma did not uncross his ankles from the desktop or lean forward in the expensive leather swivel chair. "You have been shot down over my sector. You are my prisoner."

Davis said dutifully, not making eye contact with Dalma but speaking to the wall directly in front of him, "Captain Larry Davis. United States Air Force. Serial Number—"

"Can it," said Dalma, as if bored by someone reciting an uninteresting story.

Davis blinked. The guy's diction was pure American.

Dalma nodded slothfully to the guards, who simultaneously released their twin vise holds on Davis.

This caught Davis unexpectedly. His knees wobbled,

but he stretched his arms outward from his side, managing to maintain his military bearing.

Dalma chuckled, and the pair of Serbs stepped back and joined in his mirth. Dalma swung his legs down off the desk, his boots thumping to the floor. He leaned forward, his icy eyes drilling holes into Davis. The impression of idle sloth was only image. Davis had known that from the beginning. This kid in a Serb commandant's uniform might be young in years, but he wouldn't be where he was if he had not committed more than his share of atrocities and knew how to command fear and respect among goons. Davis saw this in those cold eyes and it made him want to puke.

Dalma said, "Yeah. You heard me. Can it. You thought you were a long way from home, didn't you, flyboy? Well, you are. But so was I, for a while. Worked at my uncle's shoe store in Newark for a year and a half."

Davis decided that by-the-rules would never work with this guy. He must play the hand that was dealt him. He knew about dealing with hard cases. This Serb SOB wanted to pretend that as a downed pilot, Captain Larry Davis was not officially a prisoner of war under the international rules of the Geneva Convention? Okay, thought Davis. That's the hand I play.

The two guards stood nearby without seeming to blink or take their eyes from him. Their AK-47s were slung back over their shoulders, but their hands were ready to bring those guns around and open fire on Davis at a word from Dalma.

Sounds of work and conversation from the mechanics filtered through the open glass door leading to the garage. Beyond the repair bays could be seen the company grounds that, to any prying eye, looked for all the world like a temporarily closed-down company, perhaps for some remodeling, one that would soon be back in business.

Davis looked at the man behind the desk. "Nice place you've got here. Another family business?"

Dalma allowed an oily smile. "It is now. We liberated this factory."

"I guessed that much. And the real owner is . . . ?" Davis let the question dangle.

Dalma shrugged at what was obviously an insignificant matter to him. "Relocated."

"In other words, the rightful owner and his family are lying somewhere in an unmarked grave."

"He was not the owner," Dalma corrected him with mock earnestness. "He was the manager. The corporation that owns this facility believes it to still be fully operational."

"That would take one hell of a connection for you to have in the government, wouldn't it?"

Davis eyed the captain closely, waiting for a response. Any intel he could gather during his captivity would be passed on during debriefing upon his release. That is, of course, if he survived . . .

Dalma relaxed his posture, removing his elbows from the polished desktop and leaning back to stroke his chin and scrutinize the man before him with a crafty gaze. "I'd think that you'd be more concerned with *your* fate."

Davis shrugged. Doing so ached, but he wanted to let this little punk know that an American fighting man didn't cave quite that easily. "If you wanted me dead, I'd already be dead. That pilot your men did kill, by the way . . . he was a personal friend of mine."

The Serb didn't quite yawn, but conveyed that impression. "Too bad. Fortune or war, isn't that what it's called? Now, about you, Captain."

Davis interrupted for the same reason he'd shrugged. "I'm screwed. Obviously, you've got my ass. I'm dead meat if that's the way you want it." He tossed a contemptuous nod in the direction of the riflemen. "You think I don't know that that's what

Ben and Jerry are all about? You could order me taken outside and have them blow my brains out right now, if you felt like it."

"Or I could do it myself." Dalma's eyes glinted with amusement. "You're a ballsy motherfucker, I'll say that for you, Captain Davis."

"You stashed me in that storage room across the way for, what was it, twenty-four hours?"

Dalma leaned forward again, the amusement replaced by growing respect and wariness. "Exactly twenty-four hours."

Davis nodded. "You wanted to soften me up, keep me from raising a ruckus and making a pain in the ass of myself. It couldn't be that you want to pump me for information. Anything I have, your computer people in Belgrade have."

Dalma conceded this with a modest tip of his head. "We're supplied with NATO intelligence across cyberspace and the airwaves. This *is* the information millennium, even way out here."

"Too bad your motives are so damned primitive," said Davis. "You Serbs cloak yourselves in military jargon and uniforms and ethnic bullshit, but real soldiers *defend*. You and your cutthroats live off the land like common hill bandits."

Dalma raised an eyebrow, nodding to the guards. "Careful, Captain. I could translate for Ben and Jerry. They take offense easily."

"They won't lay a hand on me unless you tell them to. You're the big shit here. But don't worry. I know why I'm being kept alive."

Dalma's eyes hooded. "And why is that?"

"You're under direct orders from Belgrade. You wouldn't be funded or allowed to operate any other way. This ball is still in play. It has been that way since World War I kicked off the last century. Bosnia, Kosovo . . . hell, there are plenty of trouble spots waiting to explode. I'm being put on ice as a future bargaining chip."

Dalma nodded. "*If* you cooperate. *If* you do not cause trouble." He gestured as if granting a broad proclamation. "Then you may live to see your beloved America once again."

Davis remembered what he had seen before entering the garage. "I saw signs of construction when your goons dragged me over here."

Dalma chose to ignore this remark. "You will be taken to your permanent quarters now. Your permanent quarters, that is, until your ultimate fate is determined." He started to issue this command to the two guards.

Davis pressed. "I can understand you moving your command post over here to the motor pool, away from the main building, in case NATO bombers decide to make a flyover and take a whack. I'm talking about what used to be the sawmill, judging from the timber that's stacked outside. Except it isn't a sawmill. Not anymore. There are signs of recent construction all over the place. Why? What the hell's going on here?"

Dalma sighed. "I should've known that you'd be as uncooperative as possible." He turned, uttering a harsh order.

One of the guards stepped forward, rapidly unslung his AK-47, raised it, and delivered a direct blow to Davis's head with the rifle butt.

Davis experienced a blinding burst of pain that blotted out everything. His unconscious body slumped to the floor.

Dalma stood up from behind the desk. Everything Davis had said was absolutely true about Belgrade wanting this pilot kept isolated. The body of the other airman, Jackson, had been destroyed and disposed of; it would never be found, no matter what Davis's fate. Dalma snapped off another order to his soldiers, who grabbed Davis under each arm and dragged the unconscious man from the office.

Dalma watched through the glass partition as the guards disappeared from his line of vision, leaving the garage with Davis in tow.

A door in the wall adjacent to Dalma's desk opened.

Dalma turned to face the man to whom he was directly responsible, who had arrived from Belgrade by helicopter only hours ago.

Deputy Minister Viktor Tilzo appeared on record to be a minor, insignificant human cog in the bureaucratic clockworks of an obscure agency charged with prioritizing allocated monies to Belgrade citizens displaced during the '99 bombing. This "minor bureaucrat" escaped all attention of the overworked personnel assigned by NATO to deal with the Belgrade government, affording Tilzo complete autonomy in his primary assignment, which was overseeing "unauthorized" field operations such as Captain Dalma's.

Tilzo was a meek, bespectacled man in his mid-fifties. The lenses of his glasses were thick. His gray hair was thin. His East European suit fit a bulky frame that had once been muscular, but age and years as a government bureaucrat had softened Tilzo's chin line. But his eyes were hard as iron. "He will be a trouble, that one." Though physically slight in comparison to the youthful Dalma, the man from Belgrade spoke with consummate authority.

"He'll be closely guarded around the clock." Dalma's assurance was prompt and deferential.

"I did not care for his observation concerning the . . ." Tilzo paused briefly, as if searching for the proper word. ". . . the renovations that have been completed here. I doubt now that bringing Captain Davis here was the best course of action, Captain. This may be frowned upon by my superiors."

"I'll have him transferred," Dalma said.

"No." Tilzo's brow creased thoughtfully. "Let him stay. Belgrade may decide to 'find' and release him at any time. As of now, he knows nothing. To move him now would only arouse his suspicions and that would be no good for us, I can assure you, Captain. No good for *you,* I should say," he added ominously.

"Be that as it may, Deputy Minister, we do hold Captain Davis. This camp is ready to implement operations." Dalma spoke briskly, so as to impress Tilzo as a supremely efficient field commander. "May I ask then, when will we, uh, commence?"

"This killing begins at midnight tonight." Tilzo moved to settle his bulk into the swivel chair behind the desk. "Now then, Dalma, fetch me some vodka. I'm thirsty."

"Yes, sir."

Dalma appreciated that his command of this installation was a vital responsibility and therefore worth currying favor with the likes of Tilzo. He had not known the nature of this assignment when he'd first been handed it, but he was proud to be associated with this opportunity to kill more Kosovars. It was the surest route to promotion. His hope was to attain an appointment in some sort of law enforcement position in Belgrade. He would be closer to the center of Serb power and at the same time, he would then be "legitimized." Dalma would kill as many people as it took to achieve that goal.

Until now, all ethnic cleansing had been systematic in the sense that Serb soldiers and paramilitary groups had gone about the attempted eradication of the Albanian Kosovars through a strategy of village-to-village destruction, sweeping through entire communities. Alternately, the present "quiet" war in this remote mountain region was about to take on an enormous new dimension.

The sawmill had been remodeled on the inside to become no less than a mass gas chamber, linked to a crematorium. Very quietly, while no one was watching, Dalma's detachment had provided security while these renovations were made.

The tests had been run.

What was essentially a modern-day Auschwitz in the mountains of Macedonia was now ready to go operational.

Chapter 5

October 23, 1145 hours
The NATO airfield near Brindisi, Italy

The airfield was a sprawling, highly secured complex of runways, lengthy and durable enough to accommodate the F-15 Eagles and F-16 Falcons, and the enormous, Stealth-like F-117 Nighthawks that had flown countless sorties from there during the NATO bombing campaign.

General Jack Krauss held a briefing with TALON Force Eagle Team in a hangar at a remote corner of the base. The seven members of the team were assembled around a folding table in one corner of the hangar.

Each TALON Force member was leafing through a manila folder of information supplied to them moments earlier by Sam. The team was clad in civvies, except for Travis and Sam. As for Sam Wong, his rank of captain was only temporary. He was "on loan" from the NSA and so preferred to make the most of it, and with his typical youthful exuberance, came to the briefing in uniform, thus allowing him to proudly display his twin silver bars, temporary or not.

The tart scent of oil and grease permeated the atmosphere. A ground crew had been hard at work on the disassembled engine of an F-15 but were cleared out thirty minutes earlier. The grumpy protestations of their CO were mollified by the general's assurance that this briefing would, in fact, be brief. Krauss sympathized with the officer in charge of the ground crew. These guys were functioning at peak capacity to keep the NATO planes safe and in the air, and they didn't appreciate interruptions. But with something as sensitive as this, Krauss wanted a place that could not be bugged, and could not be the source of any sort of leak. After a quick scouting expedition upon his and Sam's arrival at Brindisi, they had selected this hangar.

General Krauss paced as he spoke, as was his custom during a briefing. He was fiftyish, ramrod straight, and his only nod to personal style in his otherwise strict military appearance was a carefully trimmed moustache. For anyone who might be interested stateside, he had taken a brief, personal "family matter" leave from his desk at the Pentagon. The number of those who knew he was in Italy equaled less than the fingers of one hand, just as very few, even at the highest levels of government, were even aware of the existence of TALON Force.

Krauss began. "The CIA's contacts on the ground in Kosovo have been reporting vague rumors picked up by anti-Serb factions about an American aviator being held by a renegade Serbian military detachment stationed in the mountains between Kosovo and Macedonia. And when I say mountains, ladies and gentlemen, what I mean is rugged, remote frontier."

"How recent is the intel from the ground?" asked Travis. He sat at the head of the table, wearing starched, plain U.S. Army fatigues. Travis was never out of uniform. Krauss always had to grin inwardly whenever he thought of what Travis's personnel file listed as his stated religion: *Army*.

Krauss said, "That file before you was updated less than ten minutes ago, just before we left crypto for the drive over here. You'll find in that file what the ground contact reported, pertinent maps of the region, profiles on the indigenous personnel that you'll more than likely be working with and against and computer projections of realistic scenarios and strategies."

The members who had been involved in the fire-heavy Iraqi mission had sufficient time to rest up and refresh, and looked collectively healthy and well-scrubbed and as different from each other as any seven people could be, General Krauss reflected. TALON Force was the world of covert ops at its most ultra high-tech; the highest tech force America had. As commanding officer of the Technologically Augmented, Low-Observable, Networked Force, Krauss considered his unit to be the ultimate military special team, composed as it was of a Navy SEAL, a Marine Force Recon, an Air Force Rescue and an Army Green Beret, top echelon military commandos to a man, along with a female Army medic, a female Naval Intelligence officer, and a National Security Council communications expert. Except for Sam, each force member was in remarkable physical shape.

Krauss finally stopped pacing. His eyes swept the faces of these men and women. "Your job is to go in and locate those two downed pilots in those mountains. If they're alive, bring them out. Simple, no?"

Sam stepped forward. Krauss nodded for him to interject.

"Like the general said, I've verified, identified, and assessed the intel from the people on the ground for you," said Sam. The specialist shed his glib lightness whenever it came time for serious business. Sam was skinny and nearsighted, with the horn-rimmed glasses that most techno-geeks seem born with. "But to say the least, the situation over there is fluid, which is why Kosovo pops up and down in the domestic media like a yo-yo. People don't massacre each other's families and burn their villages, then make nice and rebuild and go back to being good neighbors. What I'm saying is that the people on the ground will have new intel for you, more than likely before I can beam it to you.

You're going into a theater of operations that can best be described as a minefield or quicksand, your choice of metaphor."

General Krauss turned to Travis. "So there it is, Major. Your assignment is to formulate a workable operation and implement it."

"Yes, sir. We're on it. How long before logistical support is in place?"

Krauss resumed pacing, a man who thought better when he was moving. "I'm setting up that end now. We should have you in country within eight hours."

Jack DuBois, seated next to Travis, shrugged his six-foot-five muscular frame that made the metal folding chair beneath him seem like one made for a preschooler. "It does sound simple enough. We're going in after Americans in enemy hands, like in Iraq. That's the sort of mission this team was put together for."

"That is not precisely correct," countered Krauss. "The mission you just got back from, and the entire Gulf War for that matter, was a study in simplicity compared to what we've gotten involved with in Kosovo."

Sarah Greene sat next to Jack. She tossed him a droll glance and tapped the manila folder in front of her.

"I think that's why we're supposed to read this file." Sarah's off-duty appearance was wholesome. Although she would never have what was considered a model's figure, at five-foot-four she was the picture of casual feminine comfort in a flattering blue linen dress. "We're going into what sounds more like Vietnam than Iraq."

Sam Wong nodded in agreement. "She's right. Everyone you'll be dealing with over there has a bone to pick, especially after this past year."

Jack faked a yawn. "Sounds simple any way you slice it. Travis puts a plan together, the general approves the plan, we get our logistic, and we're on it.

Except for Sam, of course, which may be just as well. Sam's the only one of us who can stare at so many computer screens and not go batty."

Krauss nodded. "As a matter of fact, Captain, that does succinctly sum up the mission." Krauss had always appreciated the directness these people embodied, as exemplified by this conversational give and take around the table.

Stan chuckled. "And what makes Sam any less crazy than the rest of us, Jack? He's no more or less nuts. He's just smarter."

"That's not saying a lot. And you don't fool me, DuBois," countered Sam. "You're as tied up as everyone else about what's going to happen next. Even us city slickers have to get a case of nerves every once in a while."

Sam's best buddy in the group was Jack. They'd both grown up in big cities and, though they didn't often give voice to it, barely veiled their opinions of the others on the team as country hicks.

Hunter Blake was seated across from Sarah and Jack. His chiseled, suntanned Californian surfer-boy good looks were complimented with the Italian-cut threads he picked out that morning in Brindisi. Hunter looked every inch the ladies' man, from his slicked-back hair and ever-present shades down to his expensive leather shoes.

"Well then." He started to stand. "Unless my presence is vitally required, I think I'll utilize my time here in Italy to pursue my interest in the local female population. I sure did see some fine looking *signorinas* on my shopping trip this morning."

Jenny sat in the chair next to him. She leaned back and studied Hunter, clearly not impressed. "I don't know, Romeo. Dressed like that, about all you're going to attract are streetwalkers looking for a customer."

Sam couldn't stifle a chuckle. "Or a pimp."

Hunter laughed. "Hey, what's to apologize for? There *are* nice hookers in the world, y'know!"

"Belay that, all of you," said Travis. "No one's going anywhere until we fly out for Kosovo. You heard the general. We've got some lag time here. We're going to put it to good use."

Hunter sighed. "I should have known. Training, right?"

Travis nodded. "There's a training facility near here, perfectly suited to us."

Jenny chuckled at Hunter's subdued disappointment. "Don't worry, Hunter. The ladies aren't going anywhere, and you sure don't need any training where they're concerned. They need training to deal with you!"

Stan Powczuk hadn't been listening to the joshing. Instead, until now he had been perusing his file with the focus of a speed-reader. In the field, Stan was second in command to Travis. Bearded and muscular, he was generally possessed of a hearty disposition when relaxed. But he was rarely relaxed at a briefing. He palmed the file shut with an unenthusiastic snort and looked across the table at Sam.

"With all due respect, Sammy, this package of yours in based on intel provided by the same bunch of nincompoops who had our fliers mistakenly target the Chinese embassy in Belgrade during last year's bombing. Why should their intel now be any more accurate than it was then?" Stan narrowed his eyes. "Your brilliant analysis and your gizmo projections don't mean shit if they're based on faulty intel," he told Sam. "The sooner we get over there to get our own take, the better." He lightened up with a grin in Hunter's direction. "Sorry to interfere with your love life, surfboy."

Hunter pretended to be miffed. "*Playboy*, if you please."

"So how reliable is this intelligence of ours?" asked

Jenny with a sober, inquisitive expression on her super model face.

Krauss again ceased pacing, a sure sign to everyone present that this briefing was about over.

"The intel is as reliable as we can make it. You will begin improvising on your own the minute we get you on the ground, and of course there will be steady intel downlinks from Sam. Good luck, people. Right now, Sam and I have places to go and people to see, and I think we've used up all the time I promised to take from the ground crew for use of their hangar."

They stood as one from the table.

Travis glanced ruefully at Krauss. "Uh, call it a soldier's hunch, General, and I mean no disrespect." His Texas drawl was a mite broader than usual. "But I've got me a feeling in my gut that there's something else we ought to know about."

Krauss paused, facing the members of the team awaiting his response. "It's what I was talking about, passing along fresh intel as soon as it substantiated."

Jenny frowned. "I don't read the tabloids, but I think in this case, inquiring minds want to know."

"That's why I was going to hold off until we have something solid for you," said Krauss. "The problem is, there's nothing to know, only vague, unsubstantiated rumors."

Sam wore an earnest, contrite expression. "You'll get it in country before you go into the mountains."

Stan snorted again. "So what's the harm in telling us now?"

Sarah's eyes twinkled mischievously. "Come on, Krauss. Be one of the girls. Dish us some dirt."

Krauss harrumphed. He was not always comfortable with the sad fact that, among these field-tested, battle-forged mavericks, rank was not much recognized nor accorded its due. Krauss again appraised each of them in turn as he spoke.

"Okay, you want vague, as yet unsubstantiated rumors? We got 'em in spades."

Jack grunted under his breath. "About damn time."

Krauss pretended not to hear that. "There may be a new wrinkle in what the Serbs are up to in those mountains."

Hunter had dropped his playboy glibness. His mouth set into a grim line. "What kind of new wrinkle?"

Krauss sighed wearily, which was unlike him. "We have unsubstantiated fragments of intel just beginning to filter down out of those mountains that suggest the Serbs may be about to implement a new, very different, method of dealing with the Kosovar Albanians."

"What about NATO?" Jenny asked.

"That's where some of the rumors are being reported from. It's just too damn thin at this point." Frustration darkened Krauss's somber eyes. "All we have as we speak are the vaguest vibes possible. We're utilizing all of our resources to develop it, believe me."

Sam interjected, "And you *will* be updated on an hourly basis, per SOP."

Travis's eyes were on the general. "I've got another hunch."

"Let's hear it, Major."

"My hunch says that if we should happen to encounter whatever it is we're talking about, we are also expected to nullify such Serb action."

"Right as usual, Major. Any objections?"

"Wouldn't have it any other way," said Travis.

Chapter 6

At precisely noon, Ceca Keloni rose from behind her desk in the small, barren, two-person office in the government building at the center of town. She picked up her purse and, as always, nodded civilly to her co-worker, a woman of Albanian extraction who, like Ceca, was in her mid-twenties and labored diligently behind a desk.

Their desks, which faced each other, were both overflowing with paperwork. There was not a computer in sight.

Her co-worker observed but chose not to return the nod, continuing with the unending stream of forms and files that flowed through their cramped office for processing and rerouting. They exchanged words only when absolutely necessary during the course of their job, and then only in the most strained of tones. Ceca knew that her co-worker's brother and father had been murdered by Serb paramilitaries the year before. She understood the woman's barely contained hostility and had come to accept it.

As she left the office, Ceca thought, If she only knew . . .

She strolled down the central corridor of the building, past the open doors of offices that bustled with activity, with the clacking of computer printers and terse male conversations in several languages and dialects.

She emerged into the sunshine from the main entrance, which was pockmarked with bullet holes and chipped masonry from the fighting that had gone on over this small provincial town that was as strategic as it was remote. She stepped past the sandbagged machine gun placements, exchanging brief, pleasant nods with the soldiers stationed there. She had never had much difficulty gaining a smile or a second glance from men.

At five-foot-three and one hundred and seven pounds, Ceca had the strongly defined facial lines of a Serbian woman, dominated by a sharp jawline, a full, lush-lipped mouth and soulful eyes. Her dyed-blonde hair fell softly onto her shoulders, worn loose today. She wore a print dress and a light cotton blouse with long sleeves.

This town, where she had been born and lived all of her life, was at the foot of the Shar Mountains. Suva Reka was the southernmost outpost of civilization on the Kosovo side of the frontier border with Macedonia. At this elevation, a nippy, constant breeze wafted down, carrying the scent of pine and the chill of the surrounding rugged peaks that retained their snowy caps throughout the year.

As was her daily custom, she hurried along the crowded streets and sharp hills of town in the direction of the four-unit apartment house where she resided and cared for her elderly, frail father in a modest two-room kitchenette. She always enjoyed her midday visits home with Papa, relishing the pleasure of the conversation along with the meager servings of food she prepared for them. They would always eat at the table by the window, overlooking the street.

Once the street had bustled with industrious, healthy faces, people on their way to or from the market. Then, her conversations with Papa would touch subjects far and wide, from world politics to soccer (her father's passion) to a sharing of standard small-town news. These days, the faces on the street reflected a pitiable bleakness and desperation. Only the occasional ragged figure shuffled by listlessly, without destination.

Ceca found herself more and more doing her best trying to keep these daily conversations with her father light, or at least skirting the horrors that had and were unfolding in what had once been their beautiful, beloved, peaceful Kosovo. She had thought of suggesting that she and Papa move, but she knew he would never agree. Her mother, Papa's wife of fifty-one years, was buried in this town's cemetery. Mama had passed three years earlier. No, Mr. Keloni would never leave Suva Reka, and the thought of abandoning her father had never been an option to Ceca. So she continued to do her best, keeping her spirits up even as she watched her father's health dwindle away day by day. He had never fully recovered from the loss of her mother, which is why she considered it all the more important to keep Papa engaged in their daily conversations, which she also felt did him much good. Mr. Keloni was not unaccustomed to lecturing, having been the local schoolteacher until government cutbacks a decade earlier had eliminated his position. Teaching had been her father's entire life. Her father had been a learned, informed, gifted teacher . . . and still was, as far as Ceca was concerned. But a stroke shortly after Mama's passing left Papa partly paralyzed and unable to seek any sort of employment. Yet her father's mind remained keen and lucid. She often forgot to end their conversations in time for her return walk to the government building for her afternoon shift.

As she walked along now at a brisk pace, the government building disappearing around a corner behind her, Ceca made an effort to avert her eyes from the open hostility that glowered in her direction from many of those she passed by; the soulless stares of those who until not so long ago had homes, possessions; people who had gone to Pristina to go shopping at the mall, who watched soccer on television and tucked their loved ones in at night. Now they were the homeless, the shattered of mind, soul, and spirit who wandered aimlessly, some in shock, some predatory, seeking shelter where they could find it, surviving on what they could scavenge. These were people on both sides of the horrors of Kosovo; rural, civilian Albanians and Serbs, stricken by what Ceca's people had wrought.

The aftermath of the NATO bombing and occupation had not slowed the tide of vengeance as person after person, shopkeeper to clergy to student, were found at dawn, sprawled in a pool of blood, drawn from their bed or from their job and killed to settle a blood debt, or to simply "even the score."

She felt shame for what had happened, as she knew many Serbs did, but this did not differentiate her from all other Serbs in the hateful, spiteful eyes of her co-worker or the displaced Albanians she now passed as she hurried through the old town's winding streets.

Ceca Keloni held a degree in journalism from the University in Belgrade and had been employed as a government employee for five years. But the fact of the matter was that the central government was not overly inclined to trust Ceca since she was considered to be of the intellectual class because of her degree, despite the fact that she had returned after graduation to this remote region of her upbringing. The Serb campaign of ethnic cleansing had the ultimate result of only making things worse for the 10 percent Serb population within the province of Kosovo. Since before the beginning of this violence, Serb intellectuals had voiced opposition, seeing not only the eventual consequences but also being repulsed by the inhumane carnage. Ceca had been in Kosovo throughout the worst of it.

If only they knew . . .

She was secretly conducting an affair with the regional commander of the Kosovo Liberation Army. They had been lovers for more than a year. Even her own father did not know about this, and she hoped that Papa would never find out. Prejudice is emotional, not intellectual, Papa had once told her. And yet she knew that even he was not immune. Hatred ran deep in Kosovo, and never deeper than the present. God forgive us all, Ceca thought. So many had died. A single death because of ethnicity would have been too many.

She had grown up in Suva Reka, where a young woman could take for granted the simple pleasures of the rural life: a mother waiting in the doorway for her when she, a pigtailed child, would return home from school or play; a father, distinguished and respected in the community by Serbs and Albanians alike. All of it was gone now. Her mother had died from a merciless cancer. And her father seemed to be barely hanging on. At least she knew they had been spared from anti-Serb vendettas. Mr. Keloni was revered as a fine and great man by both ethnic groups of Suva Reka. For this Ceca was grateful, and proud.

She rounded a street corner, turning onto an avenue. It was a neighborhood comprised of identical buildings; drab, unimaginatively designed utilitarian structures, housing units constructed during the Tito regime. The buildings yielded to the passage of time and lack of maintenance but had at least been spared the ravages she had seen on television news reports of demolished towns and villages in other parts of the province. War had not yet come to her birthplace.

Then she saw something ahead of her in the street.

She stopped walking, knowing that she stood out because there were fewer pedestrians along this street.

This is where the people lived who, like herself, had managed to hold employment, and so the local police force felt obliged to provide them "protection" from those aimlessly wandering throngs she had passed through.

She saw, and mentally processed everything she saw, in the length of time it took for a single heart-beat.

Then she begun running forward.

An official vehicle, a panel van with provincial government markings and a flashing rooftop light, was parked in front of the apartment house where she and her father lived.

The civilians of Kosovo did not consider it prudent these days to interfere with any sort of public exhibition of authority. A smattering of onlookers stood across the street, watching from a safe distance with that relief-that-it-isn't-me look on their faces, craning their necks for a better view.

She was halfway to the building when she saw her father being led out through the main entrance. A uniformed Serb guided him with a fist gripping each of his shoulders. Her father wore a bewildered, disoriented expression and allowed himself to be guided, with no show of resistance, toward the van where another Serb policeman stood, holding open the back door of the van.

Ceca cried, *"Papa!"*

She ran, reaching the van at the same time as the officers with their "prisoner." They turned curiously at this woman who had broken from the ranks of onlookers to confront them.

Ceca sensed that if she had any hope of helping her father, it was to meet these men eye to eye. She tried to regain her normal breathing and brushed back an errant lock of blonde hair that had tumbled across her forehead.

The ranking officer—she could see that he was a

sergeant though he wore no name tag—had a burly
build. He wore a large caliber sidearm holstered at his
hip. His hand rested on the butt of the pistol, ready
to draw.

"So, you are this man's daughter. You are Ceca
Keloni?"

"I am. What is going on here?" Even before he
could respond, she rushed over to her father, resting
a hand across the back of his neck. "Where are you
taking him?"

The sergeant stretched out a callused hand, fasten-
ing it to her shoulder and forcibly tugging her away
from her father.

"You are interfering with an official investigation."

"Investigation?" She felt her face grow pale.
"You're investigating my father?"

"He is under investigation, yes."

"For what?"

The men guided the stunned and confused Mr. Keloni into the yawning, dim interior of the van.

Ceca fought to free herself from the sergeant's hold,
but did not succeed.

His fingers were like steel biting into her flesh. "This
detainment is authorized."

"I don't believe you."

"Then check if you don't believe me. It should be
easy enough for you."

She stared at him blankly. "What do you mean?"

"I mean that the only reason *you* are not also being
detained, dear lady, is because of your employment
with the government. That does not mean that you
will *not* be detained, however, if you continue to make
yourself troublesome."

Her father and the policemen guiding him were
swallowed by the gloom of the van's interior, the door
shut after them. The sound of that van door slamming
shut had a sound of finality that caused a shiver to

course through Ceca, inwardly galvanizing her like an epiphany.

She knew what she must do.

She relaxed her stance, summoning whatever feminine wiles she hoped she possessed at being able to deceive a man. "I won't cause you any trouble, Sergeant. But I don't understand. What has my father done?"

"There have been reports that the KLA is about to implement an offensive in this region. The name Keloni has been linked to that organization."

"But that's insane! Sergeant, you know very well that Keloni is not an uncommon name. And my father is a respected member of the community."

The policeman considered her. He released his hold on her. "You had best be on your way, miss." He started past her, toward the front passenger side of the van.

"But you see the condition my father is in. Please, Sergeant, I beg of you!"

"Step aside, Miss Keloni, or you *will* be arrested."

She wanted to lash out. She wanted to slap this man. She wanted to throw herself into the path of the van and dare them to run her down in an effort to rescue her father. She told herself that none of this would accomplish her Papa's release, and could well result in her own death. Behave calmly, she told herself. The only hope she had of gaining her father's release was based on her remaining out of their custody.

And so she stepped aside, casting her eyes downward in submission.

He snorted his approval. "Now you're being sensible. I warn you, don't make any trouble."

He strode to the front of the van and climbed aboard. The driver slipped the van into gear and it drove away, trailing wispy fumes from the exhaust pipe as it rounded a corner and disappeared.

The small crowd of onlookers dispersed after cursory glances at the woman who remained standing in the street long after the van with her father had departed, long after the exhaust fumes had dissipated on the cool mountain air.

Ceca stood there numbly for several minutes. Quiet, stoic tears streaked down her face. Her hands were clenched into fists at her sides. She wondered if this would be the last she ever saw of her father.

What should she do?

What *could* she do?

She was not in their custody, true. Yet this made even more bitter the knowledge that her father was under detention because of *her* connection with the KLA, through her love affair with Adem Yashanitz. Somehow word of someone named Keloni being involved with the guerrillas had filtered through. It was only natural that the Serbs would suspect her father of collaboration with the KLA given his revered status in the community. She, on the other hand, was but a lowly office worker, beneath suspicion in their eyes.

It was *her* fault that her father was under detainment; something that could very well kill him, given his age and fragile physical condition. Her first and only goal must be to get her father out of their hands at any cost. But the question remained: what could she do?

She stepped onto the sidewalk in front of the drab apartment building that was her home with Papa. One last single tear slipped from the corner of one eye at the mental image of how pitiable and helpless her father had looked as his frail body had been tossed into that van like a sack of grain.

She then discerned a peculiar sound that she first thought was a bird or an insect. Then she realized that it was a human voice, making quiet *psssst!* noises to gain her attention. Ceca looked in the direction of the sound, which emanated from behind a thicket that grew along the sidewalk between her apartment building and the one next to it.

The crowd of onlookers had vanished. It was as if the arrest, more like abduction, she thought, had never happened.

Confident that no one was paying attention to her, she whispered over to the thicket. "Who is it?"

"It's me. Adem."

Naturally she recognized his voice. Joy and relief flowed through her. Casting another glance around to make certain that she was not being watched, she crossed the pavement and eased herself past the thicket into the narrow area that ran the length of the twin apartment houses.

Adem, her KLA lover, stood there waiting for her. She threw herself into his arms, clasping herself to this man she loved as if he were the breath of life itself. He was in his late thirties, clad in black civilian clothes that would allow him to blend in better with the darkness after dusk. He was so handsome, she thought, the liquid eyes beneath the bushy head of hair and brows were pools of emotional fire that burned both with hatred for the enemy and with passion for her.

She had begun by supplying Adem with what scant information she overheard during her walks past the open doorways of offices in the building where she worked, where she could often pick up bits and pieces of information regarding policy, strategy, shifts in personnel and troops. He then saw to it that this information was passed onto the CIA.

The Kosovo Liberation Army was a ragtag band of guerrillas committed to fighting the Serbs for independence, less than a few thousand regular fighters, most of whom were lightly armed and outgunned. Militarily, though, the KLA had a well-deserved reputation as a hit-and-run band. Overseas Albanians poured millions of dollars through clandestine, laundered channels into the province to help arm the KLA. During the NATO bombing campaign, KLA guerrillas had often been responsible for drawing out Serbs for better targeting by NATO bombers. The Serbians had never forgotten that, and the blood feud had only deepened. The KLA, supposedly demilitarized, was in fact scattered across the province, battling disparate groups of renegade Serbian military factions and preventing the chance of establishing a real peace in Kosovo.

It was Adem's courage as much as the physical passion that had drawn Ceca to the man who embraced her in this narrow space between the buildings. But she wondered if what she felt was love, or lust . . . or merely loneliness. It troubled her that it was only during their moments of physical intimacy that she saw a loving side to him. When they weren't making love, he often became a person she wasn't sure she liked. For one thing, he was obsessed by the victory he felt he was destined to carry out for his people. After their lovemaking, he'd frequently drone on about how the KLA hoped to be outfitted in the near future by the West with the effective stinger missiles and antitank rockets. She wished he wouldn't discuss such matters in bed. But because of his volatile nature, she never conveyed this sentiment to the darkly sensuous freedom fighter during the times they'd slept together; stolen moments of body heat at odd hours in unusual places, which had only added to the excitement of the situation for her initially.

There in the space between the buildings, she pulled back from his embrace and told him how the authorities had taken her father. When she was done, she stared into his eyes, cold, dark, and unreadable.

"You heard what I said?"

He nodded. "Everything. I saw everything. I came to warn you and your father. I was minutes late. I'm sorry, Ceca. I can only assure you that the informer has already been . . . taken care of."

She felt a chill. "I don't want to hear about that,

Adem. It's my father I'm concerned about, and nothing else. Do you know where they've taken him?"

"They were Serb police. They have too much autonomy. They won't take him to one of their facilities."

"Where will he be taken?"

Adem glanced out through the dense thicket that concealed them. A military vehicle rumbled by, heavy enough to make the ground vibrate beneath their feet.

"They'll more than likely take your father to one of their safe houses."

"A safe house? What's that?"

"A secure residence. They're using the Avdylaga estate outside of town. We're not sure, but it's more heavily fortified than it should be, and it's a secluded place where they can interrogate people like your father, where there's little chance of anyone stopping them from doing whatever they . . ." He abruptly realized what he'd been about to say and covered himself with a faint cough followed by an uncomfortable silence. "Ceca, I'm sorry that I didn't get here in time."

"But my father knows nothing about your group!" From his expression, she knew she'd spoken too loudly. She lowered her voice, looking around the alleyway. "My father is in this predicament because of me . . . because I'm helping you."

"It's was your choice to become involved with the KLA, Ceca. You sought *us* out, remember?"

"But Adem, that is exactly my point. *I* chose to help your organization. My father knew nothing of my involvement with you, or with the KLA. He should not have been drawn into this."

"And I'm sorry that he was." Adem's voice was peculiarly flat for a man who usually spoke with fiery emotion.

A stillness settled in the narrow confines of the space between the buildings, and she felt claustrophobic, sharing this space with this man who had been her lover. She felt that she was seeing the real Adem Yashanitz for the first time.

"Adem, you know what I'm saying. You should help."

"Help? You mean that you want me to organize a KLA strike on the Avdylaga estate?" he said as if the very notion was absurd.

She nodded. "You have the resources at your command. Your people are in place in the mountains not far from here. You could rescue my father. He doesn't deserve this."

"None of us deserve this. But what you ask is impossible. A major operation is about to be initiated. Everything is in place. A situation has arisen where we can provide the Americans with direct ground support. This is the last step in forging the bonds between the KLA and the CIA, which is essential."

"Adem." She cut through his enthusiasm like a scalpel. "What can we do to help my father? Don't you understand? I *must* do something. Help me, I'm begging you. My father will never survive at their hands."

"You are the one who must understand, Ceca. There's nothing I can do. This operation I spoke of, it is an unexpected sort of thing. A covert operations unit, a tactical commando group, will arrive tonight in Suva Reka. Everything must be subordinated so that we can help them. They intend to stage a tactical strike against Serbs in the mountains. And we need you to guide them to our camp." He glanced in the direction of the opposite end of the alley. As yet no one had passed. He touched her elbows and gazed into her eyes. "I must leave. Will you help us? I was depending on you, Ceca, to bring the Americans into the mountains to join my unit."

She still could not read his emotionless eyes. She felt none of the electricity that she would previously have experienced at his touch. *Everything has changed.*

"I was depending on you, Adem, to be there when I needed you most. The people in town have not yet spoken about anything happening at the estate you speak of. The Avdylaga family left the country in ninety-eight, and now you say it is a Serb safe house. Well, if it's heavily guarded, such a security force could never be discrete enough not to arouse anyone's suspicions in town. That means it's a security force small enough for your soldiers to overcome, given the advantage of surprise. I would arm myself and accompany you. It *could* be done."

"I've explained myself, Ceca. Given the priority of the operation with the Americans, I cannot spare those resources you ask for at this time. I must be going."

"I'm glad to hear that, Adem." She couldn't keep the acid sting from her words. "You and I will never know each other again except as allies fighting a common enemy."

The sounds of moderate traffic beyond the thicket remained normal.

Adem's face became more tautly lined with a tension he'd thus far concealed. "Well, will you continue to help our cause?"

"Of course. I just said that. Only what has existed between you and I personally has changed."

"The American force will contact you," he said brusquely. "Bring them to us."

Then he was gone. Before this, they would have embraced at the moment of parting. Not this time. Wordlessly, he turned and retraced his route to the alley, where he disappeared from her sight.

And all Ceca could think about was her father.

Her world had turned upside down in the instant of time it had taken for her to round that corner and see those soldiers loading Papa into a van.

Her stomach ached. Her neck muscles stiffened in anger. She felt devastated. Helpless. Abandoned.

And angrier than she'd ever felt in her life.

She must help Papa.

She would meet the American commando force, as Adem instructed.

But there was about to be a change in plans . . .

Chapter 7

The training exercise area was built around the crumbling remains of the villa of some long-deceased, long-forgotten Italian noblemen. The facility was in fact space-age high-tech, with sectors where virtual reality seminars and training exercises were utilized by commando units sent here to train from around the world.

The sun shone in the midday sky overhead but at ground level, a smoky mist, manufactured from an unseen machine, partly obscured the view of the once grand main edifice of the estate that had fallen into sad disrepair. The windows and doors were gaping holes. This side of the building was blackened from fire. Glass shards and grenade pins littered the ground. With some of the nearby outbuildings in similar condition, and the haze drifting across the scene, this could well be a street in Beirut, or Chechnya, or Kosovo.

Or even parts of some American cities he knew, thought Travis Barrett.

The field commander of Eagle Team, along with Stan Powczuk and Sarah Greene, were advancing on the rear of the main building. They were not wearing their LOC suits this time, but standard commando camouflage fatigues, each similarly armed with a 9mm Beretta in a snap-clipped holster, an XM-29 assault system rifle, and a combat webbing of flash-bang grenades and spare ammo clips.

Although TALON Force was the highest-tech covert ops unit in the American arsenal, Travis was still strongly of the opinion, shared by his fellow team members, that with all of the smart weaponry, with all of the high-tech communications support, winning a war still came down to soldiers moving from hill to hill, from building to building, to fully secure whatever piece of real estate with whatever hardware was necessary. No less an authority than Albert Einstein had once observed that if the Third World War would be fought with nuclear arms of mass destruction, then the Fourth World War would be fought with clubs and rocks, his point being that civilizations were fooling themselves if they ever thought they could eliminate the common foot soldier, the grunt, the dogface, call him what you will depending on the war. When it comes right down to the nitty gritty, it's the foot soldier, armed with a rifle and guts, who determines the final outcome of combat. Travis enjoyed testing himself under such conditions.

He'd always found that he performed best when his limits were being tested. Same went with his team. Any further planning would have to wait for nightfall, when TALON Force had been inserted into Kosovo and connected with their KLA contact. General Krauss had placed full control of the mission in Travis's hands, which was the way Travis preferred it and the way this unit generally operated. If a mission went sour, Travis wanted it to be his fault and no one else's. His theory was that if he got them into deep shit, he needed to ensure that he could get them out. So, afforded an afternoon in which to cover all contingencies, Travis had opted for a run-through of the operation on this training course's urban combat range.

He doubted that they would have to use this drill

in their attack, but the training mattered. It was action. While he and his team were honing their skills in this fashion, his unconscious would be sublimating its ass off, working out all the angles, and when he emerged from the other side of this training exercise, "dead" or "alive," Travis knew from experience that a fully conceived plan would form in his head.

The building they were about to "sweep" was infested with highly trained members of an "enemy force." That this was constituted of some other anonymous, highly trained commando unit from God knew where, did not matter. All that mattered was that both sides were armed with special paint-pellet ammunition, and the rules of engagement were clearly defined: "kill" on sight.

Travis motioned for his fire team to spread out as they approached a blackened doorway in the rear of the building.

There didn't seem to be any enemy presence. In combat, buildings such as this often had to be cleared of pockets of resistance; snipers quietly holed up above. The taking of each such building could *not* be a haphazard affair.

Even at this time of year, the Italian sun beaming down on the camouflage netting made it hot enough for rivulets of perspiration to slither into Sam Wong's eyes, which in turn was enough to make him want to scream.

Of course he could hardly do that, or the roving enemy foot patrol would track his position and pump him full of paint bullets. And he would never hear the end of *that*! There was a man's pride, after all.

He was wearing camouflage fatigues and, unlike the others, his Battle Sensor Helmet. A 9mm Beretta was worn in a shoulder holster.

Jen, Hunter, and Jack had assisted him in securing his position, wordlessly and with well-practiced speed.

He was stretched out, prone beneath the camouflage netting on the bare ground, within sight of the old mansion, his place of concealment nothing more than an ever so slight swelling in the ground. Then they gave him the thumbs-up sign and withdrew.

Ever since his induction into TALON Force, it had been apparent to everyone that Eagle Team's information management specialist was in no way the equal of his teammates when it came to combat experience or savvy. Nonetheless, Sam's pride and discipline had seen him through the rigors of TALON Force training, earning him the privilege of serving in their ranks, to become an integral part of this team, to serve on the front lines with Eagle Team as early as their first mission, when they had gone up against that bastard, Terrek, in North Korea.

For the Iraq and upcoming Kosovo missions, his primary role was being sidelined at his comm consoles, where his secured uplinks with the TALON Force satellite network provided vital tactical intel for processing and relay to the team. Sam preferred being in the field. Yes, it was a matter of personal pride that came with the knowledge that he truly was one of this extraordinary team.

And he usually enjoyed the training exercises. Some more than others.

Any Asian genetic or Zen-ingrained patience had yielded within him to the human frailties of claustrophobia and restlessness when the sweat had first started seeping into his eyes, the saltiness stinging and glazing his vision no matter how often and rigorously he tried to blink it away there beneath the netting.

Major Barrett had clearly stated that this was to be a "bare bones" exercise. Sam could only reason that Travis, in his wisdom, sensed or foresaw the possibility on their upcoming mission of just the sort of low-tech hot encounter that this exercise was so effectively simulating, and so he wanted Eagle Team to brush up on its "primal urges," as Jack had cracked before the exercise got under way. Travis had instructed that complete silence be maintained across the comm net.

Hell, thought Sam. They might as well have been World War II commandos! But then, that *was* the point of the exercise. A trickle of sweat slithered its way down his back. His gut crawled with spiders of tension, and he knew the sweat was from more than just the heat.

As comm man for Eagle Team, his job on this afternoon's exercise was to stay hidden and field-test communications equipment that was barely beyond the prototype stage, still in development. His input, after putting any piece of equipment through its paces like today, was always valued by the development engineers.

Uncomfortably nestled as he was beneath the cammo netting, he in fact had a bird's-eye view of the surrounding area thanks to the sharp-resolution, real-time imaging being picked up in outer space by one of the TALON Force spy satellites. Knowing the precise position of friendly combatants and processing up-to-the-second updates on enemy positions would, in a similar, real-combat situation, be crucial if Sam were assisting the team across the comm net as usual. As it was, this information was presently being graphically depicted on the BSD screen of his helmet. He intended to advise the development guys that the notion of a comm man directing a low-tech insertion by monitoring satellite imagery and data could use some fine tuning, so to speak. For instance, though he naturally lost visual contact with Travis, Sarah, and Stan when they entered the crumbling old mansion, he'd also somehow managed to lose track of Jenny Olsen, Hunter Blake, and Jack DuBois, Eagle Team's "floaters," who were tasked with remaining mobile, to cover the inside team from the outside and to protect Sam's comm uplink. But there'd been no sighting of Jen or Jack for several minutes, visually or on the BSD relay from the spy-in-the-sky that was so finely tuned. His BSD could scroll down a license plate reading, for example, from outer space, one that he couldn't read with the naked eye from across a parking lot.

Yet this high-tech wizardry couldn't seem to spot hide nor hair of Jenny, Hunter, or Jack.

Either something had gone very wrong here on the ground, Sam told himself, or his teammates were wily enough to remain invisible in broad daylight without benefit of any brilliant suit stealth technology.

The four men of the enemy foot patrol suddenly appeared, striding from around the nearest corner of the mansion, in the process of sweeping the grounds. Not having seen him yet, they were relentlessly advancing on his position of supposed concealment. They wouldn't be able to *not* see him, he knew, the closer they came; within less than a minute, if the BSD data readout of their rate of approach was accurate.

Following Travis's hand gestures, Sarah and Stan continued closing in from either side. When they were poised on opposite sides of the doorway, Travis flung himself forward into a prone position on the doorstep so that only his head, chest, and arms were inside to aim his XM-29, its laser-sighted eye ready to fire at any targets identified in the shadows. He saw a tiny room with nothing in it except dust and decay. Beyond, a narrow hallway led into deeper gloom.

Stan and Sarah quickly jumped over Travis to enter the confines of the room, covering first the front corners, then the rest of the room, each moving with a nearly absolute absence of sound. Hand signals replaced conversation.

At a gesture from Travis, Sarah nodded. She replaced Travis in the doorway, assuming a prone position that presented a minimum target while positioning herself to provide cover fire if necessary.

Having ascertained that they were not about to draw fire from down the hallway, Travis and Stan threw themselves around the corner and began moving down the hallway, deeper into the musty darkness of the building. Sarah followed, scrambling along the backtrack, her eyes intensely scanning for something to shoot at.

Travis and Stan hastened along the narrow corridor. Several open doorways lined this stretch, any of which could be used to launch an ambush, so they remained wary. Storming down the corridor, they tossed flashbang grenades into each room before passing, then sprayed each room with a quick, short burst of auto fire from the XM-29s as they moved toward the front of the building. Sarah moved nimbly, stepping backward to cover any movement out of the rooms.

Thus far, though, the house seemed to be uninhabited.

Yeah, right, thought Travis. That was the one rule that did exist in this training exercise. There were enemy personnel in this building, waiting for them. The team continued on, avoiding exposure and moving efficiently. Even Sarah, as she moved backward, avoided any telltale heaves in the floor or rug that could signify a booby trap. The whole team could then be "dead" from flying shrapnel that, in real combat, would shred flesh to bloody ribbons in the confines of a hallway like this. Such a practice detonator would release a geyser of brightly colored paint that would signify death or a wound for anyone touched by the paint.

They emerged from the corridor into the foyer of what must have been a grand entrance in its day. Dirty sunlight filtered through empty skylights that might once have held stained-glass masterpieces commissioned by the duke. Errant shafts of light pierced the gloom, revealing a wide staircase leading up to a second floor. At ground level, another corridor jutted off from the remains of the foyer, leading to what must have once been the dining room with a kitchen area beyond.

Travis knew that Stan and Sarah must be thinking what was passing though his mind. It was quiet. Too damn quiet. This was supposed to be a kill zone. What the hell?

Sweating under the netting, Sam knew that he was a dead man.

Sure, he would jump up and heroically throw his "life" away as surely as if he was committing hari-kari, and maybe he would take out one of the advancing enemy patrol with his Beretta, what with the element of surprise in his favor. But even that was doubtful. This patrol would "riddle" his scrawny carcass and turn him into one paint-spattered dead guy. His only hope for "survival" was Jenny, Hunter, and Jack and, dammit, there was still no trace of them from either his line of naked-eye vision, quite literally at ground level, watching the advancing patrol, nor from the satellite feed to his BSD screen.

There was only the line of four of the enemy, striding inexorably forward.

Something had to give.

Under normal circumstances, Sam would have raised his teammates on the comm net. Jen, Hunter, and Jack would at least then know that this patrol was closing almost on top of him and would come to his rescue, like they were supposed to. But it was now apparent that he was going to have to defend himself and "die" in the process.

Damn damn *damn*!

His mind raced. Jen! Jack! Hunter! Where are you?

Then the oncoming men were calling out to each other in German, pointing in his direction, and they were tracking their rifles straight at the clump of the terrain that was *him*!

*   *   *

Sarah stood still, weaving the barrels of her XM-29 between the corridor and the staircase, the main entrance to this haunted house. She paid particular heed, however, to the grand staircase. Its bannister was tarnished where once a silver would have cast brilliant hues across the now chipped wood and spotted marble.

Now there was only decay, danger . . . and silence.

A closed door faced where they'd emerged, one by one, into the foyer. It was a simple wooden door in a shabby wall. But what was behind it?

Travis and Stan approached, each hugging the wall to either side. Stan took the initiative to be the knob-man as Travis prepared to react. Stan beat him to it. Stan turned the knob and, finding it unlocked, flung the door open so that it slammed back against anyone that was behind it, or sprung off any booby traps. Both men crouched down.

There was no return gunfire from within.

They paused for some thirty seconds, listening.

There was no sound from anywhere in the house.

Damn, thought Travis. Did they call off the damn exercise and forget to tell us?

He held up a palm mirror and viewed the inside of what looked like nothing more than a cloakroom that had long ago fallen into disuse. Travis nodded. Stan quickly angled across the doorway, to avoid being silhouetted. Travis made the same move from his side. Both scanned the room. Satisfied that it was clear, they returned to the foyer, where Sarah met them with an inquisitive eye. Travis shook his head.

She turned and continued panning the XM-29 around the foyer and staircase. The assault rifle looked as comfortable in her hands as a surgeon's instrument.

Travis motioned to Stan, and they advanced down the hallway toward what had once been the dining area. Ahead was a sturdy double door that was of considerably more recent vintage than anything else seen thus far in this crumbling, cobwebbed mansion. Travis suspected the main part of this house was located beyond those heavy doors; a spacious room for entertaining in its day.

The perfect spot for an ambush today.

Travis and Stan approached the closed double door on the run. Sarah remained in the foyer, covering the target acquisition area to their rear.

Travis and Stan stormed the heavy doors at full force, heaving their bodies against it with their combined strength. The doors smashed open, bringing a volley of hurriedly aimed, ineffectual fire that sizzled the air where Travis and Stan would have been standing if they hadn't tumbled to the floor atop the doors they'd ripped from their hinges. Several of the enemy team were rushing for cover behind desks and chairs and were firing sporadically at Travis and Stan, who trained return fire skillfully.

But this opposing force was comprised of fellow pros, and Travis knew that it would not take these boys more than another millisecond to realign their fire.

Stan unleashed a burst of auto fire, while Travis, thankful for the earplugs that protected his eardrums, unleashed a 20mm air-burst round at a group of four attackers. Exploding mini-splotches of brightly multicolored paint impacted their opponents with enough force to knock some off of their feet. Vests and goggles were worn by both teams to minimize serious injury, but the bursting pellets of paint still packed quite a wallop.

The "dead" men sprawling under this volley of fire would be black and blue in the morning, Travis knew. He'd been "killed" a few times himself in these games. Like in all walks of life, chance favored the trained and the prepared. But luck, good *and* bad, always had to be factored into the equation.

Before the walls had even stopped shaking from the hammering gunfire, Travis and Stan were on their feet to secure the room, respectively covering its back and front corners.

There was no movement.

As per the rules, the "dead" men were staying down until the game was over, although some muttered painful curses—they sounded like Brits or Aussies.

Travis flashed more signals.

Stan nodded, positioning himself sideways at the doorway so that he could keep an eye on the room itself in case of any unpleasant surprises, while Travis double-timed back in the direction of the foyer.

Just then, all hell broke loose.

Travis heard the thundering exchange of assault rifles on full auto seconds before he rounded the corner into the foyer. Few sounds are more shockingly loud than rifle fire indoors.

Sarah was on one knee, trading fire with three ambushers at the top of the sweeping staircase. Just then, the bad guys each rolled grenades, which came hippity-hopping down that once grand staircase. Half of their fuse count was eaten up when Travis came into view.

It was almost a relief to Sam when he finally gave in to his own "primal urge."

Moving with sinewy swiftness, he flung aside his cammo netting and bounded to his feet, drawing his Beretta, and he actually heard himself howling his head off like a banshee with the liberating adrenaline release of it, spurred on by the hammering of weapons that could be heard from inside the dilapidated mansion. But even in these tumbling milliseconds, Sam knew that he would "die" without taking out even one of those enemy guys because they were already laughing with their rifles aimed at him and there was nothing left for him to do now but take their fired paint bullets and hope "dying" didn't hurt too much. A guy really could get knocked black and blue by the paint pellets when struck.

At that precise moment, something extraordinary occurred.

Three clumps of earth, matching the cammo netting under which Sam had hidden, abruptly flew back to reveal Jen Olsen, Hunter Blake, and Jack DuBois, concealed, positioned to either side of Sam. They popped up from the confines of their netting like rising-from-the-dead apparitions, like activated jack-in-the-boxes, and wasted none of their time with the luxury of self-indulgent, congratulatory laughter, as their opposite numbers had. They unhesitatingly squeezed off rounds from the XM-29s.

The impact knocked those guys off their feet; chest hits that nullified them instantly. Per game rules, the fallen enemy remained where they'd fallen.

Jenny, Hunter, and Jack approached Sam from where they'd secreted themselves. Sam realized that he hadn't the foggiest notion of how long they had been lying there in wait for that patrol, so close to where he'd been fretting and sweating. His BSD screen, monitoring the spy satellite bird's-eye view, had revealed nothing to him of their movement or whereabouts or nearness to him.

And so he just stood there, holding the Beretta, unfired at his side, aimed at the ground. He snapped up his BSD screen and knew that his confusion would be evident, so he holstered his pistol and busied himself with making a production of dusting himself off, attempting without much success to disguise his relief. His heartbeat was almost back to normal.

"Well, I'll say this," he said politely, "you sure as hell took your sweet time about making your presence known!"

"Didn't mean to startle you," Hunter chided him mildly.

"Guess those high-tech gizmos have their place," chuckled Jack, "but nothing beats an old dog's sleight of hand."

"But . . . but how did you—" Sam started to ask.

Jenny smiled sweetly. "That *may* be a subject for future discussion. For now, this game isn't over. Let's get you relocated, Sam. Jack, Hunter, and I will keep floating."

Sam sighed, snatched up his cammo netting, and accompanied them, snapping his BSD back into place.

Travis dropped to Sarah's side and joined her in returning fire, turning the drabness of the foyer into a surreal fun house painting thanks to the wild, stitching "fire" from upstairs.

Paint splattered the gray walls with bright explosions of color like Day-Glo blossoming flowers.

Their combined fire raked splotches across the torsos of the guys positioned at the top of the stairway, and the impact of the projectiles sent them tumbling. One of the "dead" men lost his balance and rolled comically down the steps behind the grenades, swearing with every bounce.

Travis and Sarah blurred into movement as the three grenades reached the bottom step and bounced one last time. They dived for cover behind the balustrade of the stairway just as the grenades detonated, spraying the foyer with bursting paint "shrapnel." Travis and Sarah remained paint-free on the faded carpet of the corridor leading to the dining room. Beyond, Stan was busily engaged with a couple of guys who'd chanced stepping from behind the arched doorway to the dining room, thinking maybe they could get a better bead on Stan. Even as Travis and Sarah brought their rifles to bear, Stan Powczuk was already methodically popping the archway with a tight figure-eight pattern that took down both targets.

Before the "dead" even had a chance to topple,

Travis and Sarah left their prone position and rushed forward to join up with Stan. They met outside the double doorway to the parlor, which was filled with supposedly "dead" men.

That's when Sarah saw one of the figures move.

One of those "dead" in reality had only a droplet of paint where he'd been nicked on his wrist, not a life-threatening wound. He'd taken the opportunity to play possum and was now bolting upright from where he'd been concealed by an overturned table.

He was tracking his rifle on the three people framed in the doorway. Before he could pull the trigger, Sarah pumped a single round that splattered against the guy's chest. The impact of the round knocked him out of sight behind the table, and this time he stayed "dead."

There was a pervasive stillness about the house that told Travis they'd reached end game. They would make a complete sweep of the house in the time remaining before emerging and claiming it secured. Travis knew that the enemy force had thrown everything into one go-for-broke ambush . . . and his team had blown them all to hell and gone.

2010 hours
The NATO airfield at Brindisi

Aboard the V-22 Super Osprey parked on the remote runway outside the hangar where they had been briefed by General Krauss, Travis Barrett and his team stood near the cockpit, watching Hunter Blake, already seated at the instrument panel, bringing the big gunship to life.

The Osprey was so new, appropriations were still being wrangled over in Congress. But the powers that be had managed to divert several of the combat "super planes" to TALON Force, and this one was flown to Italy specifically for this mission. The V-22 took off and landed like a helicopter but, once airborne, could tilt its rotors and fly like an airplane. The Super Osprey came equipped with the latest in electronic antiradar and anti-SAM jamming systems. Fast and reliable, the plane had the added advantage of being able to carry an entire TALON Force Action Team. The bay area of this plane was dominated by a massive winch mechanism that could sling a vehicle in the vertical mode. The war bird's armament consisted of mounted rockets and a vicious chain gun in the nose of the war plane.

Travis addressed his unit.

"Okay, people. In Suva Reka we have the name of a KLA contact who will take us into the mountains on the border with Macedonia where the KLA is operating. They will function as ground support. The prep work for this has been set in motion by their CIA control. The contact in Suva Reka will meet us on the ground."

Jenny gave an unladylike, cynical snort. "Imagine that. The KLA still operational. So much for demilitarization."

Jack grunted morosely. "An oxymoronic concept in a war zone, wouldn't you say?" He turned to Travis. "That's what we're going into, right, Trav? The KLA and the Serbs are still duking it out up in those mountains no matter what anyone says."

Travis nodded. "Our gear is already onboard. It's going to see some heavy use before we see Brindisi again, bet on that. Questions?"

"Yeah," said Sarah. "What the hell are we waiting for?"

Travis chuckled. "Not a damn thing." But his frown returned when he seemed to notice something different about Hunter. There was a troubled cast to Hunter's naturally cool demeanor. Nothing anyone would notice normally, but Travis was a man who prided himself in knowing his people. "Okay, Blake," he said. "Share it before we lift off."

"This town you mentioned . . . Suva Reka."

"Spit it out, guy."

"Uh, is this KLA contact male or female?"

Jenny rolled her eyes, glancing knowingly at the others. "This is going to be great."

Hunter's shrug was the suave, understated gesture of a man of the world. "They were using us to chopper in supply drops to refugees crossing the mountains. I was based out of Suva Reka. I worked with the KLA for six months."

"And there was a woman involved, right?" Sarah said.

"Okay, okay, give a guy a break. It gets cold up in those mountains. Besides, she was a single girl. I always sort of wished I hadn't had to pull out of country the way I did. The rules were that I couldn't tell even her. You know how it is. She must think I'm just an American pig that boinked her and bolted."

Jenny smirked. "Wonder where she'd get an idea like that."

Stan glanced at Travis. "So tell us the contact's name."

"Her name is Ceca Keloni," said Travis.

Seated at the controls, Hunter sighed mightily. "Figures."

Chapter 8

1930 hours
In the mountains near Shar Pass,
south of Suva Reka

Davis sat on a cot across from the room's single window and watched the sun set behind the mountain range in the distance; a beautiful sunset that tinged the snowcapped peaks of the range with rouge.

He would more than willingly have traded this beautiful Kosovo sunset for a rainy or even a snowy night back home, huddled away with Carol and the kids in the simple suburban home like a million others. But it was the happiest place Davis had ever known because that's where his family was. *A life that I am damn sure going to die trying to get back to,* he told himself.

He didn't feel like a man who'd been clubbed into unconsciousness earlier that day. There was a lump the size of a hardball on the back of his head but he'd taken worse than that during his wild teen days when he'd entertained notions of going into the ring professionally. He'd been KO'd often enough to get the idea that fighting wasn't his game. But in those days, he used to be groggy for a full day or two after a knockout. It wasn't like that this time. They had given him a pair of threadbare slacks and a one-size-too-small shirt, along with a pair of socks and scuffed civilian loafers, also a size to small. The shoes made his bruised feet ache even more, but he wore them because he wanted to be ready for anything.

Some ideas were percolating in his head.

This room was a slight improvement over that windowless room where he'd endured sleep deprivation. There was the cot upon which he now sat. Also, there was a desk and a plastic lawn chair. There was a cubicle with a sink and commode. This had been the office of some lumber company executive. Now it was a cell for Davis. He hadn't seen anyone since Ben and Jerry, his two Serbian guards, had escorted him from his interview with Dalma to these present quarters.

He was in considerable danger if NATO bombers got wind of a Serb detachment working out of this industrial site. The building he was in would surely be targeted, and he would perish as that most hapless of combat casualties, a victim of "friendly fire." He tried not to dwell on the irony of being blown to bits by a fellow NATO pilot. He spent his time trying to sleep, resting up for whatever his future held. And though the door to his cell had not opened since the soldiers had tossed him in here, he was certain that guards would be posted in the hallway outside.

The otherwise deserted office building had an eerie, tomblike stillness about it that managed to permeate the walls of this office. Davis watched the sun slide down behind the mountain range beyond the window, silhouetting the jagged, foreboding peaks. He wondered what sort of person had worked in this office, what their job had been, and what had happened to them. His stomach grumbled, and he found himself wondering when they were going to bring him something to eat. He'd be damned if he'd ask for anything. They intended to keep him alive, so they would have to bring him something to eat eventually.

Davis wanted this to happen, but not because he was hungry.

He intended to escape from this box they thought

they had him in. *Fuck 'em.* He'd slept. He'd rested. He'd had time to think. And he was ready to go for broke.

This time when he'd slept, instead of having a nightmare, it had been a deep, revitalizing sleep. He'd drifted off thinking about Carol on their wedding day, with a smile on his face. They'd gotten hitched in a civil ceremony. Just a couple of friends as witnesses. Neither wanted to make a big deal about it, especially since Carol was two months pregnant.

Conversation from outside his window had awakened him; there came the repeated *thud!* and *clang!* of objects being tossed into the bed of a pickup truck.

He stood from the cot and stepped over to the window.

A half dozen Serbian soldiers were moving about in the lengthening shadows. They were doing this at dusk, Davis figured, as a protection against being spotted by overflying spy planes and satellites. The workers saw no reason to be quiet, though, as they went about gathering up discarded lumber and the last remnants of what Davis had noticed on his way to his interview with Dalma in the motor pool garage, before the underhanded bastards had KO'd him from behind. The Serb workers were yakking it up. From the way they sniggered coarsely, he got the impression that they were telling dirty jokes to each other.

Then there came a sound from behind Davis. A key turned in the door.

Okay. Time for Plan A.

He moved to the darkened bathroom and scrunched his heft into its confines, pressing against the wall and pulling the door only halfway closed after him. He stood there and did not make a sound. In the office beyond, the hallway door swung inward. Davis pressed his eye to the crack of the bathroom door. He saw a pair of uniformed Serb paramilitaries, different from the pair that had brought him here.

There'd been a changing of the guards. The younger one held a tray with a glass of water and a bowl of gruel. The other stood close behind, his AK-47 held in a firing position in case the American airman decided to misbehave. They both were obviously unprepared for there being no sign whatsoever of the airman in the office. Their attention turned to the opened doorway of the bathroom.

The older soldier snarled a command. The younger one set down the tray and brought his own rifle around. There was curiosity mixed with wariness now. The question was obvious on their faces.

Could the American pilot have escaped?

Davis held his breath. His throat muscles were so constricted that he could not swallow, and his heartbeat was like a bass drum pounding in his ears. He drew back as they advanced on the bathroom, waiting until he sensed their presence at the bathroom's threshold. A rifle muzzle nosed around like a telescopic probe, then started to nudge the door inward.

Davis exploded into action.

He gripped the door panel with both hands and smashed it outward. This was his one chance to escape. He slammed his shoulder into the door, tearing the flimsy wood panel off its hinges. He plowed into the younger of the two, who caught the top side of the door across the forehead, pitching him backward onto the floor, where he landed on his side and curled up into a groaning fetal ball.

The other Serb was in the process of trying to back out of the room, to escape this unexpected, erupting human dynamo while at the same time raising his rifle.

Davis wielded the door like a big club, swinging it around with ample power to tear the AK-47 from the Serb's hands. The weapon flew across the room, the blow knocking the trooper off balance. The Serb, stunned and fearful, looked over his shoulder just in time to catch the return arc of the swinging door, which caught him squarely alongside the head. The man collapsed unconscious, blood dripping from a gash in his forehead.

Davis considered killing these two, but decided against it. His escape would be discovered soon enough whether they were dead or alive. He knew he was pushing the odds even attempting an escape.

He snagged an AK-47, appropriating spare clips of ammo, which he secured in the waistband of his slacks. He would kill if he had to. But he had no intention of dying uselessly. His goal was to escape, not end up dead. He was aware that he was going for broke like this. If he was re-captured, he reasoned, Captain Dalma just might go easier on him if he didn't grease any more of Dalma's people than was necessary.

He searched the older one's pockets and found the keys he was looking for, then left the room, locking the door behind him. That would further delay possible discovery.

The tomblike quiet of the corridor amplified every sound. The turn of the lock and the placing of the keys into his pocket seemed to be magnified into loud, crashing noises that rumbled up and down the hallways of the office building. The mausoleum silence of the building was a blessing, in that it indicated that besides the guards, he was alone. Dalma had cleared the office building of most of his troops in case of an air strike. This hopefully meant that there would be no more human obstacles in Davis's path.

He took off on a run toward the nearest exit door at the end of the hallway, moving in the opposite direction of the glass-windowed front lobby. He stayed close to the wall, ducking down without slowing when he passed the occasional window. Then he arrived at the metal exit door. The thought occurred to him that this could be a fire door, trip-wired to set off an alarm.

But no alarm sounded. The original designer of the building had deemed such a fixture unnecessary, and

Dalma hadn't had the time or inclination—or the fore-
sight, thought Davis—to have it done.

He eased the metal door open. As he'd estimated,
the door led outside. He opened it no more than was
necessary to peer out.

He was positioned across from the activity that had
awakened him, and some fifty yards downrange.

Two dump trucks were parked near a doorway in
the facing wall of what had been the mill. The Serbian
troopers had been loudly loading the trucks with the
remnants of debris from the recent remodeling.

The garage and the converted troop barracks were
on the other side of the main building. Back here, the
workers were lighting cigarettes and leaning against
the trucks, chatting. Their voices carried clearly, though
Davis could not understand a word. But he knew the
routine well enough from his own adult lifetime in the
military, especially in the early days when he'd worked
shit details like the men he was now observing in the
gathering gloom of nightfall.

They were waiting to be dismissed, whereupon the
NCO would order the trucks to start up and drive off
with the debris, to be disposed of who knew where.

A thought crossed Davis's mind. Why did they wait
until nightfall to get rid of this stuff? Overflying surveillance would note nothing unusual in workers loading dump trucks at an industrial site. It's like they're
covering up, cleaning up the evidence of a crime . . .

The unit leader came striding out, grunting an order
of dismissal. The troopers mumbled their satisfaction
and began ambling away, conversing among themselves. They were soon out of sight around the corner
of the main building, on their way back to their barracks. The NCO stood there for a moment with a
clipboard, making notations. It piqued Davis's curiosity. Whatever this was about, it was official and being
watched from the top. That's why a low-end-of-the-
food-chain grunt like the Serb NCO had to go through

his tedious paperwork, which also allowed time for the Serbian workers' voices to fade from around the corner.

Davis felt elated. He could not have hoped for better. This could only be played one way. The NCO was about to order the dump trucks out of here. When he did, Davis would be aboard one of them. He chose the second one. The Serb could be occupied ordering the driver of the first truck to start. It would be interesting to see where they were taking this junk, but that was a secondary consideration. The trucks would have free clearance through the main gate. Night fell quickly here in the Balkans, if the briskly gathering dusk and chill were any indication. He would secret himself within the clutter of debris in the bed of the second truck, and hope like hell that the shadows would conceal him. Then he would be outbound, putting distance between himself and this facility.

And then?

He had no answer to that as of yet. But then, he was making all of this up as he went along, he reminded himself.

Sure enough, the Serb finished his paperwork. He strode toward the cab of the first of the two dump trucks, disappearing from Davis's line of vision.

Davis bunched his body, feeling like a coiled rattler. He heard the Serb bark a guttural command at the driver of the lead truck, the Serb's voice magnified in the narrow space between the trucks and the building.

This is it!

Davis bolted from his position, beelining across the distance separating him from the second, and closest, of the dump trucks.

The engines of both trucks gunned to life; new, well-maintained civilian vehicles that must have been part of the lumber company's fleet. Their full-throated bellows filled the air.

As he reached the truck, he realized that this was

the instant in which he was the most vulnerable. He could be observed by anyone in the surrounding vicinity who happened to be looking in this direction and, more importantly, the setting sun was throwing starkly etched, well-defined shadows across the wall of the building. Davis himself clearly saw his own shadow cast upon the wall as he swung aboard, leaping onto the rear bumper of the truck and grabbing hold.

The driver slipped the truck into gear. It jolted forward.

Davis heaved himself over the rear of the truck like a pole-vaulter, landing in the truck's bed. It was in that unfolding instant of time that he caught a glimpse through the open doorway in the building of something that did not make sense; that seemed strangely disjointed from this time and place.

In what he'd assumed was a mill that had been renovated into a headquarters for Dalma's staff, he instead saw shiny white tiled floors, white tiled walls, bright ceiling lights, and prominent air ducts. Sparkling. Antiseptic. *Unused.*

Then he landed in the bed, clattering onto a myriad of gathered objects, some of which poked at him uncomfortably. The sight through the doorway was blocked from his view by the sides of the truck's bed. He didn't move at first, bouncing along in an uncomfortable, jarring, prone position on his back.

The trucks continued upshifting, one following the other, moving past where the Serb NCO would be standing, observing their departure.

All it would take for everything to turn to shit would be for the NCO to have noticed even a glimmer of movement on the periphery of his vision when Davis had hopped aboard, or maybe a shadow across the wall of the building was just now beginning to register in the Serb's thick skull. Davis caught himself holding his breath again as he bumped and rode along atop the rubble. Walls knocked out to construct a massive tiled shower room? What the hell? It couldn't have been for the troops, who were already using this industrial site's pre-existing facilities. No, this was something else. Davis didn't know what. But it gave him the creepy crawly willies, suggesting something evil and unspeakable. He turned his concern to getting off this base.

In case there was anything to mental telepathy, he found himself sending a message to the anonymous Serb driving the truck. *Come on, you goddamn son of a bitch, get me the bloody hell off this frigging mountain!*

The driver seemed not to receive this telepathic command. Instead, Davis felt the dump truck being downshifted into neutral. The truck came to a halt.

Shit.

Davis lay there, just waiting for them to come and get him, relieved now that he hadn't killed anybody to get only this far. The driver had obviously been ordered to stop by a gesture unseen by Davis, or a shouted command that had been lost to him beneath the rumbling in the rear of the truck. He hoped they wouldn't kill him. He wanted to see his family again.

The Serb NCO suddenly showed himself over the side of the dump truck, standing on one of the truck's tires. He'd had to run a short distance to catch up. He was a horse-faced brute who appeared extremely agitated over the fact that he was out of breath. He'd acquired an AK-47 somewhere along the way since Davis had seen him last and was aiming the rifle at Davis's head, looking more than mad enough to kill; as if only a direct order was preventing him from blowing Davis apart there amid the litter in the rear of the truck. The Serb gestured with the rifle, with an angry shout that Davis didn't understand.

He sat there, unmoving.

Then Captain Dalma appeared, looking cool and athletic and unfettered, and certainly not out of breath. The trim young Serbian commander stood on the rear bumper of the truck.

Davis didn't say a word. He tried to make eye contact with Dalma, but couldn't seem to take his eyes off the muzzle of the pistol that Dalma was pointing at him.

"I think, Captain, that we've had quite enough running around from you," Dalma said.

And Davis thought, I am going to die in Kosovo.

2030 hours
The NATO airfield at Brindisi

The comm center for the mission was a cammo van parked at a corner of the air base that was even more remote than the hangar where General Krauss had held the briefing.

Sam Wong was the lone occupant of the comm van. He sat, the one human cog in this techno mini-universe that had been assembled to his precise specifications in the very short time since TALON Force had been handed this mission. Such was the power of General Krauss.

The lenses of Sam's glasses reflected the rows of screens as he scanned the monitors at regular intervals. The van's retrieval system was constantly receiving, sorting, and filing intel communications being down-fed from innumerable sources, from NATO AWACS planes to dozens of direct satellite feeds. Sam's fingers flicked nimbly across his keyboard, selecting and re-routing pertinent intel, beamed directly to the ground team. In this way, Sam fancied himself like an air traffic controller, routing all of the electronic intel to its proper destination, on time, without compromising anyone's safety, with the primary purpose being to avoid catastrophe.

The door behind him opened. He glanced away from the monitors for the first time in hours, looking over his shoulder.

General Krauss leaned in, concern evident as he eyed the bank of screens, not sure of which one to look at.

"How are they doing?"

Sam swung back to the monitor he'd been concentrating on. His eyes followed the blip on a radar screen that had a map of the Balkans imposed on it.

"According to the AWACS down feed, they're approaching Kosovo air space right now. ETA at the Suva Reka airfield is eleven minutes."

"What about the Wildcats?"

Krauss was referring to a key element in the TALON Force ground combat arsenal: the XM-77 light armored car. There were four such special vehicles in the force.

"A transport set two down at the airfield this afternoon. It's waiting for our people when they touch down," Sam said as he continued to turn knobs, twist dials, and type info onto his keyboard.

The transport was one of the four special heavy lift C-117 Globemaster transports in the TALON Force squadron. These birds were often used to deploy equipment to operational base sites; a major factor in facilitating TALON Force's rapid response and deployment.

Krauss grunted. "Dammit all, I hate it when this happens. Me having to sit on the bench while the game is in play." He leaned forward for a better look at the blip on the AWACS down feed. He rested a hand on Sam's shoulder. "Keep at it, Captain. I'll get out of your way."

"That's not necessary, sir."

"Maybe not, but DuBois was right. You are the only one of us who can stare at so many computer screens and not go nuts. I'll want a full progress and intel update on the quarter hour."

"You'll have it, General."

"All right then."

Krauss exited the van. The van door closed, leaving Sam alone again in his electronic universe.

His eyes remained glued to the monitors. Sam Wong was a genius and he knew it. As a first generation Chinese-American and a Buddhist, Sam Wong brought subtle, important insights into his analysis of intelligence from the ground, filtered through his firsthand knowledge of the cultures of the regions where TALON Force often worked. Sam contributed a definite advantage that had more than once proved decisive in the successful outcome of a mission. The fact that he spoke Mandarin, Cantonese, Japanese, Korean, and some Hindu didn't hurt, either. But just because he was a computer geek didn't mean that he didn't have some inkling of the human dimension of things. And he could not recall ever hearing more concern in the general's voice than he had moments earlier. He understood. The general was a commander who *cared* about the troops he sent into battle.

Sam sort of felt the same way. In a sense, it was his high-tech communications that was "sending in" the team. He eyed the AWACS monitor showing the radar blip as the jet carrying the TALON Force team crossed into Kosovo air space.

He said to the screen in Mandarin Chinese, "*Be careful, my brothers and sisters. You enter a dangerous, bloody place.*"

Chapter 9

2040 hours
At a secret NATO staging area 2.5 kilometers
north of Suva Reka

Hunter Blake was edgy as he brought the Super Osprey clipping in for a landing at practically treetop level. The darkness whistling by outside was impenetrable, though a sea of starlight was depthless. Then the stars disappeared from sight, blocked out by the surrounding mountains.

He was making an instrument landing. The Osprey was not using its landing lights, and there were no runway lights.

The NATO airstrip had been set down on the floor of a valley just wide enough to accommodate aircraft and was well concealed from both ground and air. Those who knew these mountains well certainly knew of it, but this region had long been an Albanian Kosovar stronghold and so its presence was not talked about much by the locals, and the Serbian government did not know of its existence. There would be a chainlink perimeter fence and patrols and electronic sensors, Hunter knew, but given the nature of this particular mission, their landing would be kept as hush-hush as humanly possible.

There were many obvious examples of NATO's military presence in the region, but this base was not among them. NATO had found it prudent to erect low-profile installations such as this from where they could launch hard-strike, rapid-deployment operations in these outer reaches of the province.

The previous landing of the C-117 transport had been a daytime touchdown. Military air traffic in the region was common. It was the same logic, thought Hunter, that made house burglars usually commit their crimes during daylight, when people's guard was down. Even a lumbering transport, although certainly not noticed as it flew overhead, would not necessarily seem out of place.

The Osprey, on the other hand, slipped in under cover of both the night and the V-22's antiradar jamming system.

Centrifugal force pushed Hunter back against his pilot's seat. He felt like he was in an elevator that was dropping too fast. Then he set the Osprey down with the delicacy of a butterfly landing on a blade of grass.

"All out that's getting out," he grunted to the others as he commenced shutting down the Osprey's systems.

Stan unclipped his seat belt, leaning forward for a better look through a portal at the darkness beyond.

"I can't see a goddamn thing except my own reflection."

"That's unfortunate," Travis quipped. He added, "Don't worry, Stan. There'll be plenty of things to see and do before long, I guarantee."

Hunter unclipped his seat belt. He still felt edgy. And he knew damn well that it had nothing to do with the landing. He could land any aircraft, anywhere. He found human beings, on the other hand, rarely as easy to figure out and handle.

"It's not the things down here that worry me," he said. "It's the people."

Jenny nodded with a small, Mona Lisa kind of smile. "Ah yes. Ceca Keloni."

Travis was the first to leave his seat, and Sarah was

up and moving right behind him. She reminded Hunter Blake of a caged lioness, ready to get out there and chew up some ass.

He stepped from his controls to open the door and kick down the stairs, then he stepped back to make way for the others.

As Travis disembarked, Sarah paused at the doorway to glance at Hunter. "Coming, Hunter?"

Hunter sighed. He joined Sarah at the doorway of the Osprey and looked out at the sight that greeted them on the ground in Kosovo.

A pair of mobile prefab structures abutted the runway. Standing in the doorway for a moment before he followed Sarah down the steps to the tarmac, he could discern strips of illumination peeking from behind blackout curtains covering the windows and doors. There was no flagpole, no barracks. This was a top secret site designed specifically for the in-and-out shuttles necessary to keep the ball in play in this troubled region. The C-117 Globetrotter that had brought the force's equipment had come and gone.

Two Wildcat light-armored cars sat on the tarmac midway between the buildings and the jet.

Between the Wildcats and the jet stood a small welcoming party. The airfield commander and his aide were exchanging salutes and handshakes with Travis and Sarah.

A civilian stood beside them.

Ceca Keloni was exactly as Hunter remembered her from the last time they'd seen each other . . . which, now that he thought about it, was also the last time they'd made love. Now, as then, the lady was just plain drop-dead gorgeous. She wore cammies that matched his own, and her full head of gorgeous blond hair was topped by a beret with a small KLA pin. She stood there waiting, her arms folded, paying no attention to what was going on around her. Ceca's full attention was on the doorway of the jet, and on the man who stood there.

Hunter took a deep breath, knowing from a lifetime of experience that if you love 'em and leave 'em, every once in a while you have to meet 'em again and face the music. This was one of those times.

He walked down the steps of the aircraft and strode forward. When he reached her, he decided there could be no avoiding this confrontation. At the same time, he was here on a mission. This thing between them was a sidebar that would have to be negotiated with care, so he would let her call the play.

He hesitated before her, looking down into those intelligent eyes that had once pulsated with such passion for him.

"Hello, sweet stuff."

She glared at him. "You bastard."

He saw it coming from the thinning of her lips and from the narrowing of her eyes, but he figured that he had it coming and saw no reason to stop her. Still, she moved with incredible swiftness. Her right arm swung up to deliver him a cheek-numbing slap across the face that resounded sharply. "You could have at least said good-bye."

Hunter ruefully touched his stinging cheek. "True enough. Well, I'm glad we got that out of the way. It's good to see you, Ceca."

Then she threw herself into his arms, lacing her hands at the back of his neck, pressing her slim body against him and delivering him the most passionate kiss he'd gotten since . . . well, since the last time she'd kissed him, Hunter decided.

Brief as the kiss was, her tongue slid into his like a snake, darting and caressing and encircling his tongue before withdrawing; the briefest of kisses to those watching, perhaps, but it awakened all sorts of emotions within Hunter, most of all lust. He told himself to stay focused. But the natural fragrance of her hair and the ripeness of her figure in all of the right places practically overwhelmed him. She stepped away from him, and Hunter became aware of Stan clearing his throat.

"Complication number one," said Stan, watching Ceca but addressing Hunter. "Well, you did warn us."

The commander of the NATO airfield was a middle-aged black man, a colonel named Gavin who had a severe countenance and linebacker proportions. He grunted disapprovingly.

"I don't like working with the KLA." He studied Ceca, then his uncharitable gaze swept to Hunter. "And I don't like complications. They tend to get people killed." He indicated the landing strip. "NATO has a lot to lose here, and it's my job to see that that doesn't happen."

Ceca faced him. "I am not a *complication*." Gone was the warmth of the smoldering embers of rekindled love, replaced by another kind of passionate commitment. She eyed Gavin. "Sir, you must know how the KLA helped NATO during the ninety-nine war. They launched courageous attacks, considering that they were so outnumbered. The Serbs were well armed. The KLA sacrificed many heroic fighters."

Hunter nodded, stepping to her side. "I was there, sir."

Sarah sighed. "Complication number two. The lovebirds have made up."

Gavin wasn't backing down. "The KLA are troublemakers. Some of the upper echelon deal in drug money for the cartels in Europe."

Ceca's eyes flashed with anger.

Travis responded before she could speak. "There's a bad element on every side in every war. But we're not here to launder drug money, Colonel. Miss Keloni, are you ready to lead us to the KLA base?"

Ceca cast her eyes downward. "There is a favor I would ask."

Gavin growled deep in his throat. "Favor?" He glanced at Travis. "See? I told you. Trouble." He swung back on Ceca. "We're not in the favor business, lady. These people's lives are at stake because they're here on a specific mission."

Sarah frowned with that genuine concern for humanity that dominated her personality. She'd heard something in Ceca's voice. "What sort of favor?" she asked.

Ceca took a deep breath and began talking. It was not a long story, and she did her best to make her proposal as concise and convincing as possible.

Gavin listened with building anger, but said nothing.

Sarah's green eyes darkened. Hunter remained at Ceca's side, listening with interest and fascination, as did Travis.

Ceca told them about what had happened to her father, and of his likely imprisonment at the Avdylaga estate, located a few kilometers away. She made a plea on humanitarian grounds. Her father was being held only because of her involvement. She pointed out that there would be a low-key, most likely skeletal defense force. She observed confidently that a commando unit such as TALON Force could nullify those defenses and rescue her father.

She trumped with what she knew was her riskiest card. "And if you will not help me by rescuing my father," she said, "then I will not tell you the route to the KLA base."

Gavin reared back as if he'd just been informed that the pope was a transvestite. "Are you out of your mind? We can't have this!"

Hunter touched Ceca's arm gently. "Ceca, honey, I don't think you know what you're asking."

Her spine seemed to grow as rigid as steel. "I know what I risk. The KLA could consider this a betrayal and might have me killed."

Hunter eyed her with open admiration. "I've gotta

say, babe, I've known you in the fire and I've known you in the sack. But this is the first time I've ever witnessed your negotiation skills. Damn, you *are* impressive."

Gavin whirled on Travis. "This is totally outrageous! Major, this woman should be put under arrest." He whirled on Ceca. "You're jeopardizing a mission for your own selfishness."

"Because it's her father," Sarah interrupted.

Gavin blinked, not sure what to make of this. "You're kidding, right? You're not honestly considering going through with this?"

"Uh, this isn't really your call, Colonel," Jenny interjected. "It's the major's. You're just here to make sure the planes land and take off safely. Or am I misstating the situation?"

Gavin grimaced at this united female front formed against him and started to bark an angry retort.

Travis made a placating gesture coupled with a stern glare in Hunter's direction. "That's okay, Colonel. Thanks for your cooperation. Miss Keloni isn't jeopardizing this mission. She has vital information for us, but she wants to deal. We need her information, and the humane thing for TALON Force to do is to help her." His brow furrowed in thought as he analytically processed this. "It could be done without surrendering expediency if we temporarily split up the team. One team handles the extraction of Ceca's father, the other team follows Ceca's directions to hook up with the KLA detachment and go after those pilots. We move fast in both directions." He looked at Hunter. "Then you bring in the first team in the Osprey for the extraction after we find the pilots."

Jack glowered. "I don't want to rain on anyone's parade, but what about strength in numbers? That's always been one of our major assets."

Stan nodded. "I hate it when we split up the team on a primary strike."

Hunter countered this by nodding his agreement with Travis. "Trav, fast as we hit and git, it could be done easy."

"I don't know about the easy part," Travis growled, "but that's what we're going to do."

Gavin looked as if he'd like to slug somebody. Instead he said something profane, turned, and stalked off.

Ceca swiveled grateful eyes in Travis's direction. "Thank you, Major."

Travis said, "Save the thanks for when we get back alive." He glanced at Stan, Hunter, and Sarah. "You three are Eagle Team Alpha. You will be the extraction team for Mr. Keloni. Let Ceca show you where they're holding her father. Jack, Jen, and I are Bravo Team. We're going after the pilots. You'll be called in to provide air cover and yank us out at the appropriate time. Quickly now, Ceca. Tell us what we need to know, so we can split up and get started."

Chapter 10

The ridge ran north to south, several hundred meters above the southwest corner of a high stone wall that surrounded the Avdylaga estate.

The XM-77 Wildcat armored car used only its amber lights to guide it up the rutted path to a stop beneath a cluster of trees. TALON Force's extraordinary, mobile kill-machines were equipped with mounted 7.62mm and .50-caliber machine guns, as well as a retractable, ten-round directed energy weapon (DEW) capable of blowing its way through just about anything.

It was less than thirty minutes since they'd left the base. Stan drove. Ceca sat in the Wildcat's front passenger seat, directing him on how to reach the point overlooking the estate while avoiding the main road that twisted down out of the mountains from Suva Reka.

When they'd hit a particularly wicked bump, Sarah would emit a blue curse. "My fanny's going to be black and blue in the morning! I don't mind a good firefight, but this damn seat is chaffing my ass."

Hunter gave her a laughing glance. "Relax, Greene. You'll be off your butt and killing people soon enough."

Sarah grunted. "Some choice."

The route that Ceca had selected led them downhill at an angle that would have been daunting to most four wheel drives, but the Wildcat negotiated the forested darkness easily enough with Stan at the helm. The XM-77 was particularly maneuverable in extreme, hostile terrain.

They'd followed a pattern of game and hiking trails, overgrown from disuse. Few but combatants ventured into these mountains anymore. Recreational hiking had become a thing of the past in these dangerous times. The headlights of the Wildcat had detected no living things whatsoever as Stan hurtled the vehicle through the night with the pedal practically to the metal.

He killed the lights and engine, then he, Hunter, Sarah, and Ceca left the vehicle and approached the ridge line.

They were practically indiscernible in the sparse light under the canopy of stars. Each person's face had been blacked out with a camouflage cosmetic. They wore identical commando black from head to foot.

Each member of Eagle Team Alpha carried an XM-29 smart rifle and wore a holstered XM-73 smart pistol. As for Ceca, Stan had approved arming her with an Ingram MAC Model 10 machine gun. The short, compact SMG was chambered for .45 ACP rounds with 30-round magazines, capable of unleashing an incredible 1,145 rounds per minute.

They gained the rim of the ridge, a mere ten feet or so from the Wildcat. Stan gestured and each of them stretched out upon the ground to peer over the stony rise.

The wind murmured through the trees.

It was a sound that Hunter had always thought was kind of romantic; probably because it reminded him of those times back in his surfer days in California when he'd been lucky enough to score a weekend date with some beach bunny who felt like some fun and frolic in the mountains at Lake Arrowhead. There had been some mighty enjoyable picnics that had led to some hot loving beneath those pines, he now recalled fondly. He told himself to knock it off and keep his mind on the job at hand.

But doing so was damned difficult because Ceca was stretched out beside him as they peered down at the sumptuous estate. Her naturally perfumed, tantalizing scent caressed his nostrils like silk. He remembered all to well that he and Ceca also had shared some libidinous nights under the pines—and afternoons, and some mornings as well. Hunter sighed inwardly at the memory. The "vibe" between himself and Ceca, as the New Agers back in his native La Jolla would have called it, was a palpable and distracting presence to him, though neither had exhibited any show of affection toward the other since leaving the base.

There had been many women in his life. But the woman at his side now had always lingered in his mind. Ceca was that special one. But at present, of course, the only thing that mattered was the mission. He doubted if there would be any time in Kosovo this time around for a dalliance with Ceca. Damn, he thought. He shouldn't have left her the way he had last time. She was worth more than that. She deserved the best. But what choice had he had?

The TALON Force members scanned the grounds of the estate below them with small infrared binoculars.

The owner of the estate had been wealthy enough to have his own private road cut through the trees to the main road. The lights of the estate glimmered. The high stone wall that encircled the grounds was topped with razor-wire, and if Hunter was any judge of defenses, the barbed wire would be electrified. Supposedly, Mr. Avdylaga was long gone, but the security precautions he'd left behind indicated how much a rich man had to fear in these mountains. As Ceca had suggested, there was sparse evidence of security personnel, but such evidence did exist: a three-man sentry patrol, wearing Serbian paramilitary garb, moved along the inside of the front wall. In the greenish glow of the infrared binoculars, Hunter made one final sweep, memorizing the full layout of the main two-story house and the outlying buildings.

Then he lowered the binoculars and looked past Ceca to Stan. "What do you say, Stan?"

Sarah replied before Stan could. "He's going to say let's nail the bastards and get Ceca's father out of there." She indicated the Wildcat. "If ever there was a time for this baby to prove that might is right, now's that time."

Stan grunted a whispered assent. "Hunt, you ride shotgun," he instructed. He turned to Sarah. "Greene, you operate the weapons system console. And you stay here, Miss Keloni."

Shock registered on Ceca's face.

"Stay here?" She gestured with her MAC-10. "But you gave me this!"

He nodded. "To protect yourself until we get back with your father. We're doing you a favor, miss, by helping you at all. Don't push it. You'd only get in the way and that could get your father, or one of us, killed."

"But I want to go with you! I'm not a fighter, I know. But I can provide you with cover fire during the rescue. I will not get in your way. Please. I *must* be a part of this."

Sarah reached over to touch Ceca's arm gently.

"When we do bring your father out of there, what good would it do for him to learn that his daughter died during his rescue?"

"He knows the kind of woman he raised. He would be proud of me. But that won't happen." Ceca indicated the Wildcat parked behind them. "I can see how advanced your weaponry and equipment are. It is as I'd hoped. There are only a few guards on the estate. This will be easy for you."

Stan brought his binocs back up to his eyes. "Nothing is ever easy in this business."

"I dunno, Stan," Hunter said, hoping that it wasn't too obvious that he was trying to score some points with Ceca because he was also honestly speaking his mind. "Like the lady says, it looks easy enough. But it never hurts to have extra backup on an improvised hit like this."

Stan lowered his binoculars, clipped them shut, and returned them to his pocket. His expression was contemplative.

Among Hunter Blake's many strengths that he brought to the force was that, being great with math, Hunter also was a master planner of insertions and extractions strategies. When not working a mission with TALON Force, his present assignment was working with Air Force Special Ops, wringing out their new gunships and tactics. These days, Hunter could pretty much choose which of those personas to adapt in any given situation. Because of this, he and Stan tended to get on each others' nerves from time to time. They got along because they were total professionals.

Which is why Stan paused long enough to consider Hunter's opinion. He glanced at Ceca.

"All right. You can come along."

He slid backward from the ridge, then stood erect. The others did likewise, briskly redeploying to join him at the vehicle.

Sarah asked, "Are we wearing the suits? Are we going stealth?"

The TALON Force brilliant suits' automatic medical trauma aid feature was always taken into consideration by Sarah, the surgeon and healer. The suits, stored inside the vehicle, were "charged" up before each mission and had a normal power capacity of seventy-two hours without recharging.

Stan reached the Wildcat first. "No time. I don't want to alarm Ceca, but every second counts. Let's go for broke and hit this place hard and *fast.*"

Hunter nodded. He glanced with a grin at Sarah. "Besides, as far as the suit's trauma treatment gizmo goes, let's not forget that we are traveling with a doctor."

Sarah took the ribbing with a wry smile. "Too bad I'm not a brain surgeon, Blake. You could use a lobotomy."

This made Ceca chuckle, and Hunter thought it was the sweetest sound he'd heard in some time. She'd been aloof since they'd left the NATO air base, but he could still taste the fiery heat of her tongue during that one brief kiss when they'd first landed. Women, he thought.

They boarded the vehicle, taking the positions assigned them by Stan, who turned the ignition key and coaxed the XM-77 to life. The Wildcat came equipped with a nearly soundless engine as another of its covert ops features.

The vehicle emerged from the trees, Stan upshifting as the armored car topped the ridge and began bouncing down the dark hillside toward the back wall of the estate, picking up momentum.

The bumpy ride across the rough terrain during the brief decent elicited another string of irritable curses from Sarah where she sat at the weapons system console, dividing her attention between the rapidly accelerating flow of numbers flipping across the coordinate screens and the visual sighting of the approaching target through her infrared laser guidance sighting device. Her fingers hovered near the trigger mechanisms of the Wildcat's arsenal, and inside her battle mask, she wore the tightened grimace of a warrior determined to make the best of what she'd been trained and was committed to do.

Stan drove without lights, relying on the careful study he'd made for the approach during their recon on the ridge. He'd memorized the location of every rock formation and every tree. The Wildcat bounded through the night with nothing to mark its passing except the slightest draft, which was indiscernible from the night wind, brushing a branch here and there but no more.

The rear wall of the ground seemed to be racing forward to greet the Wildcat at an alarming rate.

Hunter felt his knuckles whiten. "Damn. I, uh, sort of feel like one of those test car dummies."

Sarah laughed. "Now there's an honest bit of self analysis, surf boy."

The ten-foot-high solid stone wall was now less than a hundred meters dead ahead, racing at them faster and faster.

Hunter's knuckles grew whiter. "Jesus. Am I the only person aboard who's a little uneasy about driving into stone walls?"

Stan poured on more speed. "Relax, man." He turned to Sarah at her console. "Gunner, make me a doorway."

"Consider it done." She triggered the DEW.

The round that spat from the Wildcat's cannon was the first overt indication of their presence in the evening's quiet. With no more than seven meters to go, the portion of the wall directly in front of the Wildcat's path blew the night apart when the high-powered DEW delivered its destructive thundering fire, a blast that shook the ground and obscured the vision even through the NVD goggles, blowing mortar outward like shrapnel, blotting out everything in the spewing earth and dust.

The Wildcat hammered on through with the effortlessness of a bullet piercing a cloud. Chunks of falling brick clanked upon the armored roof, but they could have been water balloons for all the damage inflicted. The Wildcat exited the haze, ending up behind the main building in what had once been a garden area between double glass doors and a patio. The garden was long untended.

Stan wheeled the Wildcat into a dirt-spewing sideways skid that ended in a jolting stop.

At that instant, the three-man foot patrol that they'd observed earlier from the ridge came running around the far corner of the estate, drawn by the sound of the explosion. They opened up on the vehicle with automatic rifle fire. They might as well have been throwing snowballs. The XM-77 had special electromagnetic armor that acted like a force field to deflect the heaviest of antitank rounds.

Sarah unleashed a pulverizing sweep with the .50-caliber that blew their guts out of their backs.

Stan glanced at Ceca. "You stay here with Captain Greene. Do not leave her side." He nodded to the MAC-10 she held. "Shoot anything that moves."

Hunter grinned. "Except for me and Stan, of course." Then he figured what the hell. He cupped Ceca's lovely face and delivered her a kiss that was as tender as her earlier kiss had been passionate. He then became aware of Stan barking at him.

"Knock it off, lovebirds. Blake, let's go!"

Hunter felt like a million bucks when he saw the dazed, speechless, and breathless expression that made Ceca seem even more beautiful when he released her.

He tumbled from the vehicle with Stan. "Makes me glad Trav put us through that low-tech exercise in Brindisi. Let's rock 'n' roll."

At the weapons console, Sarah swept their surroundings with the laser guidance system, discerning no targets.

The dust was settling from the explosion. An eerie silence enveloped the countryside and the estate grounds, as if the explosion and gunfire and death had never occurred.

Stan and Hunter ran across the patio, each man toting his smart rifle, automatically deploying to a position to either side of the double glass doors.

Stan's NVD goggles indicated that the doorway was curtained from the inside. Knowing that Hunter was covering him, he reached across, gripped hold of the door handle, and tugged gently, hoping like hell that the door wasn't booby-trapped. His instincts told him that the original owner certainly wouldn't, and that the low-profile Serbian unit inhabiting these environs would not take the trouble. He released a sigh of relief when the door eased open. He slid the door open completely, silently mouthing a grateful thanks when there was no responding gunfire from within.

He shoulder-slung his rifle, reached to his combat webbing, and produced one of the Micro-UAVs that he had brought along. He activated the Dragonfly and sent it skimming into the structure. By the time he switched on the receiver unit, the UAV was already transmitting from midway down the main corridor of the house.

The little airborne bug zipped around a corner and zoomed up a stairway.

And there they were: a burly Serb sergeant toting an elderly, frail, apparently unconscious man over his shoulder, accompanied by a pair of riflemen in Serb police uniforms, hastening down a spacious stairway. The Serbs were evacuating, not wanting to give up Mr. Keloni, whom they thought was a valuable intel source. As they stepped past the unnoticed drone zipping up the stairs, the drone's mikes clearly transmitted the sergeant's guttural commands to his frightened riflemen.

Then the Dragonfly was past them, continuing its way up the stairs on its reconnoitering of the remainder of the house.

Stan had seen enough. He put away the receiver and unslung his XM-29.

"They're heading out the front." He spoke into the lapel mike so that Sarah and Hunter could hear him. "We're cutting 'em off at the pass."

"Right, kemosabe," Hunter muttered.

"Roger that," radioed Sarah. Stan could mentally visualize her slipping into the driver's seat of the Wildcat, taking the controls. "Here comes the cavalry."

He and Hunter bolted off in opposite directions from the patio, each rounding the front of the house moments later from opposite ends. He sensed more than heard the silent Wildcat taking up a flanking position.

At the front entrance of the house, under a decorous porte-cochere, sat a panel van with provincial government markings.

Stan and Hunter advanced on the front entrance on the run, when suddenly the front doorway of the house burst open.

The policemen fanned out to each side from within the house, under orders of their sergeant, who moved hurriedly for the driver's side of the van with the lax figure of Mr. Keloni over his shoulder.

The first order of business was the Serb riflemen, who were only now seeing and responding at the sight of forms in commando black emerging from the night. He and Hunter each picked a target. Stan triggered a stream of 5.56mm rounds from the XM-29, chopping off one punk at the neck, sending the headless corpse into a backward skid across the pavement, leaving a greasy trail of body fluids. As for Hunter, his rifle's automatic target tracker, coupled with the XM-29's laser range finder, enabled him to group three quick rounds into the second Serb rifleman's heart.

Hunter and Stan then ran for the van, training their weapons on the man carrying Mr. Keloni.

The Serbian sergeant, with Mr. Keloni still supported over his shoulder, looked more alarmed than determined. He already had the front van door open and was about to leave his human cargo inside, then pile in after him for a getaway.

He never made it.

Before Stan or Hunter could acquire a target through the XM-29s' direct view optics, Ceca triggered a short burst from the MAC-10. She stood beside the Wildcat, which was idling without sound. The small weapon in her grip chattered. The muzzle flashes illuminated her features, which were twisted with outrage and fury as she rode the weapon's recoil, squinting against the gunsmoke and ejected shell casings.

Every round caught the Serb sergeant, dotting a line across the bulky lower waist of his tunic that blossomed instantly like a red belt. His innards then started leaking through the bloody holes. His knees buckled and he collapsed. The undertow of death glazed the sergeant's eyes and he slid first to a sitting position against the side of the van before falling over onto his side. His blood spread in what looked like a growing oil slick in the starlight.

Mr. Keloni had slipped to the pavement and lay there unmoving, as if resting on his side.

Ceca ran to him, oblivious to anything else.

Sarah emerged from inside the Wildcat, carrying a combat field first aid kit. She bolted to where Mr. Keloni lay. She looked at Stan and gave a shrug that seemed to say, What could I do? Then she dropped to her knees beside Mr. Keloni as Ceca tenderly rolled her father over onto his back. Sarah performed a brief field examination of the older man's vital signs.

Hunter assumed a combat stance, tracking with his rifle back and forth, watching the surrounding gloom for any sign of danger, for any sign of something to shoot at. But the area seemed to have been secured.

Stan slung his rifle over his shoulder and raced to where Ceca and Sarah were leaning over the prone figure of the man they had come to set free. Top priority now was to get Mr. Keloni, if he was alive, off this estate and back to the NATO airstrip so that Alpha Team could wait on the call to fly in to back up and extract Travis Barrett's Bravo Team after those missing pilots were located.

Stan glanced at his watch. Less than five minutes had elapsed since he'd driven the Wildcat over that ridge and down the mountain slope for this assault.

When he reached them, Mr. Keloni was struggling up into an awkward sitting position for a man of his age and condition, supported gingerly on either side by his daughter and Sarah. He was speaking groggily in his language, as if he'd somehow fallen asleep there on the pavement and had been caught napping. He appeared rumpled but proud and undaunted.

Ceca was laughing aloud with the hint of hysteria in her voice but mostly with joy, embracing her father, hugging him to her like a child hugs a doll on Christmas morning.

Sarah rose to her feet, snapping shut her medical bag. "Ceca's dad is a tough old bird. He'll make it."

Ceca translated what Mr. Keloni had said.

"My father wondered if anyone would remember a simple old man and where to find him. He only pretended to lose consciousness."

Mr. Keloni looked at Stan with the countenance of an educated, cultured man, despite his disheveled condition, and spoke in a tone of gratitude.

Ceca translated again. "And he thanks you for coming along to assist me in rescuing him."

From where he stood eyeing their surroundings, Hunter chuckled at the old man's spunk and fatherly pride. "So we helped *you*, eh, kiddo?" He then spoke over his shoulder to Stan, indicating the illumination from the house that spilled onto the pavement where the van was parked. "Uh, Stan. What say we get the hell out of here. I don't much care for being in the limelight."

Stan was already kneeling down to ease his arms around Mr. Keloni in such a way that would loosen Ceca's hugging hold of her father, thereby allowing Stan to heft Keloni onto his shoulder for the short hike to the Wildcat.

"I guess you're right," he called sarcastically to Hunter, "much as I do like standing around getting shot at, I guess it is time to pull out." He started to lift Mr. Keloni and rise back to his feet with his human cargo.

But Mr. Keloni had ideas of his own. He again surprised everyone by rising to his feet of his own volition. Dusting off his wrinkled clothing in the process, he spoke again, his eyes on Stan.

Ceca translated. "My father says thank you, but he can move by himself."

"Great. Then let's move."

He and Hunter provided cover as they scuttled to the armored car. Hunter held open a door for Ceca, who was preceded by her father, thus allowing Hunter the opportunity to make eye contact with her.

"They have a saying in my country, Ceca. The apple never falls far from the tree. You're the real deal, beautiful, and so's your old man."

She paused only long enough to reach across and allow her fingertips to graze his cammo-blackened face. But even through the blackout paint, that old tingle of electricity crackled at her slightest touch.

She said, "My brave, beautiful warrior," in a controlled, very quiet voice, with affection but with a sadness in her eyes more than anything else,

"Ceca."

"Why did you have to be such a bastard." It wasn't a question; more a resigned acceptance of fact. Then she joined the others inside the vehicle.

Hunter looked to the heavens, as if for an answer

or at least someone to commiserate with. He sighed
mightily. "Women." This time he said it aloud.

"You're all right, Ceca," said Sarah. "Sometimes
this bunch is too gnarly for its own good."

Ceca's face twisted in a confused frown. "Gnarly?"

Sarah grinned and nodded in Hunter's direction. In a
girl-confiding-to-girl voice, she observed, "Exhibit A."

Stan assumed his position behind the steering wheel.
Sarah took her place at the weapons system console.
Hunter leaped aboard.

Stan floored the lightweight armored vehicle into a
sharp U-turn and fired the Wildcat out of there. They
stormed through the rubble from the hole in the wall
and commenced the jostling return trip across the
rocky terrain back up the mountainside toward the
ridge.

Sarah did not complain about the bumpy ride this
time. As the battle zone receded behind them, she left
her station at the console and resumed an intent field
medical exam of Mr. Keloni, who rode in a passenger
seat, seemingly unmindful of the rough ride, focused
only on the nearness of his daughter in the seat next
to him.

The Wildcat topped the ridge and the glimmering
lights of the Avdylaga estate disappeared behind
them.

2230 hours
The secret NATO base near Suva Reka

Colonel Gavin stood with the TALON Force troopers of Eagle Team Alpha, watching Ceca help her
father into one of the nearby, unlighted quonset huts.

The fact that the mission to rescue Mr. Keloni had
been a success had done nothing to eradicate Gavin's
bleak disposition. "I wonder what the general is going

to say," he grumbled, "when he gets an unexpected guest."

Hunter Blake had decided that he didn't much care for the spit and polish CO. "Colonel, Mr. Keloni is a refugee and with that bunch of dead Serb secret police we left back there, there will definitely be a bounty on his head. Wouldn't make much sense to rescue the old guy and then not get him to safety and to some decent medical treatment."

"I thought you guys were supposed to be elite troopers," Gavin sneered. "You endangered the whole mission."

"Colonel, your general will not mind," Stan assured him. "Mr. Keloni has spent his entire life in this region. He can and is willing to provide invaluable on-the-ground intel. And that will make both you and your general look good, whoever he is."

Sarah eyed Gavin sternly. "I thought things were over, over here in Kosovo. I'll bet nobody back home knows what's going on in these mountains." Then her pixieish smile turned on a hint of charm to deliver the next statement with the vocal equivalent of a velvet glove. "If you'll forgive me for pointing it out, Colonel Gavin, I'm not so sure that our people on the ground over here couldn't use the intel that Ceca's father will provide."

Their attention then collectively shifted to Ceca, who approached from the direction of a quonset hut.

"Father is resting peacefully," she reported. She turned to Sarah. "The sedative you administered during the flight is working. Thank you."

"He'll receive proper medical treatment soon, in Brindisi," Sarah assured her.

Hunter cast a sideways glance and saw Ceca brush away a tear. He slid an arm around her shoulder and gave it a tender squeeze. His only indication that the hug had a positive effect was in the way her back straightened, regaining her resolve.

Gavin was glowering at Ceca. "And now are you happy, miss?"

"Extremely." Ceca's chin was up, her eyes clear, taking in the three TALON Force troopers. "Thank you so much."

Sarah was always embarrassed by praise. "I'm just glad that we got to your father in time."

Stan was pretending that he hadn't observed any of the displays of affection between Ceca and Hunter. Interpersonal relationships nearly always managed to screw up a mission, in his opinion. He had another thought, but Sarah gave voice to it before he could.

"Now we hold our breath and watch the clock," she said, "until we get that call from Bravo Team."

Chapter 11

The mountains began rising sharply within one kilometer of Suva Reka.

Travis drove his XM-77 Wildcat, following the precise directions he'd jotted down from Ceca. The directions routed them around the town.

He and his partners of Bravo Team, Jack and Jenny, wore their Battle Ensemble suits and, like Stan's Alpha Team, each was armed with an XM-29 smart rifle and an XM-73 smart pistol.

The NATO base had disappeared into the darkness behind them. Colonel Gavin and TALON Force had been equally glad to be rid of each other. It was unusual that there should even be the need for a secret military base in a region that was supposedly pacified, but such were the shifting dynamics of this remote border region between Macedonia and Kosovo. Despite U.N. peacekeepers, even when this war was over . . . it wasn't.

At first, the drive along the trails around Suva Reka had been relatively comfortable. Jenny Olsen sat at her control console, next to Travis, her fingers tapping keys and deftly turning dials, as if mesmerized by the ongoing imagery and radar readouts that were among the armored car's defense features.

The Wildcat's engine did not display even the slightest slackening of power as the night-shrouded terrain began its sharp climb. The Wildcat was insulated against external sound.

The trails they followed became more winding and treacherous. From time to time, the vehicle's amber lights would reveal that a trail was no more than a ledge with a wall of a mountain abutting one side and a sheer, bottomless drop-off a half-foot from the opposite side of the vehicle.

The problem was that much of this mountainous frontier was virtually unmapped. It was the remoteness of this frontier that accounted for the disappearance of the two American pilots, and the reason why this route had been one of the only avenues of escape given to the "evicted" Albanian Kosovar refugees during the height of the ethnic cleansing.

The KLA was locked in an ongoing guerrilla war against the Serb paramilitaries in this region. At the upper levels of international diplomacy, it had been unilaterally deemed in the best interests of everyone involved to keep this a dirty little secret. But the fact of the matter was that the United States continued to use the "disbanded" KLA as a kind of proxy ground force in the mountains, despite the KLA's less than savory aspects in other areas. It was much as the American military had used the poppy-dealing highland tribes most effectively as scouts and a guerrilla force during the Vietnam War.

The trails taken by the Wildcat were long since overgrown with vegetation, not being much used either by humans or animals. Noncombatants of all species had learned to give this killing ground a wide berth if possible. Along with increased narrowing precipices along rocky shelves where a trail would take another dangerous turn, the steep route mostly worked its way through heavy timber alternating with meadowlands that lay flat and exposed beneath the starlight.

Jack was leaning forward, closely monitoring what he could of the route they were taking as revealed in the vehicle's lights. They were in the process of traversing yet another of the narrow shelves, and his body was pushed back in his seat against the steep incline up which Travis was piloting the Wildcat. Jack couldn't help but notice that there seemed no bottom to the gaping maw of murkiness beyond the ledge.

As this occurred to him, the ground at the edge of this earthen shelf began to crumble. The vehicle tilted wildly to the right with the alarming abruptness of a chair collapsing.

Travis goosed the accelerator. The vehicle rocked ahead like a punted football. He steered into a swerve as the solid ground behind the armored car continued to disintegrate under the vehicle's weight. The Wildcat barely outraced the evaporating shelf, launching into a crazy skid, Travis swiveled the steering wheel around like a kid doing doughnuts on a snow-packed schoolyard parking lot. It worked. The rear wheels of the Wildcat swung up and grabbed hold of the solid ground of the far ledge. Travis upshifted and pumped the Wildcat into a climb that rejoined the trail, and they were back on track.

Jenny pretended as if she had been barely distracted from her console. "Nothing like a close call to sharpen the senses. Well done, Trav."

"Thank you, Jen." Travis's fists remained gripped on the "ten and two" position of the steering wheel, his eyes intensely probing the night ahead.

Jack wasn't thinking about anything right now except getting his combat boots back on solid ground. "Uh, pardon me for asking." He did his best to keep anxiety out of his voice, but wasn't quite sure he succeeded. "Any way of telling yet how close we are to this KLA base?"

"We may be in Macedonia by now," said Travis. "According to Ceca, who's lived in these mountains all of her life, no one knows exactly where the borders are."

Jack took a measure of comfort in the feel of the XM-29 rifle resting across his lap as he eyed the dense, oppressive terrain beyond the bullet-proof windows. He saw nothing but his own reflection.

"We've got to find our men and bring them home. This is a no-man's land."

Without shifting his attention from the path ahead, Travis said, "This route is far safer than the roads that survive in this region. They're salted with land mines."

Jack couldn't think of anything to say in response, so he kept his mouth shut, and the concentrated quiet resumed among the trio within the confines of the armored car. Only a fool underestimated the enemy of his own field of battle. Jack knew that the Serbians were a tough lot. They came from that East European gene pool that had produced one of the strongest warrior tribes known to civilization before splintering off through the centuries into the fragmented, in-fighting ethnic groups of today. But that toughness was still there. The Nazis had learned that the hard way when they'd fought in vain to pacify Serb guerrillas hiding out and fighting from these same mountains in World War II. Even in '99, the Serbs had hardly shown themselves to be a passive adversary. The Serbs controlled this high ground consisting mostly of passes too narrow for tanks.

The weather over the Balkans was turning murky. The Wildcat became shrouded in mist.

Travis had to activate the windshield wipers. Yet he resisted the impulse to switch on the spotlights, not wanting to make more of a potential target of their vehicle than it might already be in the scope of some Serb artilleryman at any point along the treacherous journey.

The higher they followed this trail, the more it became a nearly impassable dirt track for anything but

the Wildcat. The Cat started really jouncing now, staying the course per Ceca's instructions. The trail had
long ago been eroded by the elements and by the farm
tractors that had hauled loads of ammunition up this
slope. The path led through light green scrub oak,
connected with a slightly wider but similarly rutted
dirt road, which in turn soon tracked deep into the
cleft of a narrow valley.

Without saying a word, Travis braked the Wildcat
to a halt. He shut off the lights and ignition and
opened his door, already exiting the vehicle before it
had even come to a complete stop, observing casually
over his shoulder to the others, "We're here."

Jenny registered surprise and some confusion. She
and Jack had also jotted down Ceca's directions.

"This isn't where Ceca said to stop."

Jenny glanced at Jack, who shrugged. They followed Travis.

They stood in what seemed to be the middle of
the trail that was lined with trees whose thick trunks
disappeared overhead in the dark. There was a chilly
dampness in the heavily pine-scented air.

"Her directions were helpful getting us to a point,"
said Travis, "but after that I pretty much read sign by
myself and made a little detour. Ceca's friends, or anyone keeping them under surveillance, won't be quite
so prepared."

He unslung his rifle and accessed his Battle Sensor
Device on his helmet to scan the night.

Jack and Jenny did likewise.

When Travis's BSD's thermal view revealed a
crouched—or cowering?—human shape, he called out
to that shape, who would be thinking that he or she
was hidden by the night.

"If you speak English, I advise you to step out
now." There was a stony quality to his tone that made
the suggestion into a command.

After the briefest pause, a youthful-sounding male

voice replied, "I speak only little English. Who are you?" There was the quaver of apprehension in his query.

"You know who we are."

Another pause.

Then the quavery voice said, "But you are early. They say you don't come this way."

"They say wrong," said Travis cordially. "It's all right, son. I'm Major Barrett. We're TALON Force, Bravo Team. Take us to your commander."

The young sentry at last revealed his position by switching on a flashlight. The beam of illumination was half expected by the team, who instantly separated from each other, knees bent, prepared to spring for cover.

Travis's Battle Sensor Helmet registered no other hidden human presence in the immediate area.

The sentry was savvy enough to keep his flashlight aimed at the ground so that only suppressed, weak voltage shone, revealing a footpath where the sentry stood, having concealed himself from the trail by a cluster of branches.

"I am Jarmi," said the sentry. He could not conceal his interest in the high-tech appearance of the team member's battle suits. "It is an honor to meet you, Major. Come, I will take you." He trudged off.

Travis gave his senses and his gut a heartbeat or three to appraise the situation. Pretty much what he'd expected. So he nodded to Jack and Jenny, and the three of them fell in behind the Albanian, automatically assuming combat intervals.

The Wildcat was left to itself on this chunk of mountain. Travis did reach into his pocket to activate the car's tamper-proof precautions. Anyone who touched the Wildcat would be knocked onto their ass with a near-fatal jolt of electricity. Anyone who managed to nullify that impediment and somehow miraculously managed to attempt jimmying a door would be zapped into oblivion by a directed blast of lethal gas. It never paid to mess with a wild cat.

Jarmi led them to higher ground. The mist made the rocky ground slippery beneath their boots and would have soaked them to the skin except for the special fabric of their fatigues. As it was, Travis found the light mist refreshing after the confines of the Wildcat.

A few meters from the road, a couple of huge boulder formations nearly abutted each other. A person had to stand sideways to ease between them. The rock formation had been indiscernible from the road, but now loomed like monolithic structures against the black, cloudy sky. The rock formations formed an entrance, Travis saw when they rounded a bend in the footpath and left behind them the heavy timber.

Suddenly, before them, was the KLA base.

The intel printout, passed around to Travis and his troopers that afternoon during the briefing by General Krauss at Brindisi, had provided the recent history of this real estate. It had been a Serbian military outpost until very recently, ostensibly situated here to monitor this zone of lingering blood feuds. A single small, bullet-flecked building, which until the week before had ben a Serbian army barrack, was nestled in a hollow and surrounded by flower beds full of dead tulips. Before the building was a flagpole bearing the Albanian flag.

Their small group made its way through the camp toward the barracks. They naturally drew attention as they passed through the compound. They passed clusters of soldiers, some of whom slept in sleeping bags. Others huddled near fires made from empty wooden crates.

Travis noted that there were both male and female soldiers. He estimated an approximate three to one ratio. Although he had not always been crazy about the concept of women being assigned to combat units in the American military, Captains Greene and Olsen notwithstanding, he did appreciate the long and noble history of women fighting beside their men in armies of insurgency like the KLA. Rebel groups living in the hills, on the run, subsisting off the land, functioned on a whole different set of conditions and priorities wherein a sense of community, of a solidarity crossing gender lines, bonded the outcast rebels with a cause. Anyone who could pick up a gun and contribute to that cause was needed. But within the disciplined traditional units of the American military, Travis interpreted the sexual dynamics introduced with gender integration as only a destabilizing influence on a combat unit. Of course, he always had to remind himself when such thoughts crossed his mind that the female troopers of TALON Force had often enough displayed the fierceness and efficiency that a woman can bring to combat. Hell, thought Travis, those two gals have saved my life more than once!

Some of the soldiers they passed, grouped around the fires, were in uniform. Others wore track suits. As the new arrivals passed, conversations ceased. Expressions smoothed impassively, cast in the shadowy golden illumination of the meager flames of communal fires. Soldiers were armed with everything from bolt-action carbines to Kalashnikovs. Travis's intel was that about half of those present were seasoned fighters while the newer KLA recruits were "flea-market soldiers." It was easy to spot the difference, but the common denominator was that every person here was a combatant for the cause. They all wore the KLA shoulder patch.

Travis saw ammunition boxes stacked here and there, along with bulging tarp-covered equipment.

Now walking at their side, the sentry said, "When we took this barrack, we also captured ammunition." Jarmi indicated the largest of the tarp-concealed heaps. "Mortars. More trucks are hidden. We are lucky. In other battalions, five soldiers sometimes share a single weapon."

"Adem Yashanitz," said Jack. "That's the dude who's honchoing this outfit, ain't he? Read about him in the file on the flight over."

"That is his name, yes," said the young man. "He is a great man."

"How has this outfit been doing since you took over here?" Jenny asked gently.

Jarmi grimaced. "Our luck has not all been good. One day last week, Commander Yashanitz sent out a patrol of twenty-four men. Twenty of the men were killed."

"Another damn war of attrition," Jack muttered.

Eventually, the sentry drew up. "Good luck to you," he said in his best faltering English. "I leave now."

"Thanks for bringing us in," said Travis. "Watch your back, son."

Jarmi nodded politely and left them, returning down the footpath in the direction of the perimeter guard line. He walked away looking over his shoulder, unable to take his eyes off the Americans, so openly fixated with these strangely and heavily armed new arrivals that he practically stumbled over his own feet before hurrying on to no doubt relay this encounter to his fellow sentries.

Jack chuckled. "Maybe you should have told him to watch where he's going."

A pair of sentries stood one to either side of the barrack's entrance, their AK-47s held at port arms, their backs ramrod straight. One of them was what you'd expect: a muscle-bound, permanently five o'clock–shadowed fellow in cammies who looked like he could chew up and spit out chunks of Serbs without working up a sweat.

But the second sentry was something else in more ways than one: an energetic teenage girl, small-boned and pretty. Her budding, nubile figure was encased in army pants and a black jacket. She looked more like a cheerleader than a soldier with her frizzy hair poking out from under her KLA hat.

Neither sentry made an attempt to interfere with their passage into the building. They were expected, after all.

Travis paused on the threshold as he passed the teenage girl.

She was his daughter's age.

Rarely did Travis Barrett think about his personal life while on a mission, but he thought of Betty Sue now as he looked down at this scrappy kid who met his gaze directly but respectfully, here in a war zone halfway around the world from Texas. Travis never missed an alimony payment but that didn't keep his daughter from hating him. His son, Randall, adored him, but Travis's ex had thus far successfully poisoned Betty Sue totally against him. Betty Sue was excelling in academics and sports in high school. Travis closely monitored this through Randall, who updated him whenever they spoke. Like any self-respecting absentee father, Travis missed being a part of his little girl's day to day growing-up life. But right now he found himself thankful that his sixteen-year-old baby was safe at home with her mama, not stuck here in these mountains toting an AK-47.

He asked, "Miss, do you speak English?"

She nodded, beaming with a youthful pride. "I do, sir."

"What is your name?"

"Katrina, sir."

"How old are you, Katrina?"

She blinked at the unexpected question, reminding him of a startled fawn.

"I am sixteen, sir."

"Have you had much training, Katrina?"

She arched her shoulders with pride. He retained eye contact, knowing that Jack would be eyeing the

pert, outward thrust of her breasts accentuated by the
gesture. Travis had other things on his mind. Getting
a reading of the human factor on the ground from this
sort of exchange was invaluable in augmenting and
interpreting intelligence gathered by impersonal electronic eavesdropping or by satellite overflights.

"I've had two weeks of training, sir." Some of Katrina's idealistic pride dissipated as she seemed to become aware of the inadequacy of her response, but
she added quickly, "We were trained by the best, sir;
by veterans who fought the Serbs during the war."

Travis liked this kid. That's why his heart ached.
Katrina should have been playing on the soccer team
and dating and doing her homework, the way his own
kid was.

"I'm sure they were good men and I'm sure you
learned a lot. But two weeks is a very short time,"
he said.

Her jawline set, determined. She indicated her rifle.
"This is a dead man's weapon. I inherited it this morning. Yesterday I went into battle with a single-shot
rifle and forty bullets." She spoke in a tone of new-
found confidence, and of bravery. "We lost four people, but I killed two."

Travis rested a hand on Katrina's shoulder and gave
it a squeeze. "Good luck, miss."

Then he nodded for his troopers to accompany him
into the building.

Chapter 12

2200 hours
The secret KLA base near Shar Pass
on the Kosovo-Macedonia frontier

They entered an open area of the building where a young orderly, who was not much older than Katrina, sat behind a metal office desk.

Jack and Jenny fanned out to either side of the entrance as soon as they were inside, each of them assuming a strategic position so as to enable intersecting angles of fire while diminishing the potential of creating a cross fire . . . just in case an extreme predicament arose. TALON Force was an invited guest here, after all, even if they had shown up earlier than expected. But they were in enemy territory, and so they followed SOP.

The orderly jumped to his feet. He was the only occupant of the open area. He had a pasty complexion that accentuated a horrendous case of acne, and a moist lower lip. His expression was a mixture of surprise and alarm.

Travis duly noted this. Less than a minute had elapsed since their arrival at the camp. Though they'd left a buzz of curiosity among the troops in their wake, word of their arrival had apparently not preceded them. The orderly had certainly been told to expect them. But again, the time that Travis had shaved off their drive time here had its desired effect. Travis's primary tactic in unfamiliar surroundings was to stir things up. When you pushed people in such a way, when you created the unexpected for those you were not sure of and watched them deal with it, you more often than not could more effectively assess what their inner mettle was, which was always useful information in a combat situation.

"You . . . you are TALON Force?" the orderly stammered in an accent as heavy as the sentry's.

"We are. My name is Major Barrett. Please inform your commanding officer that we have arrived."

The orderly hesitated, his Adam's apple bobbing. "Commander Yashanitz meant to greet you personally at the main gate. The commander is presently engaged in . . . a very important meeting."

Travis directed a commanding glare at the orderly. "Inform your commander that we're here, please."

Jack was eyeballing the interior of this low-ceilinged structure, which was brightly lit with overhead florescents. A hallway bisected the length of the building, leading in opposite directions from the open area.

"Seems like the Serbs had one wing for administration, the other for living quarters," he said.

Jenny's line of vision followed his, and she picked up on the thought. "So why are KLA troops bivouacked outside?"

"That's easy enough, ain't it?" Jack was experiencing an escalation of battle awareness; that tightening of the gut, that tingling along the spine. Being inside like this made him feel cooped up. He didn't like it.

Jenny nodded her understanding. "The commander has something going on in this building that he doesn't want his troops to know about."

A nearby office door was yanked open at that moment and two men emerged before the orderly could follow Travis's directive.

The first man strode forward. He was Adem Yashanitz. Travis recognized the handsome KLA commander from the intel file. As the file had indicated, the Albanian radiated an aura of intensity. The tightly controlled muscles of his face registered surprise.

"Which one of you is Barrett?"

"You're looking at him," said Travis. "Thanks for your cooperation, Commander."

"You were not due until later," Yashanitz observed.

Travis's attention shifted beyond the KLA commander. The man who had emerged from the office made no effort to follow the KLA leader into the well-lighted open area. Instead, he lingered in the shadows where the hallway florescent lighting had not been turned on. Travis glimpsed a figure wearing a styleless East European suit, a mousy, bespectacled man in his mid-fifties with thinning gray hair.

Yashanitz made a placating gesture. "My apologies, Major Barrett." The Kosovar commander's English bespoke tutoring by an Eatonian at some point in his life. "I am in the process of concluding a most important meeting." He started to turn away in the direction of the man waiting in the shadows. "Please wait."

"My apologies, Commander," said Travis with identical civil firmness. "TALON Force does not wait."

"But I will be with you shortly."

"Commander, we're here as your guests, so I feel uncomfortable reminding you of the urgency of our mission."

Yashanitz paused, considering this. He obviously made up his mind about something. He returned to face Travis, wearing a more cordial expression.

"Of course, Major. Of course. It is good that you have come to help us. I was only caught . . . unprepared for your early arrival."

Travis could not ignore his gut feeling that something was out of joint here. He spoke to Yashanitz, but his eyes were on the man in the shadows.

"Commander, who's your friend?"

The man in the shadows stepped back with surprising spryness.

Travis reached up and used his index finger to snap down the Night Vision Device goggles affixed to his helmet. He did not like the unknown at this stage of a mission inside hostile territory. The shadows of the hallway morphed into the shimmering green of infrared vision.

There was a door with a push bar at the far end of that corridor. The door slammed shut.

The mystery man was gone.

Jenny started down that corridor. "I'll get him."

"No," Travis commanded.

She halted in her tracks with a puzzled frown. "But he'll get away."

"We've spent enough time getting here. We're here to bring those pilots home."

"Yes, sir."

She and Jack assumed standard combat positions, back to back, their rifles scanning the open area and the hallways.

"But let us be aboveboard and clear with each other," said Yashanitz in a reasonable tone. "The man was a Serbian official. He is willing to sell arms to the KLA in exchange for cash. Your country may have branded him a war criminal, but he helps us."

"Don't be too sure about that, pal," said Jack. "A traitor is a traitor."

Jenny frowned. "You're making deals with the enemy?" she asked Yashanitz.

"The heavier weapons have always been difficult for the KLA to obtain," Travis interjected. "That's why a catch like this base is so valuable."

Yashanitz nodded. "Exactly. You understand."

"I know that what the KLA does get is imported from Eastern Europe," said Travis.

Yashanitz nodded again. "At considerable risk,

Major. I have hopes of eliminating that risk at least as far as my detachment is concerned."

"So okay," Jack said grudgingly. "I can see where a local source would come in handy. But you ought to know, guy, that there's usually a price to pay when you sleep with the enemy."

"But of course I know that," Yashanitz growled with some irritation. His voice, his eyes, his demeanor were like granite. "Do you dare to question that I hold the KLA cause above all else, including my life?"

"Maybe we just don't want your overzealousness interfering with your judgment," said Travis in a cooler voice.

He continued to keep their primary objective at the forefront of his mind, along with the fact that TALON Force was dealing with this Kosovar and his KLA detachment as a step toward achieving the primary objective. He shared the frustration of Jack and Jenny over Yashanitz's dealing with a Serbian official. But the fact of the matter, Travis knew, was that the KLA and Bravo Team were allies. The Kosovar guerrilla commander was a cool-headed, Machiavellian warrior. Travis always trusted his own instincts. Yashanitz's attempt at brokering a deal with a Serbian official was, for Travis, one more indication of the shifting and unexplainable alliances that made this whole Balkan situation so tenuous.

"Can you tell us about your dealings with that Serb?" he asked Yashanitz. "You owe us that much, Commander, for the sake of our own safety."

"What I am doing is honorable," Yashanitz said coldly, obviously not caring for this notion of explaining and defending his actions to an interloper in his domain. "We need arms and we need them quickly to launch an attack. Time is of the essence, Major. You will understand this when I tell you that a renegade Serbian force has built a death camp to exterminate the Albanians in these mountains."

This caught Travis off guard. "Say again?"

Yashanitz nodded earnestly. "Like the Nazis had for the Jews in World War Two."

"Wait a minute," grunted Jack. "That sounds pretty damned far-fetched. What about NATO?"

"There are many Albanians still in these mountains." Yashanitz remained adamant. "They hide out of fear because of what happened only last year during the slaughter by the Serbs."

"This death camp?" Travis pressed.

"The Serbs are rounding Kosovars up to be sent to there. They operate with impunity. Picture it, Major. You have seen the newsreels of Nazi atrocities, have you not? The piles of discarded shoes and clothing. The truckloads of charred bones buried in mass, unmarked graves. Entire families, grandparents to infants, marched into a facility to be gassed, to be put to death, screaming and clawing for air, fighting for life while their captors laugh and watch them die. The corpses burned to ash in ovens. Not a pretty picture, eh? And yet it is about to happen again; genocide against our people, right here in these mountains. And if my intelligence reports are correct, this installation, wherever it is, will become operational at any moment if it is not already. As we speak, detainees are already being bussed to that place, sent to a camp of death. That is why I deal with whoever will best serve the cause of the KLA, be it yourself or a treacherous Serb minister. Would you not do the same?"

"I don't know," Travis said with a sigh, thinking, goddamn all inhumanity everywhere.

"When the facility has been located, we will need firepower to attack it," said Yashanitz. "I do not ask you to forfeit or in any way delay your reason for being here. But if you can, Major Barrett, will you help us?"

Travis didn't have to think this one through. He said the only thing he could say, without hesitation.

"If we come across anything on that, Commander, we'll do what we can."

Yashanitz nodded, the coldness of his demeanor melting. "It is good that you remember, American, that we are on the same side."

"I can pass the word on to the right people and help get you what you need," said Travis. "Ammo, large caliber guns, and mortars. I'll see that the right people requisition. But first things first."

"Your mission." Yashanitz nodded reasonably. "But of course. The American pilots. I understand that. We are to provide you with tactical support."

"I'm thinking it's time to improvise," said Travis. "I'm thinking it's time to change the plan. I'm not so sure we need your help."

Yashanitz's eyes and mouth tightened. "What are you saying, Major?"

"He's saying that American pilots were shot down by the people you're double-dealing with," put in Jack.

"And what makes you so sure," asked Jenny, "that this Serbian buddy of yours wasn't just paying you a visit to get an idea of the layout here before ordering in an air strike to have you wiped out?"

Yashanitz continued to address Travis. "We have offered him a generous payment. Believe me, he has much to lose if he's apprehended by his own people. But what of us? It was my understanding that our forces would be cooperating. You do not wish us to provide tactical support?"

"All I want from you at this time," Travis said mildly, "is whatever you know about where we can find those pilots, Davis and Jackson. We'll take it from there."

Yashanitz chose that moment to avert his eyes, avoiding Travis's direct gaze. "I regret to say that I have nothing to tell you about them at this time." He was visibly uncomfortable. "However, I believe that will change."

"What do you mean, Commander?"

The Kosovar drew himself erect and resumed eye contact with Travis. "We have captured and are presently interrogating a Serbian soldier."

"I see." Travis nodded. "That's why you had the barrack cleared and your troops sleeping outside."

"That," added Jenny, "and the fact that you were playing hanky-panky with your Serbian friend." She glanced at Travis. "I don't like it, Trav. I don't like death camps, either. This mission is taking on a lot of wrinkles."

"This Serb prisoner you're interrogating," said Jack, addressing Yashanitz directly. "Have you gotten anything from him yet?"

Yashanitz glanced in the direction of the living quarters, where entranceways to the sleeping bays yawned from either side of a hallway that stretched from this open area to the opposite wing of the building from where the Kosovar and the Serb had conducted their business.

"When I last checked, the prisoner was being interrogated by my best men at that sort of thing."

Travis's eyes tightened. "I hope that by interrogation, you don't mean torture, Commander."

Yashanitz drew his head back, genuinely startled. "But of course that is precisely what I mean. You surprise me. This is war. I was led to believe that you were a highly trained, technically superior covert force whose only mandate is to get the job done. And yet you play by *rules*?"

"We make our own rules," said Travis. "But there are standards. TALON Force doesn't torture people, and we don't allow it for the sake of a mission or for any other reason. If that were to happen, we'd be no better than the bastards we're going up against."

"Noble sentiments indeed, Major," said Yashanitz with a trace of sarcasm.

The KLA man started to say something else, but was interrupted.

Because that's when they heard the first scream.

Chapter 13

The scream arrested everyone's attention.

It was impossible for Travis to tell whether it was emitted by a man or a woman. For that matter, it was difficult to tell if the scream was even human. But the awful shriek that originated from within this barrack building was the type that would make anyone's blood run cold. It ended abruptly, as if a hand had stifled it, and was followed shortly by a muffled groan that originated from the same direction before tapering off altogether.

Travis wheeled from his conversation with Yashanitz and stormed off in the direction of the hallway that housed the living quarters.

Yashanitz kept pace. "Major, this is KLA business. I must demand that you not interfere."

Jenny and Jack followed, backpedaling with their narrowed eyes and XM-29s covering their backtrack.

"Maybe you didn't hear the major so good, Commander," said Jenny. "TALON Force doesn't go in for torture."

Jack concurred with a grunt. "Sorry, pal, but that does mean any time, any place. It doesn't happen when we're around, get it?"

Yashanitz began to voice more strenuous objection,

but by now Travis was striding into the nearest arched doorway to their right.

Jack followed them. Jenny remained at the door, keeping an eye on the hallway. Jack staked out a position just inside the doorway where he could cover everyone present.

The high-ceilinged room was designed to house a half dozen bunk beds. Heavy shades were tightly drawn across a row of windows. The bunk beds that normally formed two rows, running the length of the bay, had been pushed against the wall, leaving room for a single bunk bed in the center of a cleared area.

The overhead florescent lights harshly shone down upon three men in the room.

Two of them wore KLA patches. They were bull-necked, with crewcuts. One had a cigarette dangling from the corner of his mouth.

The third man lay on his back, nude and tied spread-eagled to the bed. A Serbian army uniform was bunched-up in the corner. The prisoner, an in-shape fellow in his mid-thirties, was covered with bruises. There were cigarette burns on the bottoms of his feet. He was bending his back like a bow because of something one of his interrogators had just done to him.

The Kosovar who was smoking a cigarette was roughly holding a calloused hand over the man's mouth to muffle any further scream. The second KLA interrogator glanced around casually when their commander stepped in with the TALON Force troopers.

Jenny swept the room with her eyes to rapidly register the tableau, then turned her back on the scene to watch for any human presence in the hallway. She felt inwardly relieved that she didn't have to view what was happening behind her. Women could be real bitches, she thought, but male cruelty had a hideousness that repelled her despite her understanding of the circumstances.

The man who had muffled the prisoner's scream

straightened, practically ignoring the Americans. He spoke to Yashanitz.

Yashanitz heard him out. Then without a glance in Travis's direction for explanation, confirmation, or permission, went over to a table and picked up a combat knife. His men stepped away from the bed. He sorted through some items on the table beside the knife—a wallet and its contents that had been removed from the crumpled-up Serb uniform. Yashanitz found what he wanted, plucking up a photograph that the prisoner must have been carrying in his wallet. He crossed to the bed, holding the knife in one hand and the photograph in the other.

As he passed by, Travis got a glimpse of the snapshot. Universally mundane and yet somehow glaringly humane in this stink pit of a human hell, the photograph was one of the prisoner posed beside a grinning woman with a happy child on his lap.

Yashanitz's mouth was a tight line. His eyes glittered with utter ruthlessness. He started toward the man on the bunk, the wholesome family photograph in one hand, the knife in the other.

Standard technique, thought Travis. The carrot and the stick approach. He touched Yashanitz's arm.

"Hold up there, Commander. We need to talk."

"You dare to question my methods and efficiency?" Yashanitz bristled. "We of the KLA do not have your so-called 'high-tech' wonders, Major. We must rely on more primitive methods. This man has verified that there is a death camp and that it is about to become operational tonight. But he claims not to know where the facility is located."

Travis listened, his eyes appraising the tableau of the man and the interrogators standing indolently to either side of the prisoner, the Kosovars prepared to resume at the first indication from their commander. The prisoner's mouth and eyes were open wide at the sight of these new arrivals, but he said nothing. For a few moments, the only sound in the bay was his ragged, gasping breathing, watching in helpless fear as his fate unfolded.

"I understand," said Travis to Yashanitz, "that there is imperative urgency here, believe me. But I will not sanction torture."

"It is hardly your place to sanction or not to sanction," Yashanitz rasped. "Time is of the essence. These mountains are combed with isolated estates and lumber mills, any of which could be renovated to become the death camp that this man knows about. These are the lives of *my* people at stake, Major. I must learn what he knows. He has already verified the rumors that brought us here. Now he will tell us where the facility is."

Travis grit his teeth, appraising the pitiable condition of the man on the bed.

"Has he said anything about the pilots?"

"I intend to find out about that also."

Yashanitz turned with grim determination and knelt on one knee beside the bunk bed where the prisoner was restrained. The man's mouth snapped shut but his eyes grew even wider, his breathing more ragged as he seemed to try to shrink into the mattress, away from the man leaning over him. Yashanitz placed the blade of the knife against the naked man's neck. The razor-sharp edge of the blade glinted dully in the harsh light. Yashanitz leaned in so that his face was inches from the battered, bloodied face of the prisoner. He held up the snapshot so that it was less than an inch from the man's eyes and began hissing questions in Slavic.

Travis knew the SOP that the KLA man was following and could read their vocal inflections well enough to decipher the exchange. Yashanitz was demanding to know where exactly the death camp was located, and where the American pilots being held were. Threats were interspersed with demands for more information, Yashanitz telling the man that they would take a photograph of him moments after his death and send the picture to his wife and daughter. Yes, Travis knew field interrogation procedure. The idea is to make the torment so hellish and unimaginable that it ultimately extracts information. Travis knew the procedure, but could take no more of this inhumanity.

"Stop," he said in a quiet but commanding voice.

Yashanitz removed the blade from the man's throat. He took the photograph away from the man's eyes and ceased hissing vilely in the man's ear. He swung eyes, cold as marble, in Travis's direction.

"I beg your pardon, Major."

Travis indicated the interrogators. "Get these men out of here."

Yashanitz rose, his face an amoral mask. "Major, it is you and your people who should leave. I am surprised at you, truly. Surely you understand that there is a very good chance that your pilots are being held at the same facility that this man knows about."

"I understand that, Commander. And you understand that I will not abide torture."

The moment hung heavy between them. Icy stares interlocked like the cold parry of dueling swords.

"I do not want trouble over a detail like this," said Yashanitz after a lengthy hesitation. "Nor will you run roughshod over my command."

"I have no interest in doing so," Travis assured him. "Look at it this way, Commander. The real issue here is that we need information from this man, and your way isn't working, now is it?"

"And what do you propose, precisely?"

Travis stepped away from the bunk, out of earshot of the prisoner, gesturing for Yashanitz to join him.

"In my country," he said, "the police practice a common interrogation technique that's very effective. It's called good cop, bad cop."

"Good cop, bad cop?"

"One member of the interrogation team puts on the pressure. Not as heavy as your boys have done, but with threats of consequences and badgering. That's the bad cop. You're the bad cop."

Yashanitz nodded. "And the good cop? He takes the side of the person under interrogation, *against* the bad cop, is that not so? Yes, I see it."

"I knew you would." Travis indicated the prisoner. "I want to work it on that guy."

"You are the good cop," said Yashanitz, warming to the idea. "Yes. Yes, we will do as you suggest. What what is the first step?"

Travis viewed the battered condition of the prisoner. He winced. "You've already done that part."

Yashanitz idly tossed aside the knife. It clattered onto the table. He crumpled the photograph and tossed it to the floor like a discarded candy wrapper and commanded his men in their language.

The interrogators cast disappointed glares at Travis but withdrew, leaving Yashanitz and the TALON Force troopers alone in the bay.

The prisoner sagged upon the bunk as if his soul had been drained from him, as if his pain was forgotten, yielding to his humiliation and shame. His expression remained taut, apprehensive eyes darting from Travis to the man who'd just held a knife to his throat and back again.

"Now what?" Yashanitz asked Travis curiously.

Travis extended a hand. "The keys to his shackles."

Yashanitz started toward the prisoner, reaching into his pocket. "I'll do it."

"No," said Travis under his breath, loud enough for only Yashanitz to hear. "Good cop, bad cop, remember?"

"But of course," the KLA man whispered, stopping where he was. He handed the keys to Travis.

Travis unlocked the padlocks manacling the prisoner's shackles to the frame of the bunk bed.

The prisoner watched this with growing dread. When he sat up, Travis nodded to the pile of clothes in the corner. The man practically threw himself into his uniform. Minus his hat, with his face bruised black and blue from the beating he'd endured, his general appearance was a mess. But his relief at no longer being naked was obvious.

Travis called over his shoulder, "Commander. Cigarettes, please."

Yashanitz responded by tossing a pack of East European cigarettes, which Travis caught effortlessly with hardly a glance, busy establishing eye contact and nonverbal communication with the prisoner.

The man stood in a corner of the room, looking frightened, but no longer a cowering naked man. Rather, he was now a captured soldier. There is a difference to the military man, and his nonverbal response to Travis was one of unspoken appreciation.

Travis extended the package of cigarettes. "Do you speak English?" Many people did in this part of the world.

The prisoner nodded haltingly, nervously accepting the offered cigarette. "A little . . . yes, I think so." He nodded appreciation again and stepped forward for the light Travis offered him.

"You know what Commander Yashanitz has in mind for you," said Travis.

The man cast a fretful glance at the Kosovar who hovered nearby, listening. "Yes, I know." The prisoner exhaled a plume of harsh, foul-smelling gray smoke. "Please, American. I do not know who you are, but help me. I beg of you. Help me!"

Travis recalled Ceca's entreaty earlier at the secret NATO air base and was struck again with how dicey this whole mission was, what with both sides in this ethnic war pleading for his assistance.

"You understand that the commander and I are allies," Travis told the prisoner. "I can only help you, my friend, if you will agree to help us." The man started to speak. Travis saw evasion coming. Travis shook his head. "No. Don't even think about bull-shitting me."

The man mentally stumbled over this new word in his limited vocabulary of English. "Bull . . . bull-shitting?"

"I want the truth," said Travis, "and I want it now. Is that clear enough? I can help you, but only if you cooperate with me."

"You can save me?"

"You're a prisoner of the war. You'll be treated as such under the rules of the Geneva Convention. I give you my word on that. No harm will come to you." Travis nodded to Jack and Jenny. "I have the fire-power to back up that promise, and it's made on be-half of the United States of America. You can live to see your wife and child again. That's the deal, soldier, *if* you cooperate. You know what we want. Tell me where this death camp is . . . or I'll let the KLA have you for dinner."

That was good enough for the prisoner.

There was no more resistance left in him after his torture, his rescue, and the promises of this "good cop." Words, mostly in Slavic, poured from him in a torrent, as if he could not speak them fast enough.

Yashanitz produced a spiral notepad and began jot-ting furiously.

Travis regarded the Kosovar from the corner of his eye while centering his attention on the prisoner, gleaning as much as he could from the prisoner's de-meanor and tone even if he didn't understand the language.

It was obvious when the prisoner had divulged all that was demanded of him. The torrent of words abruptly trickled away to nothing and for a moment a pregnant silence permeated the cavernous room. The man sank onto the bunk bed, leaning forward with an air of complete mental and physical exhaustion, physically deflated, his feet planted on the floor, his head drooping, hands clasped before him and the cigarette, unlighted and forgotten, dangling from his mouth.

"It worked," said Yashanitz with smug satisfaction. "Congratulations, Major. Good work."

Travis waved aside the compliment. "What did he say?"

The Kosovar referred to his notes. "The site we want is a civilian lumber concern that the Serbian paramilitaries took over not long ago."

"Is it far from here?"

"No, but the terrain is difficult. It is partly why it was chosen by them for their camp of death. He confirms that it is to become operational at dawn."

"What about our pilots?"

"This prisoner is of low rank," said Yashanitz. "That is how we were able to capture him. We ambushed his platoon when they became lost near here."

"The pilots, Commander," Jenny pressed impatiently from her position at the doorway. "Are they at that lumber company?

Yashanitz nodded. "He confirms that one of your pilots is there."

Jack frowned. "Only one? Two of our guys went down."

"I repeat, the man only knows what he has heard," said Yashanitz. "Rumors within the ranks. He claims he has never been to that facility."

"Well, that's where we're going," said Travis decisively. "And we're leaving now."

Yashanitz gestured for Travis to join him beyond the prisoner's earshot.

"This technique of yours," he said in a hushed voice. "It's a good one, American. You have done well. Good cop, bad cop. Yes, I will remember." The

KLA man's icy gaze settled on the prisoner, who remained seated on the bunk. Yashanitz reminded Travis of an undertaker measuring a man already dead for a coffin. "There is now the question of what to do with him. Will your people kill him, or mine?"

"You still don't get it, Commander," said Travis patiently. "You just heard me promise him safe passage out of here."

"But surely you were only lying to him to get him to talk. We cannot afford to let him live. He would tell the Serbians about our troop strength, our weaponry, everything."

"Not as a NATO prisoner, he won't," said Travis. "I told him that he would live to see his wife and child again, and he will. I didn't say when. All I said is that NATO is in charge on the ground in Kosovo, or they're supposed to be. This prisoner will receive safe passage. Besides, the Serb military is far more likely to learn things from that man you were entertaining when we got here."

Yashanitz furrowed his brow, considering, and when he nodded it was without enthusiasm.

"Very well. I owe you for getting the prisoner to talk so that we can move against the Serbs." His tone of voice lightened to something approaching camaraderie. "And I owe you for what you have taught me. Good cop, bad cop. Okay, it shall be as you say. But keeping your word to a prisoner? Why keep your word to one who slaughters my people? I confess, Major, it goes against my grain."

"Sooner or later, word of what happened with this man will filter its way down to the Serb foot soldier, just like rumors about that lumber yard. And when a soldier is captured and he's offered a deal if only he'll talk, if he knows that he can trust the word of his interrogator, the threats *and* the promises, then it gets easier every time to make the next one talk and the one after that. A pattern of trust is part of the technique."

Yashanitz stroked his chin. "Again you make sense. You are a wise man."

"I want your guarantee, Commander, that the prisoner will reach a NATO base alive. We're moving out against that Serb installation, your people and mine. That means that some of your personnel will have to transport him. I'm counting on you."

Yashanitz bowed slightly with deference after only a minimum of hesitation. "It shall be as you wish."

"Trav," said Jenny from the doorway. "I've got to speak my mind."

"Let's hear it, Jen."

"I sincerely recommend that we consider going the rest of the distance on this one alone, without tactical support from the KLA." She added for the KLA man's benefit, "With all due respect, Commander. Trav, this is getting too complicated. Aren't we putting our mission objective at risk?"

Yashanitz balled his hands into fists. "But that would be unacceptable. Major Barrett, the KLA will attack that Serbian installation tonight to prevent the slaughter of our people."

"And we're here to bring home two American pilots," said Jack. "Don't screw up our mission, we won't screw up yours, how does that sound?"

"Cool it, the three of you," said Travis gruffly, as if quelling a school yard dispute. "We are your guests here, Commander. I appreciate that. We will work together. Jen, I appreciate the input but that's my decision. We don't know these mountains. We need the KLA."

Jenny nodded. "And we share a mission objective. We can't very well let Serb paramilitaries slaughter those people. I understand. All right, all right. Guess I was just letting off steam."

"Ditto," said Jack. "Sorry, Trav, but I'm getting the itch to get something *done,* man."

Yashanitz's mouth remained a taut line of anger. "But why do you Americans not trust me? You have come into *our* country! Is not the KLA commitment to your mission beyond question?"

Jack replied before Travis could.

"I don't know about commitment. I'm just not too crazy about you double-dealing with the enemy."

Jenny nodded. "You're going to pay, Commander, for getting into bed with that Serb."

Yashanitz frowned, genuinely perplexed by this colloquialism. "Into bed? The minister and I have not done that!"

Jack couldn't contain a horselaugh. "Relax, pal. She's not questioning your lifestyle."

"Lifestyle?" The Kosovar's frown deepened. He spoke cultured English. These phrases were foreign to him. And he did not care for being laughed at. "Would you Americans not call what I have done 'covering all of your bases?'" he asked, mildly defensive.

"You're letting yourself get *too* committed," Jack said in a surprisingly nonaggressive, sympathetic tone. "You're losing perspective."

Jenny added in the same tone of voice, "You think you're playing both ends against the middle. Playing that game never wins."

"I said cool it, everybody," said Travis. "Commander, do we have an understanding regarding treatment of the prisoner?"

Yashanitz nodded. "We do."

"Fine. In that case, please have someone take charge of the prisoner. How long will it take for us to get to this lumber company?"

Yashanitz paused to consider. "It will be a difficult drive by night, but it can be done in an hour, perhaps slightly more, I would say. My troops will follow in the trucks we have hidden near here."

"I'll ask you to ride with us in our vehicle," said Travis, "to show us the way." He was already pivoting toward the archway leading out of the sleeping bay. "Okay, everyone. We're moving out. Are there any questions?"

The attack began before anyone could respond.

Chapter 14

A Soviet-made Mi-24 Hind gunship, heavily armed with sidewinder missiles and air-to-ground rockets, swooped out of the darkness. A cacophony assaulted the night, the droning rumble, as if out of nowhere, the unmistakable thumping of the helicopter's approach at first muffled and muted by the mountains as the gunship sped in through a network of mountain valleys.

Then came the shouts and cries of alarm from the sleepy compound outside the barrack building; the sudden awareness and panic of the incoming assault. But it was too late.

The attack left no response time whatsoever. The Serbian Air Force was infamous for being populated with renegade officers whose true allegiance was to the paramilitaries in these mountains. Contrary to every postwar regulation, they supplied the Serbian troops with aircraft diverted through creative bureaucratic paper shuffling, then hidden at strategic points.

There were frantic shouted commands from KLA soldiers outside the building. Then the droning of the gunships became an ear-hammering, earth-shuddering, wall-shaking quake. And then the explosions began.

The Mi-24 positioned itself above and away from the base, as the Serb gunner in the Hind lay down a carpet of fire that ate up practically every square centimeter of the compound from front to back, sweeping across the bivouacked soldiers like a blanket of hellfire.

The scattered, wholly ineffectual return fire could barely be heard beneath the booming, fiery detonations that pulverized the compound.

It was only seconds before the incoming fire chewed its way up to the barrack building.

"Out!" Travis shouted above the uproar. He swung his XM-29 around and fired off a single 20mm airburst round that blew out the nearest window, leaving a gaping hole that revealed the night beyond.

They moved with blinding speed.

Travis rushed over to the stunned prisoner, who had remained seated on the bunk. The man was numb, traumatized. Travis grabbed the man by his collar and harshly tugged him to his feet, giving a push with the palm of his free hand to the center of the prisoner's back, propelling the man toward the hole in the wall.

The jolt startled the man at least somewhat to his senses, and he shambled forward of his own volition.

That's when the rockets hit, obliterating the end of each wing of the barrack building.

Travis was flung as if caught within a tornado, the concussion of the nearest explosion lifting him from his feet as if he were a puppet whose strings were violently jerked. He hit the ground outside with painful, bone-jarring force. He managed to hold onto his rifle and kept on somersaulting from the momentum of the impact, rolling up onto his feet. He felt something wet on his cheek and wiped it away with the back of his raw, battered hand. It was blood from a razor-thin slash made by flying shrapnel. It felt like a bloody but superficial paper-thin flesh wound. At least he didn't feel as if he'd broken any bones, and for the moment that was good enough.

Echoes of the explosions and the thunder of the

gunship began to recede as the pilot of the Mi-24 drew
back in a hover to literally allow the smoke to clear
and see how much damage had been wrought before
selecting targets for the final mop-up sweep.

Travis estimated that this gave him and his people
a window of some thirty seconds to get the hell out
of here. He looked around.

Jack was the first one he spotted through the roiling
clouds of battle smoke. Jenny stood nearby. Each held
securely onto their rifle, and neither had been knocked
off their feet but they did look winded. Jenny was
helping an unkempt Adem Yashanitz to his feet.

The KLA commander nodded his thanks to her,
shaking his bushy head to clear it. Like them, Yashanitz remained crouched, getting his bearings in the confusion of the attack. Pieces of wood and mortar were
still raining down.

The prisoner lay nearby, sprawled motionless, face
down, arms outflung. The back of his head sparkled
like strawberry jelly where a flying piece of metal had
cleaved away the top of his skull.

The narrow confines of the terrain magnified the
chopper's rotor blades pummeling the air.

Travis spoke into his comm net. "The Wildcat. It's
our only chance. Go go *go*!"

"I copy that," Jenny responded. "Best idea I've
heard all night!"

"Gone gone *gone*!" replied Jack.

Jenny took point, her XM-29 probing the darkness
before her. They sprinted around and through flaming
debris, leaving what had been the barrack building.
Yashanitz kept apace, holding the pistol he'd worn
holstered at his hip.

The rubble of the structure was a fiery inferno. The
roof had disintegrated. Most of the building had been
obliterated, leaving only a gutted mass of charred rubble. Flames licked the night sky.

They left the burning ruins, skirting what remained of the compound.

Cries for help and the moans of the wounded and dying stabbed the air through smoke that drifted across smoldering craters. Bodies were scattered everywhere. There were a few stunned soldiers, wounded yet walking around in a daze. These were not fully trained, vastly experienced combatants, and there was nothing but stunned confusion in the immediate aftershock of the air assault.

They dashed past a man pleading for help in his native tongue, shuddering upon his back, holding onto his intestines like pieces of shiny bloody rope.

When Yashanitz saw this, his pace faltered. Emotion twisted his features with agonized indecision, and he started to turn toward the injured man.

Travis hurried alongside Yashanitz and shoved into him roughly, his palm pounding against the center of the Kosovar's back much as he'd shoved the prisoner moments earlier.

"It can't be that way, Commander. Keep moving. You've got medical people to tend to your wounded. We've got the mission."

Travis then drew up short when he spotted a crumpled figure near the remains of the barrack ruins.

It was Katrina.

The teenage girl lay on her back. Most of her torso was a pulpy, ragged mess. She had died holding her rifle, no doubt aiming it at that advancing, fire-spewing gunship, knowing she didn't have a chance in the world. That's the kind of soldier she'd been, thought Travis. Even facing certain death, she was ready to take on the enemy.

Damn, he thought.

"My God," said Yashanitz solemnly, reverentially. "That what a waste of human life . . ."

They were halfway to the outlying rock formations where the Wildcat sat when the Mi-24 gunship pilot decided that the smoke had cleared enough to allow his gunner to destroy anything left moving on the ground.

The oncoming gunship blotted out the sky, its whirling rotors catching the flicker of the ground fires, lending the helo a hellish halo of flame. The gunship's crew sailed in this time, expecting no real resistance, prepared for a procedural flyover. They did *not* expect troopers on the ground who were ready and waiting for them with XM-29s.

This was exactly the sort of combat situation the smart rifle had been designed for. Priority number one had to be the helo swooping in.

"Jack. Help me out," Travis called across the comm net. "Jen. Back us up."

Travis and Jack swung their rifles toward the incoming chopper. They unleashed a sustained barrage of armor penetrating smart bullets, launched unerringly by the millimeter wave sensor and aiming device located beneath the rifle's barrel. Jack threw a couple of 20mm airbursting grenades at the helo for good measure.

Round after sizzling round from the XM-29s pierced the Mi-24 fuel tank. Jenny triggered a sustained burst that seared the sky with a blinding detonation of destructive fire.

The gunship blew apart in an eruption far more forceful than any thus far, igniting the night like a nuclear fireball that hung suspended in midair for several seconds. Secondary explosions sent rockets shooting in all directions overhead, showering sparks like fireworks. Then the fiery wreckage plummeted to earth with a crash that spewed flaming fragments in every direction.

Travis and his group continued on to the rock formations, hurrying through the niche between the rocks that led to the footpath. He assumed point position, and was the first to dash through the opening in the direction of the Wildcat.

Yashanitz accompanied them, casting regretful glances over his shoulder at the smoldering remnants of his command. The air hung heavy with thick smoke and the stench of destruction.

Jenny and Jack brought up the rear.

Once through that crevice in the towering rock formations, an eerie silence pervaded the mountaintop. The fires, the cries of agony and suffering, were shut off by the dark, thick pine forest.

Suddenly, footfalls came rushing in their direction from below, advancing on the base.

"Fade," Travis whispered.

Without hesitation or response, his group fell back into the inky blackness beside the path.

The KLA base, behind the wall of rock and trees, could have been a million kilometers away, thought Travis. There was only silence, broken by the pounding of combat boots on the footpath. They emerged on Travis's NVD sight.

It was Jarmi, the youthful sentry from earlier, along with several other KLA troopers, hurrying in from their stations.

Travis stepped onto the footpath along with the others. The soldiers drew up short. Yashanitz stepped forward. With a nod to the American commandos, Jarmi and the other two sentries listened raptly as he concisely reported the situation to them in their language. They then hastened on their way, vanishing into the darkness.

Yashanitz turned to the TALON Force troopers.

"I have sent them to the trucks and to select a handful of my best surviving fighters. I gave them directions. They will follow. We will rendezvous at the Serbian base. I told them to hurry, and they will."

"Let's do the same," said Travis.

They dashed down the footpath and when they

reached the Wildcat, undisturbed, parked in the grove of pine trees, Travis reached into a slit pocket in his combat suit and produced the matchbox-sized device and clicked off the armored car's locking and defense systems.

The doors automatically unlatched, popping open.

Jenny climbed aboard, assuming her post at the computer console. She set aside her rifle, her fingers flying across the keyboard to summon up an array of maps of the region that were stored in the computer.

"I hate machines as much as the next woman but I've got to admit, there are times when this high-tech stuff does come in handy."

Travis sat behind the steering wheel, motioning for Yashanitz to lean forward to better see the maps on Jenny's monitors.

"We're ready for you to show us those directions now, Commander."

Yashanitz concurred.

Jack and Travis also leaned forward grimly, ready to memorize the route that Jenny would be entering into the guidance computer.

Jack gave voice to the apprehension in his gut. "If even one of our pilots is at that Serbian base, and if that death camp is set to go operational, then our time's running out damn fast."

Chapter 15

"I don't like it either," said the President of the United States, "but the TALON Force mission into Kosovo is aborted." He looked across the interior of the presidential limousine at one of the two passengers who rode with him. "You're going to have to pull the plug on this one," he instructed General Freedman. "Buck, you're White House liaison for TALON Force. I want you to stop Barrett and his team in their tracks, is that understood? They are to take no further action, and the matter is closed to debate."

The commander of the government's Special Operations Command frowned deeply. "But, sir, there are still two missing American pilots over there."

"I'm well aware of that," said the president with a weary sigh. "But there is still also the fact that Kosovo is a NATO responsibility. The supreme command in Brussels retains the right to issue directives to member nations concerning ground operations and that is the case here."

The presidential motorcade was traveling smoothly through midtown District of Columbia traffic that could often be gridlocked, but never for a presidential motorcade. The leading Secret Service vehicle worked its siren, sailing unimpeded through an intersection, with a second Secret Service vehicle, a van—the "war wagon"—right on its tail. The president's limo was sandwiched by two identically matching vehicles. Each of the four of the Secret Service cars carried four agents apiece.

Two agents and a chauffeur rode in limo one, separated from the president and his guests by an opaque, soundproofed window. This was the president's "private time." Recording machines and other monitoring devices had been deactivated, leaving the limo's main compartment a cocoon of privacy.

General Gates, Chairman of the Joint Chiefs of Staff, seated beside Freedman facing the president, grunted an expletive.

"Mr. President, with all due respect, we're the most powerful nation in the world. I advise that we start acting like it."

"Your respect for the office is duly noted, as is your opinion," said the president dryly. "Fact of the matter is, George, I am in full agreement with you on this."

The chief executive was on his way from delivering an innocuous address to a youth club group, heading back to the White House for a high-profile Rose Garden photo op with the visiting king of Jordan and his wife. There would be no questions allowed from the press at that event, naturally.

"NATO insists that ongoing negotiations with Belgrade concerning return of the American pilots is about to bear fruit," continued the president. "They insist that it is a very delicate matter and that if any covert action, mounted by us, were to go sour the same way as, say, President Carter's botched rescue of those Iranian hostages in the 1970s, then the whole thing could go to hell, both any chance of us getting our pilots back safely or of NATO maintaining a meaningful dialogue with Belgrade."

"Meaningful dialogue," grunted Gates irritably. "I'm sure the everyday civilian in Belgrade wishes this whole mess would just go away, just like the rest of us. America has no quarrel with them. But as for the bosses in control over there, why, they're nothing but a bunch of murdering hairballs, Mr. President. My recommendation is that they're not worth having a dialogue with.''

"And don't forget, sir," added Freedman, "Jimmy Carter didn't have TALON Force. They do have a one hundred percent efficiency rating since their inception.''

"There's a first time for everything to turn to shit, unfortunately.'' The president stared at the passing street scene wistfully, as if he wished he were a part of it, not sharing this short, crosstown trip with the grim-faced, uniformed men seated across from him. "Well I guess I was wrong. Apparently the subject is open for debate.''

Freedman leaned forward earnestly. "Sir, it's never too late to reconsider canceling a viable option. If we abort this operation, we're giving up the best chance we have of getting our pilots back. And since Major Barrett and his people haven't fumbled a mission yet, and they're now poised to put their lives on the line for this mission, don't we owe it to them to allow them to continue with the job they've been handed? I think we owe that to everyone involved.''

The motorcade swung onto Pennsylvania Avenue.

"We owe an allegiance to NATO," said the president, but there was the hint of doubt in his voice.

"Mr. President, you chose me as chairman for your Joint Chiefs because you want my opinion,'' said Gates gruffly, "so here it is. The world owes *us*. It's American fire power, resolve, and moral fiber that's made this planet a safer place for people and fledgling democracies all around the planet, and then they come around whining about the way we get things done.'' He snorted another expletive.

The president swung his eyes back to the men riding with him. "The NATO directive was not specific," he conceded. "TALON Force is far too deep cover for the Pentagon to know about, much less NATO. But NATO command claims they have picked up something in the wind about us initiating a covert operation to extract those pilots. That's why their shorts are in a knot."

"NATO is shooting in the dark," said Freedman. "'Those Americans, what cowboys. Better let them know that no monkey business will be tolerated.' Heck. They don't know a thing about our Kosovo mission, sir. They couldn't."

"Given the nature of the NATO posture," said Gates in a more conciliatory tone, "is there any wiggle room whatsoever that we can work around?"

The president sighed. "You want the God's truth just between us girls? The mood I'm in thanks to those lying sons of bitches in Belgrade, I've got half a mind to nuke them back to the stone age if they don't give us our men back."

The lines softened in Gates's leathery face. He chuckled, relieved. "You might want to be careful with two-gun talk like that around your chief of staff, sir," he said. "He'd have an aneurism if he heard you say anything like that. And uh, sir, you're, uh, not seriously considering taking any sort of military action like that, are you?"

The president chuckled with scant humor. "Relax, General. This is my place to vent, remember?" He shifted his darkening gaze out again through the heavily tinted, bullet-proof windows. "So what have we got so far? We've lost a twenty million dollar aircraft. We don't know if it went down in Kosovo or Macedonia. We've lost the crew of that fighter plane, their location presently unknown. *And* we haven't bothered with the nicety of informing the American people because all of the polls show that we're on thin ice as it is. Belgrade is lying their asses off, with NATO being hung out to dry, spread too thin and not having a clue."

The president swung in Freedman's direction. "And you report to me that this top-notch covert ops unit of yours delays action by illegally interceding in Kosovo's internal politics, not to mention NATO's jurisdiction, when they rescue some young woman's father! I mean, I appreciate their success ratio thus far, Buck, but excuse me for asking just what the hell sort of cowboys did you send on this job?"

During his tenure at his duty station in the basement of the White House, Freedman had learned early not to pay too much heed to the president's mood swing into petulance, especially when things weren't going well.

"Cowboys and cow*girls,* sir," he corrected in his best polite tone, "thanks to one of your illustrious predecessors integrating the genders in combat units. But to answer your question, sir, I repeat, TALON Force is the only sort of crew that has any chance at all on a mission like this. They have the best in equipment and backup, and they play by their own rules. Sometimes improvisation is necessary."

The president sighed again, the anger vented, his mood swinging back to the middle as it always did. "You've never let me down yet, Buck, so I'm cutting you slack on this one. But I hope to hell that you know what you're doing."

"I understand, sir," said Freedman. "And TALON Force *is* the best we have in covert ops. This is precisely the sort of operation they were designed for."

"I just don't like the idea of not having radio contact between Travis's people on the ground and their backup at Brindisi. I know, I know, the terrain. The mountains. Communications will be restored as soon as their progress permits. Yada yada. But the fact remains, dammit, that at this point in time, we have no contact with the people we've sent over on this mission. And when the shit hits the public fan, if it does,

I can assure you, gentlemen, that we will be the ones
hung out to dry."

"Those pilots are the only priority TALON Force
is concerned with, sir," said Freedman respectfully.
"Major Barrett and his people are the best we have.
And we've outfitted them with the highest level technical and tactical support of any unit in military or
covert ops history. Sure, anything could be happening
over in those mountains right now. Believe it, sir,
that's driving me nuts too. But this is their operation
and this is what they're the best at."

The president studied Freedman. Then he nodded.

"Thanks for reminding me of that fact. That's why
I like having you around, Buck. You cut through the
bullshit."

"Yes, sir," said Freedman dutifully.

The limo began slowing as they approached the
White House. The president tapping his fingertips
upon the plush upholstery was all that belied his outward demeanor of confidence.

"Sometimes, guys, it really sucks being the president," he said with feeling. Limo one braked to a stop.
These were the final seconds before Secret Service
agents outside would spring open car doors. The president pinned Freedman and Gates with the look of a
man hoping for a miracle. "Okay, debate's over. There
is some wiggle room and I'll milk it for what I can,
but that won't be much, gentlemen."

"What can you give me, sir?" asked Freedman.

"Two hours, Buck."

Gates growled. "But, Mr. President, that's as good
as giving those commandos no time at all."

"Not if they're half as good as Buck claims," said
the president. "Believe me, gentlemen. With the uni-
fied force of the NATO countries breathing down my
neck, for two hours I can con them with smoke and
mirrors, but not for much more on something as big
as this. TALON Force is the best, as I understand

it." The president eyed Freedman. "Can the Kosovo mission possibly be a done deal within that kind of severe time frame?"

Freedman nodded. "TALON Force has another opportunity to prove what they can do, and they will."

"Thank you, sir," said Gates to the president. "Hope I wasn't speaking out of turn before."

"Let's save the thanks for after those pilots are home," said the president. "And you're right, General. I keep the both of you around to help steer me through troubled waters like these." The commander in chief added soberly, to Freedman, "And I sure as hell hope that you're right, Buck, about Barrett and his people. Because right now, the truth of the matter is that the only hope our pilots have is TALON Force."

**2230 hours
The Serbian installation on the
Kosovo-Macedonia frontier**

Davis had not been presented with a second opportunity to attempt an escape.

Captain Dalma had naturally taken it as an extremely personal affront to his ego, an assault on his honor, that this upstart American prisoner should actually implement his escape to the point of having hidden himself in the bed of the truck that was about to leave the Serb base.

As long as he lived, Davis knew that he would never forget the sensation of lying there on his back in the bed of that truck, holding his breath, his heart frozen in his chest when he saw Dalma leaning over the side of the truck, aiming a pistol at him.

Dalma supervised Davis's capture and subsequent "processing" by his Serb strong arms, step by mali-

cious step. Throughout, Dalma's cammo fatigues had
remained clean, pressed, and sharp. So had his manner. He issued commands as Davis was roughed up
and hauled away by the Serb paras back to this single-
window executive office in the lumber company's otherwise vacated administration building.

Dalma ordered his men to tie Davis's hands behind
his back, and his ankles to a plain wooden chair that
had been brought into the otherwise well-appointed
office. Then two Serb troopers were posted on either
side like bookends, each of them holding an AK-47,
glaring fiercely at their quarry.

Dalma appeared satisfied. He stood there for a moment between the pair of guards, his arms folded before him smugly. He swayed back and forth on his
boot heels, a smirk on his face, vast satisfaction and
enjoyment in his eyes.

"You see, Captain Davis? Even that famous American ingenuity you people are so proud of fails you
now. I'd say that you are again my prisoner and that
you shall remain here until it is decided otherwise."

Davis tried to shrug, but his bonds didn't allow it.
He managed a smirk of his own. "And I'd say you're
a sorry sack of shit, Captain Dalma. I'm not going to
die here."

"We'll see," said Dalma with a malicious glint in
his eyes.

Then he hauled off and delivered Davis a widely
swung backhanded slap to the side of the head, pack-
ing enough of a wallop to pitch Davis's senses into
orbit and send his body toppling over backward, chair
and all. The Serb guards hastened to right the chair
and the prisoner and they were none too gentle
about it.

Dalma made a production of examining the knuckles of his hand for any damage that might have been
caused by delivering the blow. Finding no scrapes, he
eyed Davis with a sneer. "It might be best for you if

you hold your tongue, Captain, and thank your god
that you're not dead."

Davis felt the trickle of blood seeping from where
his split lower lip was already swelling. "Maybe
you're right."

Dalma coughed up a chunk of phlegm and spat. His
aim was good. The gob caught Davis square on the
cheek. Davis braced himself, wishing like hell that he
or someone could brush the foulness away.

Dalma laughed. Then he turned and walked out,
leaving Davis alone with his two Serb playmates. The
guards laughed at the dripping slime on Davis's cheek.

They left Davis sitting there for a while. He lost
track of the passage of time. At one point, his chin
tilted forward and he drifted off into a fitful but merci-
ful sleep, tied up right there in the chair.

He dreamed again. Another incredibly vivid dream.
Real enough to walk through. It was more of a memory than a dream, because in it he relived the first
time he'd ever met his weapons systems officer, Jack
Jackson.

*Stateside. First training exercise flight together over
the Arizona desert range to push an F-16 through its
paces and size up each other's capabilities.*

*Jackson had a big man's expansive good nature; a
fun-loving, woman-adoring bachelor with a contagious
laugh. But it was equaled by a serious side, tempered
by skill and instinct, displayed that first day over the
Arizona bombing range. From the start, Davis had
known that Jackson would be a topnotch WSO.*

*On the ground after that flight, when they were
changing from their flight suits to their civvies, Davis
had been glad to see that the professional respect and
personal acceptance was mutual. They decided to
socialize.*

*After dinner that night, the happy-go-lucky Jackson
had stated a preference for one of the topless bars in
town. Davis had declined, being a family man. Jackson*

said he understood. Besides, the WSO said, it was just
as well. Davis would be a good influence on him. As
Jackson ruefully put it, "I always seem to end up in
scrapes when I go into them titty bars. Don't know why
I keep going back. Must be the titties, I guess." And
so instead of a topless bar, after dinner at a Thai restau-
rant frequented by servicemen and their families, Davis
and Jackson had taken in a movie and had ended the
night at a Baskin-Robbins . . . where Jackson had got-
ten into a scrape by getting irritated at a drunken off-
duty Marine who'd been harassing a brace-toothed high
school girl working behind the counter. Jackson had
KO'd the offensive jarhead through a plateglass win-
dow and had offered his buddies a taste of the same,
but they had declined to participate. Jackson and Davis
had withdrawn before the police or the MPs could
show up, and Jackson had been contrite as hell all the
way back to the base. "Guess I just have a thing for
getting into scrapes. Sorry, man, but next time I'm
going out by myself. If I'm going to get in a scrape,
might as well be able to watch some titty while it's
happening . . ."

Davis had always found himself smiling at that
memory over the years, and he dreamt smiling at it
now, until another head-pounding backhand slap to
the head shattered his reverie and jolted him back to
the land of the living.

He gave his head a shake to clear his vision and
tried to focus on the bleary image of the man who
towered over him.

"Well well, Captain Dalma. You've taken a liking
to slapping the shit out of me. That's not good news
for me." Clarity of thought returned with his clarity
of vision. "It is still captain, isn't it? Or was I out long
enough for this horseshit excuse you call an army to
promote you to something like a ten-star general for
recapturing the American pilot?"

Dalma appeared to contemplate hauling off on him again.

Davis didn't give much of a damn. The blood on his chin and the spittle on his cheek were both caked and so forgotten. His guards must have let him nod off for a while then.

Dalma made up his mind. He drew back his hand for another angry swipe.

"Captain!" A new voice in the office snapped like a whip from beyond Davis's line of vision. "Stop. I wish to speak with him."

Dalma lowered his hand and stepped back.

"Of course."

The speaker stepped forward, positioning himself directly in front of Davis.

He was a meek-looking fellow in an ill-fitting gray suit, in his mid-fifties. The lenses of his glasses were thick. His silver hair was thin. His eyes were flat as gray slate. "I am Viktor Tilzo. I am in charge here." The man's accent was thicker than Dalma's. He looked like a pale-skinned bureaucrat who rarely went outside of his office, much less out of Belgrade.

"I, uh, sort of guessed that, Viktor, what with the way you've got the captain jumping and all."

Davis took satisfaction in the reddening he saw in Dalma's features.

Tilzo also seemed displeased, "I am an official of my government. You will address me as Mr. Tilzo."

"Go screw yourself, Viktor."

Tilzo's eyelids lowered once over his slate eyes and if his eyes registered any response to the insult, it happened during that instant when his eyelids were lowered. Otherwise he revealed no reaction. "You have been a considerable inconvenience for us tonight, Captain Davis. You will forgive Captain Dalma. He is rather displeased with you at the moment."

Davis snorted. "He ought to be. I made an ass out of him and of his security, didn't I?"

Hearing this, Dalma blew up in heated Slavic curses. He started around Tilzo, charging at Davis in blind anger, his hands reaching out like claws for Davis's neck, looking pissed off enough to throttle the life from the wise ass tied to the chair. But again he forced himself to draw to a halt when Tilzo raised a hand.

Tilzo otherwise ignored Dalma and studied Davis, stroking his chin reflectively as if he had an invisible beard.

"Captain Davis, I would not be quite so self-assured if I were you. It would not do to overly agitate Captain Dalma. He is your host, after all."

Davis made a vague, vain show of struggling against his secure bonds. "Yeah, right."

"Captain, you are in a most precarious position."

Davis took a moment to scrutinize Tilzo in return. He thought, Meek, hell. This son of a bitch from Belgrade will outlive Dalma by decades. The meek inherit the power if they are cunning and slick and deadly. Davis sized up Tilzo as being all three.

"You must be one of those cogs in the Belgrade government that slipped right through the cracks after the war. Now they send a suit. I should have expected you, Viktor."

Tilzo blinked with a flash of genuine confusion, momentarily caught off guard. "What is this you say about my suit?"

"Figure of speech. I wasn't talking about your suit. I was talking about you. You're a long way from Belgrade, Viktor. Why did they send you all the way up here into these godforsaken mountains? You sort of look out of your element, pal."

Tilzo glowered, somewhat taken aback by the prisoner's flippancy. He snarled nastily, "I am not your pal, Captain Davis."

Davis snarled right back at him. "I heard that. So where's the body of Jackson, my weapons officer? My government is going to want him back as much as me, dead or alive. That's why you're here, isn't it? To handle me?"

Tilzo's scrutiny became a scowl of displeasure. "Partly. You are insolent, Captain. I think that first I must cure you of that."

"Well go ahead and give it your best shot, Vik."

If the shortening of Tilzo's first name offended him, as Davis intended it to, the Serb gave no indication.

"You think that simply because you are an American, that your life has special value," said Tilzo. "You believe that we will not kill you. You seem to be secure in that knowledge."

"I hope you don't kill me," said Davis truthfully. "And no, my life's not special to *me* because I'm an American. Uh-uh. That's what makes my life special to *you*. There are a lot of areas that need settling between the NATO alliance and the U.S. and Belgrade. It's an ongoing process and there's a lot of bargaining involved. And I'm the best bargaining chip you've had in a long time, aren't I, Viktor?"

Dalma sneered where he stood next to Tilzo. "You mean nothing to your country. They have not even made public the fact that you and that other pilot were shot down. And there is something else."

Davis's throat went dry. "Something else?"

Tilzo nodded with satisfaction at the sobering effect Dalma's statement had in curbing Davis's attitude. "That is correct, Captain. You see, your country doesn't even care about you. The full military resources at their command, and they have not even publicly announced that you've been taken prisoner. They have not launched cruise missiles or air strikes."

Dalma snickered. "They sent in one commando unit, that's all. Just like your President Carter thought he could use one commando unit to rescue those hostages in the heart of Iran during the 1970s. Well, the team they sent after you is already finished just like that Delta Force team of Carter's."

Davis looked at Tilzo. "What the hell is this moron talking about?"

He was trying to get a rise out of Dalma, out of pure spite and nothing else. And he got one. Dalma's fists clenched as he muttered curses. But Tilzo's icy look held the Serbian in check.

Tilzo studied Davis.

"The Captain is referring to the fact that, before I arrived here, I was a guest at a base not far from here." He paused for dramatic emphasis before adding, "A base camp of the Kosovo Liberation Army."

"It's no news that you are still fighting a war up in these mountains that's supposed to be long over. That's what the targeting of that Serb facility was about when me and Jackson were shot down."

Tilzo nodded. "Your grasp of our internal struggle with the rebel holdouts is admirable." The gloating came mixed with sarcasm. "Then you may also be interested to know, Captain, that while there as a guest of the KLA commander, I had a brief encounter with an American commando unit that happened to arrive at the KLA base at the same time that I was about to depart."

"Do tell." Davis tried to swallow, but couldn't."

"Your NATO surveillance knew about the installation that you were sent to destroy, obviously. But they did not know about *this* installation. However, the KLA knew. They were amassing a force, not far from here at the base of which I speak, to attack us."

"So you went to visit them?"

Tilzo smiled an unpleasant smile. "Pilots and commandos are not the only ones who go behind enemy lines. Although it was a new experience for me, I admit. We played on their greed, you see. Another reason I am here is to investigate the matter of some of our paramilitary commanders, and officers of the regular army, selling arms to the rebels for cash. In this case, it was easy enough to persuade the local

KLA man that I was of such a persuasion. We met tonight. In his mind, we were concluding a business arrangement. He arranged for the cash transfer. In reality, I was there to make sure that *he* was there, if you understand."

Davis regarded Tilzo. This guy was a cold-blooded viper who liked to look a man in the eyes before sending him to his death.

"We call it target confirmation, Viktor. A preemptive strike."

"Precisely." Tilzo sighed with self-satisfaction. "I must say it was an exhilarating experience. I mean, after the normal routine of my office duties in Belgrade."

Davis forced himself to swallow, feeling his Adam's apple bob. "You said something about Americans coming to get me."

"Ah yes, indeed we did."

Tilzo produced a cigarette, placed one in his mouth and tilted his head slightly.

Dalma promptly extended an arm, holding a lit match to the tip of the cigarette and not appearing overly happy about being expected to provide this service. He held the flame steady until Tilzo was able to exhale a long drag.

Davis winced at the acrid fumes of the foul smelling East European tobacco. "Damn, Vik. You make me glad I gave up smoking."

Tilzo took an exceptionally protracted drag on his cigarette, then pointedly exhaled a stream of the harsh gray smoke directly into Davis's face, making him cough.

"Your bravado does you little good, Captain. Those Americans that I saw at the KLA base were in commando garb and were heavily armed. They could only have been there for one purpose. The KLA commander was a fool to begin with, doubly so for scheduling my visit so closely to theirs. He acted nervous throughout our transaction. More nervous than I, and I was a Serbian who had been secretly smuggled onto a KLA base."

"And you think I'm the reason those commandos were there?"

"But of course. The KLA knows about . . ." Tilzo took the briefest pause, visibly concentrating on selecting his words. ". . . about what is happening here. The KLA wanted this to be their victory, you understand? But they are dependent on America for supplies and protection in this dirty war in these mountains, and so they must have been contacted by your government when your plane was reported missing near here. They were told to cooperate with the commando unit sent to locate you."

Davis nodded. "Our people would need some ground support and intel. We're in one of those terrain blackout pockets, aren't we? There's dozens of them in these mountains. That's why no one responded to our emergency locator signal when we went down. The signal never made it out of this valley, after we'd gone way off course, before we bailed and the plane went down. That's why you chose this place, right, Viktor? Terrain blackout. So okay, I'll bite."

Tilzo frowned his deepening irritation. "Bite?"

"These American commandos you say you saw at the KLA base. What about them?"

"Ah. I regret to say, Captain, that when I referred to those Americans, I spoke in the past tense."

Dalma was snickering again. "That base was hit tonight. We leveled it. We sent in two gunships, which Deputy Minister Tilzo was good enough to requisition. Your American commandos are as dead as every other living thing on that base, Captain."

Tilzo concurred with a nod. "You understand, Captain Davis? A preemptive strike."

Davis saw something in Tilzo's eyes and acted on his intuition.

"Simple as that, eh? Bim bam boom. Viktor, what happened to those gunships you sent in to do the job on that base after you left?"

Tilzo drew his hands together, both thumbs to his cheek. He regarded Davis solemnly over steepled knuckles that he cracked loudly. "You may want to choose your words carefully, American."

"I am." Davis knew he'd gone too far. He thought about backpedaling and decided against it. "That KLA camp may be burnt to a cinder, and those KLA troops may have been cut to ribbons. But if that was all, you'd have crowed about those gunships making it home safe and sound to wherever you have them hidden. But you didn't, Deputy Minister."

Tilzo regarded Davis blankly through the thick lenses of his eyeglasses. "And what have you surmised, Captain?"

"You mean before you proceed to pronounce my death sentence?"

Tilzo turned to snap angrily at Dalma.

Davis managed a half-hearted laugh. "Hell, Vik, don't blame the Dalma for anything. I'm only reading between the lines. If you're invisible enough to slip through the cracks in Belgrade, and important enough to divert military hardware and oversee renegade paramilitary operations like this one, then it must be something real important to bring you up here. Right, Viktor?"

"What are you saying, American?"

"I'm just letting you know that you can stop the song and dance if you think I'm going to cough up anything new. You think that I haven't figured out that my number is up? I now know the name of a Serbian government official who's breaking every international civil rights law in the book and doing it with his government's sanction. Dalma's cretins didn't kill me outright because Belgrade had to approve it.

So you paid a visit to size things up before a decision about me was made."

Tilzo looked uncertain. "Size things up?" he echoed impatiently.

"You decide whether I live or die, don't you, Deputy Minister? That's all I'm saying. You were sent here for three reasons."

Tilzo's eyes flickered with interest. "Indeed?"

"Uh-huh. You were sent to stop the sale of Serb weaponry to the KLA, like you said. And you were sent to decide if I should live or die, like I just said. I mean after all, Jack Jackson really *is* dead. I'd say that you've seen to it that his remains will never be found, thereby allowing you to legitimately assure NATO and the United States that they honestly have no idea where he was."

The interest remained in Tilzo's slate-gray eyes. He strode across the office to the single window and looked out at the night. He spoke to his reflection in the glass.

"My grasp of your foolish American slang may be lacking, Captain, but I have no problem with mathematics. You're quite right. I have already seen to the execution of three of our generals caught selling arms to the Albanian Kosovars. And yes, your life is in my hands. By my count, that is *two* reasons that you have correctly guessed regarding my presence here. You said that there were three."

"If your government was intending to admit to my presence here and say that I was being well cared for by your compassionate government, et cetera et cetera . . . well, you'd have already buzzed that call to your pals in Belgrade, and you'd be standing there right now telling me that I was going home so why don't I just behave and cooperate. But you haven't done or said those things." Davis sighed with sincere regret. "My escape attempt was a bonehead move, but it sounded like a good idea at the time."

Tilzo snorted peevishly. "Again you resort to slang. I do not know this term, 'bonehead move,' but I can assure you, Captain, that you did commit an act even more stupid than you thought when you attempted to escape."

Davis nodded without enthusiasm. "A bonehead move. But as an American serviceman being held prisoner, I have a code I am obliged to adhere to. Trying to escape was worth a gamble."

Dalma laughed, a nasty sound, as if he wanted to spit again at Davis. His hand hovered near the handle of his holstered pistol.

"It's a gamble you lost, sucker. When you tried to escape and made it as far as that truck, I didn't have to pull the trigger on you. I wanted to see you tied up and sweating bullets. You signed your own death warrant."

Davis turned to address Tilzo, the man in charge here, as a way of further insulting Dalma. "You should have Dalma here teach you some good old American slang while you're here, Vik. He tells me he spent time living in the States. Anyway, Deputy Minister, you've made your decision about me, haven't you?"

Tilzo turned from the window to confront Davis across the width of the office. "Tell me honestly, Captain. What did you see between the time when you broke free from this office and the point in time when Captain Dalma apprehended you in the rear of that truck."

Davis said promptly and with as much conviction as he could muster, "I didn't see anything."

Dalma laughed, but said nothing.

Tilzo said, "You are correct in your assumptions, Captain Davis. I have reached my decision."

"I have spoken to the soldiers involved," Dalma informed him like a prosecutor in a court presenting evidence. "A door was left open after the workers finished. You could not possibly have climbed into the bed of that truck, Captain, without looking in through that doorway. You saw enough, didn't you?"

"I didn't see anything."

"Unfortunately for you, Captain, the operation at this installation is to be activated . . ." He glanced at a wristwatch. ". . . within the next hour, I should say. In fact, the first busloads of detainees are presently en route here. And so you will appreciate that I can ration little time for further contemplation of the matter. Yes, Captain Davis, you are about die."

"You're here to supervise the implementation of a death camp, aren't you, Deputy Minister? Like Auschwitz, where the Nazis gassed the Jews in the showers." Davis's words dripped with loathing and disgust. "You're doing it up here in the mountains where no one can see, and you're going to do it to all those Kosovars unfortunate enough to fall into your hands."

Tilzo continued to stroke his chin. "We Serbs fought the Nazis in World War Two. But that does not imply that some of their means and methods were not . . . without merit. But let us return to the more immediate matter of you, Captain Davis. You're quite right in everything you say. Since you cannot be permitted to tell anyone else what you have seen and what you know . . . well, I'm afraid that you have signed your own death warrant. I am truly sorry."

"Sure you are."

Dalma drew his pistol and drew a bead on the man in the chair. "Now all that remains is for the sentence to be carried out."

Davis forced himself to pretend to ignore even this. He retained eye contact with Tilzo. "Viktor?"

Tilzo had already raised his hand to Dalma yet again. "Captain, no."

Again Dalma obeyed lowering his pistol, again with disappointment and anger. "But Deputy Minister, this man—"

Tilzo's mouth tremored as if wanting to smile. "This man will die. All that remains is to determine an appropriate manner to dispose of him. A simple bullet seems to me to be far too mundane considering the trouble he has caused us."

Dalma may have lowered his pistol, but the knuckle of his index finger was still white around the trigger. "Begging your pardon, sir, but a bullet would rid us of this American scum nicely, I should think."

"Not so," said Tilzo contemplatively. "Something more fitting is necessary. Something particularly humiliating for Captain Davis."

Davis knew he was a dead man, but he was damned if he'd give these sons of bitches the satisfaction of seeing his inner resignation. "We have a line that's been used a million times in old movies, Vik. Maybe you've heard it. It goes like this: You'll never get away with it."

"Oh but I think we shall." Tilzo spoke with smug assuredness like a hawk as it eyes a wounded field mouse. "And I believe I have concocted the perfect end for you, Captain. These Albanian mountain people you are so fond of, that you would fly halfway around the world to drop bombs on us on their behalf . . . well, the first busload will very soon be entering the shower facilities. Mass graves await them. You will be among them."

Dalma laughed loudly, and this time the Serb commander wasn't kissing ass. He actually found the irony amusing. "I like it, Deputy Minister. I like it very much."

Tilzo bowed slightly at the waist. "I big you adieu then, Captain, until we return to take you to join the others to meet your end. May you enjoy this last hour of your life."

Dalma responded likewise.

They left the office as if Davis no longer existed,

speaking language that he did not understand, leaving him in his plushly padded cell.

The pair of Serb paramilitaries stood as before, rifles at the ready from several paces away, their eyes riveted on him.

Davis closed his eyes and again rested his chin on his chest, doing his best to shut out the hell outside of his head. This time he did not sleep. He prayed.

And he thought about the only hope that he might still have for making it out of this alive. There had to be hope. That's what his mind, his soul, his being was based on. And right now, in addition to his God, his hope rested on the extremely improbable possibility that the American commandos, who Tilzo reported having spotted, had not died when that KLA base was firestormed.

Whoever they were, *they* were his only hope.

Had they survived?

And if so, where were they now?

2300 hours
The secret NATO airfield near Suva Reka

At the far end of the runway, the V-22 Super Osprey sat ready for takeoff.

At the co-pilot controls, Stan Powczuk glanced up from the weapons computer system, having completed a second full system's check.

"All we need now are target coordinates from Sam and it's rock and roll time. Shit!" The expletive popped from him. "We're supposed to be such a high-tech whatchamacallit, and here we sit in this expensive piece of space-age machinery but we might as well be sitting on the crapper. I'm a *boat* pilot, for crissakes! I like to do my fighting on the ground."

In his pilot seat next to Stan, Hunter Blake feigned extreme interest in checking his shoulder harness.

"Save it, SEAL man. You know it doesn't pay to be restless."

Stan harrumphed. "But damn, we've got less than two hours and counting to pull this thing off, according to Wong. Terrain blackout. Shit."

Sarah Greene sat at the comm console just aft of the cockpit.

"It's been a reality in the Balkans since this thing started," she said.

"Sure would be nice if somebody had some coordinates for us," Stan griped, having already monitored that incoming data. "I feel like blowing something up."

Hunter grinned. "Don't worry, guy. We'll be rocking and rolling soon enough."

Sarah turned to Ceca Keloni, who was the fourth person seated in the Osprey.

"Maybe I should explain the word, gnarly," she considered aloud with a girl-to-girl roll of her eyes in the direction of the men. "Behold, exhibits A and B."

"This gruff exchange of camaraderie," said Ceca, "it is a good thing. It heartens the spirit, does it not, for what lies ahead?"

Sarah nodded, impressed anew by the forthright intellect of the young Kosovar woman.

Ceca sat, strapped in by her seat belt, near Sarah. She somehow managed to look stunningly pretty, Sarah thought clinically, even outfitted in fatigues, with a MAC-10 submachine gun cradled in her lap. A steely hardness in Ceca's intelligent eyes was the only discernible indication that Sarah could detect of the inner emotional trauma any civilian would naturally feel at violently taking their first human life, as Ceca had done when she'd gunned down the Serbian police sergeant during the rescue of her father. Otherwise, the beauty of Ceca's lush-lipped face, highlighted by that determined jawline, framed by blonde hair that fell onto her shoulders, was such a picture of composed beauty that Sarah was grateful for Hunter Blake's professional discipline and focus as he sat at the controls.

Considering the apparent intimate history between Hunter and Ceca, Sarah at first had concerns about Ceca being allowed to accompany them on the upcoming extraction phase of the mission, but it was Stan's call and he had granted Ceca's request.

As for Colonel Gavin, he had continued to so disapprove of the whole notion of TALON Force using his airfield for their autonomous, free-wheeling operation that he'd physically distanced himself from the team's presence altogether and was busy somewhere else on the night-shrouded base.

Sarah had shared a private, silent nod with Stan who, for all his wiseguy bluster, could be sensitive to nuance and in fact did not miss much that went on within the ranks of TALON Force, part of his job description as Alpha Team's leader and Talon Force's second in command. Sarah sensed that she and Stan were both relieved to observe no romantic emotional underplay between Hunter and Ceca before or after Ceca made her request.

The one emotion evident in Ceca's entreaty had been her desire to place herself directly on the front line.

After hearing her out, Stan said, "Okay. Here's the deal. The KLA is providing support and you're KLA. *And* you've proven yourself under fire."

"Then I can go?" said Ceca hopefully.

"You can go," nodded Stan.

Sarah hadn't said a thing. But if anything, she was glad for some shared female energy aboard this boy's club aircraft.

"I wish something would start happening," Sarah grumped to the others, her eyes remaining on her monitor screen, her fingers busy on the keyboard, summoning up a continuous stream of channel surfinglike data and imagery from the sources made available through the wizardry of Sam Wong. "Listening to you boys hem and haw," she continued, "is enough to make anyone restless."

"Uh, Hunter," said Stan, "maybe you should tell us again how it doesn't pay to be restless."

Everyone present ignored this.

"And let's not forget General Krauss," Sarah added, passing along incoming information as it scrolled down the screen. "An update, gentlemen. The general is presently cooling his heels in the middle of the Adriatic aboard the *Theodore Roosevelt*. Captain Davis's wife and children are with him, awaiting our triumphant return."

"I've been following that," said Stan grimly. "They couldn't find any next of kin for Jackson."

"Doesn't surprise me." Hunter spoke with a quiet respect. "I don't know Jackson, but his file said he's one of those soldiers who makes the military his family."

Stan grunted pointedly at Hunter. "Takes one to know one, Hunt."

"Guilty as charged," said Hunter. "Anyway, with the general and Captain Davis's family sailing around out there waiting for us to bring Davis and Jackson home, I would say that failure is not an option."

"Is it ever?" asked Sarah rhetorically, her eyes keen on the screen, her fingers busy at the keyboard.

"What's got me worried," Hunter groused, "is what if the reason we've lost communications with Bravo Team is not this terrain blackout that everyone's talking about?"

"Stop it, Hunt," said Stan. "We don't need *what ifs*. Therein lies the road to madness." He swung around in his swivel chair. "As a great philosopher said, 'War *is* madness.' I mean, yeah, strategically speaking, war is the application of force when diplomacy fails. But Travis and Jenny and Jack . . . it's not just the loss of communications that's got me feeling antsy." He nodded to the Stygian gloom beyond the cockpit windows. "It's our people out there tonight, out there in uncharted territory, not knowing who to trust."

Hunter grunted agreement. "I don't like it much either, but there it is. When everyone you have to work with—in this case the KLA *and* the Serbs—has an axe to grind and a blood debt to settle, well . . . that's the madness the philosopher was talking about, right? Where the line blurs between who's good and who's bad."

Ceca cleared her throat. "I can assure you of this much. Commander Yashanitz, myself, and those who have sacrificed everything to fight in the KLA . . . tonight, you *can* trust us."

Sarah nodded. "Know something?" she said to Hunter and Stan. "I believe the lady."

Stan sighed. "Okay, Ceca. Welcome aboard." His eyes swept those around him. "Now am I the only one here who wants to get into the air and kick some ass or what?"

Before anyone could respond, Sam Wong's excited voice intruded across the radio linkup.

2305 hours
The NATO airfield at Brindisi

Inside the TALON Force comm van, Sam Wong had been laboring feverishly at his bank of computers monitoring the primary satellite down feeds that formed rows of pinpoints of light reflected on the lenses of his glasses.

His usual wise-ass demeanor had yielded to intense personal involvement and frustration. For the first time in longer than he could remember, the self-proclaimed computer genius had been grappling with technical problems that had seemed insurmountable for a mad-

deningly protracted length of time. This made him all
the more ecstatic when everything finally, suddenly
linked into place.

"I've got it, I've got it," he found himself crowing
across the audio linkup to Eagle Team Alpha. Sam
emitted a victorious hoot of a laugh. "The damn machines thought they had me fooled, but I outsmarted
our own goddamn technology. Fucking A!"

"Calm down, Sam," Sarah said. "I'm not so sure
that even you have machines yet that can think."

"Let's save this conversation for later," suggested
Stan. "And yeah, Sam. Calm down and give us what
you've got."

2306 hours
Aboard the TFV-22 Super Osprey at the
secret NATO airfield in Kosovo

From his pilot's seat in the Osprey cockpit, Hunter
Blake grunted, "Terrain blackout."

"Exactly," Sam enthused. "I finally jockeyed in
their signal the same way that the ancient Egyptians
illuminated the interior of their pyramids. The Egyptians set up this network of mirrors, see, so that if
even the tiniest beam of light caught in one mirror, it
was refracted and magnified by the other mirrors and,
voila, you have indoor lighting. Well, I did the same
thing with our satellite network except that I used
about half a dozen satellites instead of mirrors and
their sequencing codes instead of . . ." Then he hesitated, exercising a valiant attempt at self-restraint.
"Anyway, to make a long story short—"

"Too late," Sarah interrupted dryly.

"I had to go out of the TALON Force satellite loop,
essentially, and brought in some mirrors. That is to
say, I hacked into key private sector comm satellites,"

Sam went on. "That's where it got sticky. It's sort of illegal, so I—"

Stan interrupted. "Sam, you listen up. If you don't cork the computer babble and give us what you've got, I'm going to steer this aircraft around and fly it back to Brindisi and right up your ass. Has that got your attention, son?"

Hunter chuckled into the comm set. "I'd do what he says, Sam. I'm sure you don't want to rile a short man."

Stan's five-foot-nine height, and his self-acknowledged overcompensation about it, was a time-honored source of reference among TALON Force members.

"Okay, okay." Sam's voice finally became cool and professional. "I've made contact with Travis."

"What!?" Stan grumbled. "Well, come on, dude. Patch him on through to us."

"I can't."

"You can't?" Sarah repeated as if their comm man was speaking another language.

"But the major did tell me to tell you that Eagle Team Bravo has reached the target site."

Hunter's eyes narrowed. "Target site. I like the sound of that."

He commenced initiating the sequence procedure for firing up the Osprey's engine. The darkness of this outlying corner of the airfield throbbed loudly to life.

"They've been trying to contact us," said Sam. "Like you said, Hunter, terrain blackout was the bitch."

Stan's fingers hovered expectantly over his navigation system keyboard, ready to program in the new information.

"Yeah, yeah. You're such a genius, Sam. So what else did Travis say?"

"He's allowing you flight time to get there," said Sam. "He said to tell you that Bravo Team is going in, and he wants radio silence maintained for security. Your target coordinates are as follows . . ."

Chapter 16

A single blacktop road wended its way perilously
down from the mountains and dipped into a narrow
little valley ringed with ominous, snow-capped peaks.
The road ended at an installation that was pocketed
snugly, cupped by the curves of the terrain at the foot
of one of the mountain slopes that formed the valley.

Travis, Jack, and Jenny had concealed themselves a
quarter of a kilometer uphill from the main gate of the
installation. They were uniformly clad in their black
synthetic armor and Battle Ensemble brilliant suit, and
were likewise uniformly armed, each with a shoulder-
slung XM-29 rifle. They crouched, reconnoitering from
a stand of pine overlooking the lumber company.

They had separated from Adem Yashanitz minutes
earlier, just after arriving at this position. The KLA
commander had exchanged a hasty "good luck" with
Eagle Team Bravo, then vanished into the night to
rendezvous with his men, who would hopefully be arriving per schedule in trucks from the KLA base.

From a distance, thought Travis, the sight below
appeared to be exactly what it had been until very
recently: a thriving lumber concern. A six-foot-high
chain-link fence surrounding the perimeter had not been
designed with defense in mind. What need had there
been to defend a lumber yard? The fence was to keep

out the wildlife. The main office building was in the
center of the property, adjacent to a vacant parking
lot. There were a few outlying buildings and one extended garage. Tapered lawns and well-maintained
shrubbery lent the place a pastoral tranquility. What
should have been the sawmill was near the administration building. The main gate was chained and padlocked. The grounds appeared deserted.

Travis was the first to spot human activity down
there. "Look," he said.

"Well, I'll be a son of a bitch," Jack muttered.

Five figures had exited the admin building and were
angling across the compound. Three of the men wore
the uniform of the Serbian paramilitary force. Two of
them carried AK-47s. The third man was a young,
lean-muscled guy who strutted with an arrogant
swagger.

Travis knew, though, that it was the man in civilian
clothes who was in charge down there, a bespectacled
man with thinning gray hair who wore a bulky East
European suit. He'd seen the man once before tonight, darting out of Yashanitz's office; the highly
placed Serb official from Belgrade.

But it was the fifth man who drew and held Travis's
attention. Davis walked with the somber resignation
of a condemned man being led to the electric chair.
He strode upright and with an air of innate dignity
despite the shackles that bound his wrists and ankles,
causing him to move with a snuffling gait. Even across
the distance magnified by the infrared binoculars, the
ugly, purple bruise across the pilot's face was pain-
fully evident.

"Bingo," said Jenny.

Jack lowered his binoculars. His narrowed eyes
glowed with anger. "And we've found the weasel who
set up the KLA. There's the guy responsible for that
little girl Katrina dying, and all those others."

As they continued to observe, the cocky young Serb

commander snickered something to Davis, then unexpectedly extended a leg. Davis tripped, pitching to the ground. The Serb threw his head back and howled with snide laughter.

The man from Belgrade looked on, saying nothing. But there was smug satisfaction on his bland features.

The Serb riflemen grabbed Davis by each arm, yanking him harshly to his feet, and the small group continued in the direction of the renovated building that would until recently have been the lumber yard's sawmill.

Travis whirled from the sight and jogged without further hesitation to the Wildcat. "We're hitting that place hard, and I do mean right now." They reached the Wildcat together and flung open its doors. "I don't know what they're about to do to Davis down there," said Travis inside, in the process of adjusting his Battle Sensor Helmet, "but we're going to break up that party before it gets started."

Jenny started toward her station, then drew up short when she glanced out through one of the Wildcat's windows.

"Oh, oh," she said.

Travis and Jack followed the direction of her gaze. Both men murmured heated curses in unison.

A convoy of battered, mismatched buses was clanking and wheezing its way down the treacherous mountain road, about half a kilometer away from what was supposed to have been a new Auschwitz.

"If I were a betting woman," said Jenny, "I'd bet that those buses are bringing the first batch of Kosovars for mass execution."

"Well I am a betting man," grunted Jack, "and I'm betting you're right."

"Looks like we've got here just in time," Travis snarled, gunning the Wildcat's silent engine to life.

"Showtime," muttered Jack. He assumed shotgun position.

The armored vehicle rocketed from the tree line, storming down the gradual incline, chewing up the distance between their observation point and the padlocked front gate of the lumber yard.

"Can't you get any more steam out of this buggy?" Jenny groused.

2320 hours
Outside the Serbian installation

Approximately one quarter of a kilometer away, Adem Yashanitz lowered his binoculars at the sound of a single truck braking noisily to a stop somewhere in the darkness above and behind him.

He pulled back from the lip of the ridge over which he'd been peering, studying the lumber yard. He hurried to the narrow game trail that was hedged in on both sides by towering trees that melded overhead with the blackness of the night sky.

The game trail forked at this point, continuing onward along the rim of forest surrounding the installation, or landing upward to higher ground that marked the western flange of the outer reaches of Shar Pass. The trail was beyond the line of vision of either the wending road below or the Serbian base beyond, which is why Adem had guided the Americans to that approach and why he had designated this fork in the trail as the rendezvous point for his men.

Their truck was a quarter-ton of indeterminate age, rusted and battered. It wheezed and clanked as the driver doused the lights and engine. A half-dozen KLA troopers leaped from the rear, and the driver alighted. Each of them carried an M-16. They hurried over to Adem.

The driver was Jarmi, the sentry. His youthful face bore a worried expression discernible even down here where moonlight and starlight barely penetrated. He glanced in the direction of the ridge beyond, which was the Serbian installation.

"Commander, the truck is old. I hope the sound didn't carry."

"I doubt it, not across this distance and through the trees," Yashanitz assured them. "You made good time." He turned and they followed him to the ridge. "But I had hoped that there would be more of you."

"We suffered heavy losses at the camp," said Jarmi somberly. "A few men had to be left behind to guard the wounded."

Then they crouched along the ridge, staring down across the broad sweep of blackness separating their position from the lumber yard, the darkness bisected by the barely discernible winding road that hugged the mountainside.

"It does seem deserted," observed Jarmi, scanning the lumber yard through his binoculars. "Could we be wrong?"

"No," said Yashanitz. "I saw the American only moments ago. The pilot is down there."

The Wildcat suddenly appeared, rocketing down the incline from a point further along the ridge, heading straight toward the front gate of the lumber yard. The armored car's headlights pierced the night like the blades of twin stilettoes.

Then, more movement to their right, on the road. The acrid bite of exhaust fumes and the clanking, huffing, and chugging reached them well ahead of the ancient buses, now emerging into their view from around the mountain.

"Those buses," said Jarmi, dawning horror in his voice. "Do they carry our people?"

Yashanitz nodded, fury building within him. He sensed the same ferocity in every man there on the ridge with him.

"They've been rounded up, detained elsewhere, and

are now being brought here in the dead of night. We've arrived not a moment too soon, my brothers." He glanced at his wristwatch. "The prisoner said that at midnight, the camp is commencing operations on schedule. We must intercept them. Quickly now!"

He sprinted away, his men hurrying alongside and directly behind him. They rushed through winter-stripped thorns and thistles that slowed but never impeded their progress, though scratching raw the skin of face and hands. Occasionally a man would tumble in the dark, curse, regain his footing, and storm on.

With Jarmi running at his side, proud and brave and young, Yashanitz discovered himself to be oddly removed from the immediacy of what was unfolding. He found himself consumed by guilt. He dared not speak of having seen Tilzo, the Serbian official, the man he had been dealing with, on the grounds of the lumber yard moments before. Yashanitz felt nothing but sorrow and shame. A death camp to exterminate his people, and he had dealt with one of the key men involved! The Americans had been right. Tilzo's only objective had ben to target the Kosovars for the Serbian air attack that had decimated his force. Heavy losses, Jarmi said. The blood of those brave, dedicated men and women, who had trusted him and paid the ultimate sacrifice, was on his hands. The American woman commando, Jenny Olsen, had been right about something else. He regretted what he'd done more than words could ever describe.

Strangely, an image of Ceca, the woman who loved him, came to him unbidden. His shame would be unspeakable when she learned of what he had done. He clearly recalled her disappointment when he'd denied her request to mobilize KLA personnel to rescue her father. He should have realized then that he was losing his grip on humanity, he now told himself. Ceca had seen then what he clearly saw now. He had become one who would stoop to the barbarism of physical torture, who would sacrifice lives entrusted to him, for unyielding blindness to a cause. Was he no better than those he fought? He must atone for his folly, with his life if necessary. His cause deserved no less. There were many, like Jarmi and Ceca, who would carry on the fight if he fell tonight.

He gestured for his men to spread out.

They swooped down on the convoy of buses.

2320 hours
Inside the XM-77 Wildcat

Travis was hoping like hell that they weren't already too late.

The Wildcat jolted from the rough terrain onto the road for the final head-on assault. A gatehouse stood to one side of the main entrance to the grounds.

Jenny closely eyed the heat sensor imaging on one of her screens. "Two sentries," she reported. "Twenty meters."

Jack stared through the bullet-proof windshield. "And there they are."

The gatehouse spewed forth two guards who stormed from it at first sight of the oncoming armored vehicle tearing toward them. Panic flared in their faces. One was screaming into a walkie-talkie even as he tried to bring his AK-47 around while the other did manage to trigger a burst that bounced bullets off the Wildcat like tossed kernels of popcorn.

"Take them," snapped Travis.

"Consider them took," Jack said coolly. He triggered the Wildcat's .50-caliber machine gun.

The Serb paras were blown off their feet in bloody sprays of red.

The armored car plowed on through the padlocked iron gates, violently severing the gates from their hinges, tossing iron in either direction like discarded pieces of kindling.

Travis wheeled the Wildcat into a skidding stop in the center of the compound.

Jenny confirmed, without looking up from her screen, "We're in a hornet's nest, gentlemen."

The garage area and several buildings of the lumber yard were vomiting forth Serb troopers, responding on the run to this assault, firing their AK-47s at the Wildcat as they charged from points around the perimeter where they had been bivouacked under cammo netting. Again the bullets bounced off the car's armor plating.

Jack and Travis were popping open the doors of the Wildcat.

"Give those hornets a swat," Travis instructed Jen.

"Done," she assured him.

She slung herself across the interior to take the spot vacated by Travis behind the controls.

Travis and Jack alighted in unison. They hit the ground running in pumping, fleeting strides, crossing from their vehicle to the building.

Jenny opened fire with both the war wagon's .50-caliber and the forward mounted 7.62mm machine gun. The Serb paras were wholly unprepared for the incredible dual fire power of this strange-looking vehicle. Some of them dropped and kept firing from the ground. Others scrambled to return fire from cover. But far more of the Serb paras jitterbugged grotesquely as heavy-caliber slugs tore through them. The wave of soldiers dropped away under the Wildcat's sustained burst, which cut through their ranks like a scythe chopping down a field of wheat.

Travis and Jack gained the nearest entrance to the sawmill. Each activated his suit's stealth camouflage and became virtually invisible, the microsensors woven into the tough, bullet-proof fabric functioning perfectly, automatically determining and duplicating the visual qualities of their background. Each man became shimmering vapor in the dim light. They'd left their XM-29 rifles behind them in the vehicle. Travis reasoned that, on this extremely delicate, hot insertion, it would be dangerously counterproductive to render the body invisible and then draw everyone's attention to a seemingly airborne rifle. Instead, Travis and Jack were each armed with another key item in the TALON Force high-tech arsenal, the Offensive Handgun Weapons System, a .45 caliber Special Operations Forces pistol equipped with a silencer. The OHWS was worn beneath the suit, thus assuring complete invisibility until the pistol was unleathered for action.

Halfway between the vehicle and the structure, a series of explosions rocked the compound, drawing the attention of the invisible men.

A few Serb soldiers were unleashing shoulder-held stinger rockets. The bursting shells rocked the Wildcat.

Inside the Cat, Jenny triggered off a line of swift return fire that swept the Stinger-wielding Serbs off their feet into tumbling deadfalls.

Travis's BSD picked up another trooper, thus far undetected, to the rear of the Wildcat, firing a Stinger. He barked across the comm net to Jack, "Down!"

They threw themselves to the ground, Travis drawing his .45 OHWS from its concealment beneath the LOC suit. The newly designed SOF pistol came equipped with a flash suppressor and a Laser Aiming Module. From his prone position, Travis squeezed off a round just after the Serb had triggered the Stinger.

The Serb was knocked off his feet by Travis's round, which sped through the man's open mouth and evaporated the back of his skull.

The missile whizzed past the Wildcat, missing it by inches because, in an unrelated action, Jenny jolted the vehicle forward for a better angle of fire. So rather than hit the Wildcat, the missile instead struck the far end of the renovated building, raining down mortar and shrapnel.

A flying piece of shrapnel sliced open a quarter-inch stretch of Jack's Battle Ensemble suit, plowing a furrow across the top of his left shoulder.

Travis leapt to his feet in alarm and rushed over to Jack, holstering his pistol. Travis re-zipped his suit to re-establish the effect of invisibility. These suits were bullet proof, but flying shrapnel could eat through just about anything this close to the blast.

This section of the building remained intact even though the rocket had blown away most of the far end.

Jenny was doing her job with the armored car's full arsenal on auto, first drawing enemy fire, then blasting them to smithereens.

When Travis reached him, Jack was already on his feet. "Better living through technology!" Jack's shimmering aura said to Travis.

The Battle Ensemble's Automatic Trauma Med Pack, a micro-engineered medical system that transmitted vital information to the ensemble's bio-chip health sensors designed to provide first aid fluids and stimulants to the wound, automatically sealing minor or superficial wounds like the one Jack had sustained, kicked in.

The Wildcat's twin machine guns continued firing, breaking apart the outlying buildings behind which Serb soldiers sought cover to return fire. This further scattered them, and those who continued firing at the Wildcat saw absolutely nothing when Travis and Jack passed them. But the Serbs were far too distracted with survival to note anything else anyway.

The invisible men, creating only a shimmering, whispered suggestion of movement, bolted for the rocket-damaged building.

2325 hours
Inside renovated building on the Serbian base

They had Davis standing in a corner where a length
of exposed pipe joined the tile wall of this aseptic,
sparkling clean communal shower room that could
have been transplanted here from any gymnasium in
the world.

Except that this was no gymnasium, thought Davis.
The two Serb guards had stepped back, training
their AK-47s on him.

"Aren't you guys rushing things a little?" He didn't
feel the bravado in his voice, but Davis was determined not to die begging or bargaining for his life. He
indicated the gunfire and explosions booming in the
compound just outside the building. "Aren't you even
a little worried about them coming to my rescue?"

Tilzo laughed. "Your rescue? But no one knows
you're here! We are protected by elite troops at this
facility." The Serbian official may have appeared
meek, but he was unflinching at the nearness of the
raging sounds of warfare from outside. "The KLA will
often launch futile attacks against us." This assault,
too, will be repulsed and their force annihilated."

"The deputy minister and I," said Dalma, just as
calmly, "have decided that it would be appropriate if
the last thing witnessed by our first group of, er, detainees, would be their sharing in the death experience
with one of those sent to save and protect them."
Dalma chuckled smugly at the thought.

Tilzo nodded, indicating a glassed-in partition in the
wall facing rows of shower nozzles. "It shall be most
gratifying and interesting to observe."

Davis hadn't thought he could be more appalled by
these sickos than he already was, but his jaw gaped.
"You're going to *watch* men, women, and children die
while you gas them?"

Dalma sniggered. "And enjoy it." He produced a set of handcuffs and gestured to the exposed pipe. "Extend your hands."

"Fuck you."

Davis swung his shackled arms like a club, striking Dalma across the side of the head, not hard enough to knock Dalma off his feet, but the blow flung the Serb against the wall. Davis started toward Tilzo, but one of the guards stepped in and clobbered him in the back of the head with a rifle butt. Davis dropped to his knees, his senses reeling, hovering between unconsciousness and the self-determination not to topple over.

He heard the cruel laughter of Tilzo. He heard Dalma curse and sensed a vicious personal assault about to befall him. Maybe they would just beat him to death, he thought. There was tremendous pain at the back of his head where he'd been struck.

He shook his head and his senses cleared. He opened his eyes. The tiled walls stopped spinning. Then he saw something strange. He thought he saw the daylight, filtering in through the outside doorway, sort of waver.

A collective sensory shift somehow told everyone in that shower facility that they were no longer alone, that they had suddenly been joined by more than one human presence. Dalma, Tilzo, and the guards momentarily hesitated, sweeping their attention around to the doorway.

Despite the fact that they were theoretically invisible, Jack and Travis fell away to either side of the doorway immediately upon entry. Indoors, Low-Observable camouflage has its drawbacks. People's sixth sense will often detect a new presence within the confines of an enclosed space, particularly in the sense-heightened atmosphere of combat.

That's what happened now.

The tableau that confronted them in the corner of the communal shower held for only an instant.

Davis was now convinced that he could see subtle, bizarre, moving *sparkle* shapes approximating the proportions and dimensions of men positioning themselves one to either side of the doorway.

Dalma shouted a command. The guards tracked their rifles toward the door.

Then the most bizarre thing of all happened.

A pair of oversized .45 automatics suddenly materialized out of nowhere and hung there suspended in the air! Each laser-sighted, silenced .45 quietly chugged once, and each Serb rifleman spun around like a human top, the heavy caliber slugs splattering gore across the tile walls as rifles clattered to the floor.

Dalma snarled, grabbing for his holstered pistol.

Tilzo dropped to his knees, facing those alien glittering images against the far wall. "Please . . . whoever you are . . . *whatever* you are . . . please, *don't*!"

Each suspended pistol chugged once again. A ragged crimson hole bloomed in the forehead of Dalma, an identical third eye simultaneously centering itself in the forehead of Deputy Minister Tilzo. The back of each man's head exploded, massive exit wounds splashing tile.

Davis rose shakily to his feet. He may have had trouble grasping that glistening auras were rescuing him with suspended pistols, but he was quick enough to believe the reality of four dead Serbs, their dark life fluids spreading pools on the otherwise spotless floor.

The savage firefight outside continued to roar.

Jack maintained his position near the door.

The other aura said, "I'm Major Barrett."

Davis's eyes grew wide. "Uh, I'd like to say it's nice to see you, Major. But, uh, I *can't* see you . . ."

That brought a grim chuckle from Travis. "You don't have to see me. I'm here. Hold your hands up as high as you can."

Davis obeyed without question or delay, separating his shackled wrists as far apart as he could. The hovering pistol blasted again, and his shackles burst free. The pistol next aimed at the shackles between his ankles. Davis planted his feet as far apart as the shackles would allow. The laser sight dot tracked to the middle link. The silenced .45 coughed, freeing him from his confinement.

The apparition asked, "Where's Jackson?"

"He didn't make it." He stared with bitterness at the pile of fresh corpses on the tile floor. "Thanks for taking care of those bastards. You settled a score."

"Right now we're taking care of you, Captain." Travis's shimmering hand extended around Davis's wrist, clamped and tugged. "This way."

Then the apparition was moving through the doorway with Davis trotting along, willingly in tow.

They were followed out by Jack, whose pistol continued to search for targets.

2335 hours
Outside the Serbian base

As soon as the lead bus rounded the mountainside, the driver got his first view of the firefight raging within the perimeter of the lumber yard. The driver applied his brakes, as did the drivers behind him.

The wheeze of air brakes screeched, unnaturally loud in the night air.

Adem Yashanitz reached the road with Jarmi and the other KLA men at his side, their footing more sure now because of the refracted illumination from the buses' headlights spilling onto the side of the road.

"Headlights and tires!" Yashanitz commanded. "Aim with care!"

He and his men opened fire. Faces behind the windows of the buses were illuminated in the bursts of muzzle flashes. Frightened civilians cried out in alarm, diving for safety within the buses where panic and pandemonium could be heard even through the chattering of rifle fire. The night became black again after the headlights were blown out. The gunfire stopped.

In the instant of heavy silence that always follows gunfire, the only sound to be heard was the wheezing of air from flattened tires.

"Now what, Commander?" asked Jarmi breathlessly.

Yashanitz signaled for his men to separate, directing them in the direction of each bus.

"Carefully!" he cautioned again. "There will be soldiers. Not many to guard the helpless," he added sarcastically, "but they will fight."

"They'll be in radio contact with the base," said Jarmi from where he remained at Yashanitz's side. "They'll be calling for reinforcements!"

Yashanitz thought of TALON Force, presently attacking the base.

"*If* there are any reinforcements left," he said, then raised his voice emphatically for each of his men to hear. "The most important thing is that no refugee be injured. That above all! No more innocent blood!"

The door of the nearest bus burst open, spewing forth a pair of Serbian paramilitaries who plunged from the bus into the night, frantically tracking their rifles toward the guerrillas as other guards stormed from other buses.

The guerrillas opened fire from behind trees and boulders, whatever cover they could find. Their sustained, well-directed salvo pulverized the Serbian paras before any of them could fire a shot or take more than a step, the patterns of fire directed so as not to riddle the buses and injure those inside. Serbian troopers were spiraling to the ground as sizzling projectiles shredded flesh.

"Cease fire!" Yashanitz shouted.

When the echoes of rifle thunder rippled away this time, only the lingering scent of burnt gunpowder remained, and the pitiful moans of a few of the fallen who had not yet died.

Then, more movement from the doorway of the first bus. The atmosphere was stretched as taut as were Yashanitz's nerves. It was one of those razor's edge, anything-can-happen moments. He straightened from his place of concealment, revealing himself from where he had crouched with Jarmi behind the trunk of a tree.

Jarmi covered the bus with his rifle, nervously eyeing their surroundings.

Yashanitz approached the bus, where a figure poised tentatively, fearfully; a civilian, a male who would be the elder of this busload, Yashanitz reasoned. The man peered out nervously, not certain of what to do. Adem slung his rifle over his shoulder and extended a friendly gesture to the bedraggled figure in the doorway.

"I am Commander Yashanitz. My men and I have come to rescue you and your people. Come with us, quickly please. We will lead you to safety."

"Commander, look out!" Jarmi shouted frantically.

It was the last thing Yashanitz heard. He did not hear the shot that killed him. He experienced only a sudden explosion of all-consuming brilliance that yielded to total *nothing* as the bullet, fired by a fallen, mortally wounded Serbian, blew apart the back of his head.

Jarmi's snarl of rage was drowned out by the yammering of his M-16. He rode the recoil with practiced precision, stitching the man who'd fired the fatal shot. The Serbian's body shuddered, fragmenting messily into an unrecognizable, burbling pulp. Jarmi lowered his weapon and ran to Yashanitz. He rolled his commander over and saw that Yashanitz was dead.

And he knew then what he must do. There would be time to grieve later.

"Cover me," he instructed the guerrillas who remained concealed. He stood erect, as Commander Yashanitz had, and addressed the man who had drawn back a pace in the bus doorway. "Please, sir, we must hurry," Jarmi said in the same tone that his commander had used. "Instruct your people that we are KLA. We have come to rescue you. You will be safe with us, but we *must* hurry."

The man observed Jarmi's demeanor as much as the entreaty. He turned then and spoke to those in the bus, and the unwilling passengers filed out in an orderly fashion, numb shock and fear etched deeply in their expressions, though this was already giving way to grateful glances in the direction of the KLA rifleman who had stepped forward.

Jarmi could not help but notice that even the older men of this unit appeared to be now silently deferring to him for direction. And so he motioned them to guide the stunned collection of refugees back along the road, back along the route from which the buses had come. They would hear any approaching vehicles in the night, he reasoned, and could then seek cover in the forest. The important thing right now was to get these people out of harm's way.

The body of Adem Yashanitz would be recovered once the refugees were safe. A fearless martyr of the cause, thought Jarmi. A hero, and an inspiration.

Jogging alongside the mass of humanity that was beginning to collectively shuffle down the road, he had time for a backward glance. Jarmi cast another glance, this time at the lumber yard. He wondered how Major Barrett and the commandos of TALON Force were faring.

That's when he first heard the unmistakable, mighty throbbing sounds of a fast-approaching helicopter.

2340 hours
Inside the Serbian base

Hunter Blake flew the Osprey in through a narrow cut in the mountains, banking for a pass straight over the lumber yard, delivering blistering rocket fire.

Long wispy lines of white-trailing rockets demolished the garage, the remaining outbuildings and, for good measure, the administration building. Each erupted in multiple fireballs while the Super Osprey's chain gun cranked away like a sonic typewriter, cutting down the remnants of Serb troopers attempting to flee before they made it past the perimeter. The only structure spared was the building next to where the parked Wildcat was so busily engaged on the ground.

At the controls of the V-22, Hunter provided copilot/gunner Powczuk with a full 360-degree sweep before banking into a lowering hover over the parking area.

"Had your fun, two gun?" Travis asked over the comm net.

From his armory systems console, Stan grunted, his complete attention on his radar monitor. "Yeah. But I'm keeping my eyes open."

The gunfire from the Wildcat ceased.

From her communications/armory console, Sarah Greene saw a single man down there, shambling along from the building toward the Cat.

The man walked strangely with his arms extended, led by an invisible hand. He leaped into the armored car.

Seated near Sarah, Ceca saw this also and frowned in consternation. "What a strange sight. It is as if that man is walking upright, but not of his own strength!"

Sarah knew well enough what Ceca was seeing.

"It's called high-tech," she explained, but diverted her attention to say no more.

Ceca nodded, satisfied, shifting her attention out through one of the Osprey's windows, looking at the flickering of gunfire on the ground from where, moments earlier, she had discerned headlights from forms that were vague, considering their helicopter's speed and altitude. But she had the impression of buses on a mountain road.

Emotion surged through her at the realization that it could only be Adem's unit of KLA guerrillas down there, exchanging fire with the enemy beyond the perimeter of the lumber yard; the KLA ground support, she had assured these Americans, would be forthcoming. She clasped the MAC-10 in her lap, wishing that she could be on the ground in that firefight, where her presence would truly count. But there had not been adequate time to travel the distance from the NATO airfield to the lumber company, and her primary concern had been the rescue of her father. Now, with her index finger curled around the submachine gun's trigger, Ceca's stomach muscles were cramped with frustration and anxiety.

In the cockpit, Hunter commenced easing down the Super Osprey to rooftop level. The beating twin rotors palpitated the air, creating a backwash that disturbed the glittering of the LOC suits.

"Don't you invisible men get blown away now," he warned across the comm net.

"If the Serb punks don't blow us away, a little wind won't," growled Travis's voice from within his LOC suit. "Nice to see you made it, Alpha Team, and thanks for the hand. Now get us the hell out of here, would you, please?"

"We're five minutes by air from Colonel Gavin's airfield outside Suva Reka," said Sarah. "I'm sure he'll be overjoyed to see us again."

"We won't be there long enough to get on his nerves, or him on ours," said Hunter. He glanced over his shoulder. "Do your thing, Sarah."

"Doing it," Sarah assured them from her console. Her fingers floated sprightly as butterfly wings across her keyboard.

The doors of the Osprey's bay opened. The heavy

winch began to hum. The winch's sling rope lowered. The sling was made of a special NASA-derived alloy with the pliability of rope but with the strength of reinforced steel.

Stan found nothing more to shoot at.

Ceca got another opportunity to see in the direction where she'd previously seen headlights and the flashes of gunfire. There was only pitch blackness down there now. She hoped that Adem and every man in his unit had survived.

When the rope was lowered far enough, Travis and Jack went about systematically looping the rope through the appropriate eyehooks that lined the roof of the Wildcat. Travis then secured the clamped end of the rope.

The moving "vapor" that was Jack was already bounding into the vehicle.

"Drive on, Jeeves," Jenny instructed Hunter via the comm net from within the Wildcat. "And remember please that the lives you save could be ours."

Travis was the last one to leap aboard the armored car, slamming the door after him.

"Hey, I frankly don't care how the hell safe your driving is," he replied. "Just get us the hell out of here, flyguy, like *now*!"

"Hang on," Hunter deadpanned. He yanked back on the twin throttles. "You guys down there get the fun part. Pretend you're on a ride at the carnival."

"Whoopee," Jenny deadpanned right back up to Hunter across the net.

Then the Osprey was climbing, the armored car rising beneath it, securely suspended to well above rooftop level.

Blake tilted the V-22's rotors, and the aircraft's nose dipped forward as it flew off, leveling out and tearing forward in conventional flight toward the cut between the mountains from whence it had come.

The Wildcat trailed along, towed gracefully by the length of metallic rope with all the tenderness of a mother hen leading home an errant duckling.

Epilogue

October 24, 0015
The *USS Theodore Roosevelt,*
somewhere in the Adriatic Sea

On the helo deck, General Krauss and Sam Wong stood side by side.

As Hunter settled the Osprey down gently on the landing pad, they caught his attention and reminded him, as always, of the original military odd couple.

Krauss stood ramrod straight. Sam, two heads shorter than the general, was his usual disheveled, computer-nerd self. The only similarity was in their shared expression of relief at observing the arrival of the big gunship.

There had been a brief touchdown inside Kosovo. They'd deposited the Wildcat at the NATO air base near Suva Reka for retrieval, with the second Wildcat, later that day by a C-117 transport and had picked up Ceca's father. Mr. Keloni was grateful but subdued, mildly sedated as well as exhausted from his ordeal. Colonel Gavin had not expected to see the maverick unit so soon and was just as happy that TALON Force's layover was a brief one.

During the layover, Travis, Jack, and Jenny shed their Battle Ensemble suits for standard fatigues. The Osprey then followed the extraction route at high speed, out of the Balkans.

Hunter reverted the aircraft to its vertical helicopter

mode upon their approach of the *Roosevelt*. After landing gently on the foredeck with his charge safely touched down, he shut down all systems and snapped loose his flight harness.

The others likewise freed themselves from their seat belts. Sarah was first to the bay door, which she heaved open.

With a parting wave of appreciation to TALON Force, Captain Larry Davis, USAF, wasted no time in bounding from the chopper's doorway. He hit the ship's deck running, right into the open, welcoming arms of the jumping-up-and-down-with-joy family awaiting him; one lovely but visibly stressed adult, and a trio of overjoyed children. Despite his bruises and cuts, the pilot had held up well during the hardships he'd endured. He scooped up his wife and children together in his arms, lifting them off their feet in a reunion of joy and tears.

Then the military handlers—smartly uniformed, efficient, polite, and impersonal young male and female officers—moved in to firmly but gently steer the happy little family away from the aircraft. They were whisked from sight through a nearby doorway.

Travis, Jenny, Hunter, Stan, Jack, and Ceca appeared in the doorway of the V-22, alighting from the Osprey to join Sarah on the deck's tarmac. Sarah supervised, and Ceca stood nearby watching, as Ceca's father was placed onto a gurney.

The elderly man remained dreamily sedated as he was wheeled off to the ship's medical area.

Ceca touched her father's arm lovingly and leaned over to place a kiss on his forehead as he was wheeled past her. She watched the corpsmen steer the gurney from view, then turned with gratitude to the assembled members of TALON Force.

"Thank you for what you have done, all of you. The people of Kosovo could never repay you enough for your good deeds of this night."

"Thank you for helping us," said Travis. "As for us, well, I'm afraid the people of Kosovo and very few others will ever hear anything about this unit."

"Then I am that much more privileged to have fought with you." Ceca turned to Sarah. "My father?" she asked.

"He'll be fine," Sarah assured her. "I'll see to it that you get clearance to stay with him for as long as you want."

The TALON Force troopers, except for Hunter, started walking, carrying their flight helmets, across the landing pad in the direction of Krauss and Sam.

Jack began mildly ribbing Jenny.

"My guess, Jen, is that you'd like to get that beautiful mug of yours on the cover of *Time* and *Newsweek* next week for what we just pulled off. What do you say, gorgeous? Am I right or wrong?"

Jenny's shoulder-length blonde hair framed a cover girl face that was presently marred by resignation and, perhaps, some wistfulness.

"Well, it would be sort of nice to be recognized as a woman for a change instead of as just another soldier. But I know that's impossible. Goes with the job."

Jack pondered this with genuine befuddlement, scratching his regulation crewcut. "Uh, I tried to read a book once about guys understanding feminist issues, *Men Are from Mars, Women Are from Wherever.* I didn't get it then and I don't get it now."

Stan laughed heartily with an eloquent shrug. "Hey, it's the mystery of women, pal. Ain't that why we love 'em?"

"Don't you monkeys irritate us womenfolk," said Sarah, with a conspiratorial wink to Jenny. "We're liable to kick some macho ass, right, sister?"

Jenny smiled sweetly at Jack. "Just for the fun of it," she concurred.

As their joshing voices drifted away, Hunter and

Ceca were left standing there alone, watching the others approach Sam and General Krauss on the opposite side of the wide deck.

There was a moment of uncertain hesitation between them, the moment underscored by the lapping of waves and shipboard noises.

"Well then, I guess it's good-bye again, Ceca," said Hunter after some length. "At last this time I hope we're doing it right. Saying good-bye, I mean, without any hard feelings like the last time I had to leave."

Her smile was a faint but lovely thing that brightened her intelligent features, framed by her full head of blonde curls.

"How could I ever have anything but fond thoughts in my heart for you, Hunter, from this time forward to the end of my life? You and your friends risked your lives to help victims, my people, in a fight that was not your own. I will always think of you as one of the finest, most gallant, *best* men I have ever known."

He was somewhat taken aback by this. He gulped.

"Uh well you know, Ceca, uh, now that your father is in safe hands, you know that you could always catch a ride out of the war zone with us, don't you?" He indicated the towering Osprey. "After the help you've given us, Travis would make sure that the general clears it. Travis knows lots of generals. The U.S. government would relocate you and your father to a new, comfortable life."

"No, Hunter. Thank you, but no." Her words softened but steely resolve remained in the look she shifted to beyond the ship's deck, across the murky, choppy seas of the Adriatic, in the direction of Kosovo. "I have nothing to lose now. My father is safe, thanks to you. I cannot leave. I will spend a day or so with my father, to help him reorient to being here, to these great changes. At his age, such changes will be difficult. He has spent his whole life in Suva Reka. I will see him often. But I must return to the mountains. My place is there. Until there is a real peace in Kosovo, I will serve in the KLA." She regarded him with sad, moist eyes. "Please, Hunter. Tell me that you understand."

"I understand," he said truthfully. He chuckled with scant humor. "Don't know what I was thinking, kiddo. It couldn't be any other way for a person like you, could it? I guess that's why I love you, Ceca."

She tenderly touched the palm of her hand to his cheek. An intimate, sad touch.

"Love, Hunter? That word sounds so strange, coming from you."

He cleared his throat. "I, uh, hope this isn't the last time that we see each other, Ceca."

"Me too, my darling bastard. Until another time, then."

And they met them in a spontaneous, passionate clinch that lasted a long, long time but not nearly long enough, as far as Hunter was concerned.

They broke the clinch with a brief, sweet kiss.

And then she was gone, striding off in the direction taken by the corpsmen who had wheeled off the gurney with her father.

Hunter watched her walk away, admiring the view and wishing like hell that he understood himself better sometimes, like now. Then he squared his shoulders and got back to business. He crossed to where the others had gathered around Sam and the general.

Sarah seemed to glimpse a hint of sadness in his eyes. "Luck of the draw, Hunter," she said matter-of-factly.

Jenny nodded agreement, not particularly sympathetically. "You're the one who's used to breaking hearts and going off to fight, isn't that right? Well, you met your match, Hunter. Welcome to the woman of the new millennium, bub."

"What the hell?" groused Hunter. "You couldn't

have overheard our conversation from way over here."

"Yeah, that is kind of scary," agreed Jack. "Having a pair of chicks along can be troublesome as is, but if they're *psychic* chicks, well, I don't want 'em reading *my* mind!"

Stan grinned. "Yo, Jack my man, what exactly makes you think you have a mind? That may be going too far."

Jenny joined in with, "And if Sarah and I *could* read your minds, well, I dunno. I gave up reading comic books a long time ago."

Jack harrumphed with the resignation of a man who know's when he's been bested.

Sam Wong smiled at General Krauss. "Sounds to me like the group dynamics are intact, sir."

Krauss nodded approvingly to those assembled before him. "Good work, people."

"Thank you, sir," said Jenny. "Glad to hear you feel that way. But is there by any chance a shower onboard this boat?"

"Jen does have a point, sir," added Sarah. "It's been that kind of a night."

Jack grinned. "Call me a simple man, but I'd settle for a cup of coffee and breakfast."

Stan nodded with satisfaction. "At last. A jarhead with a brain, and one with at least one good idea."

"All right," laughed the general. "Dismissed. I'll want a briefing in full at 0600. In the meantime, thanks again on behalf of Captain Davis and his family. And your country."

Travis Barrett remained behind with Krauss and Sam, watching the others casually disperse.

"You're awfully quiet, Major," Sam noted.

Krauss read something in Travis's expression.

"Your troopers have the right idea, Trav. Captain Davis is safe. That marks another successful mission logged by TALON Force, even if it will never see the light of day."

Travis glowered. "I wish we could have brought them both home, sir. I wish we could have recovered Jackson's remains. I'll bet I know what happened. Dalma had Jackson incinerated. They scattered his ashes from the first completed oven at that Serb facility."

Krauss sighed, then threw his shoulders back. "But I repeat, Major, you and Eagle Team delivered the way TALON Force always does. No one could have delivered more."

Travis took a deep breath and exhaled it slowly, considering this. Then he glanced sideways at Sam, feeling a fresh, renewing surge of inner strength.

"Computer man, what say we catch up with Stan and Jack and see if they'd like some company for breakfast?"

"Yes, *sir*!" Sam beamed, always ready for an opportunity to be "one of the guys."

With salutes to the general, they ambled off in the wake of the others.

Krauss remained behind, standing alone, lingering near the deserted helo pad, near the looming, impressive Super Osprey.

He thought that it was a mark of Travis's character that his first response upon his return had been dissatisfaction that the mission had not been a total success.

True enough.

There would be one more name, Jack Jackson, added to that list of valiant American servicemen lost in battle, seemingly forever catalogued and forgotten as missing in action.

Krauss found himself wondering where and when TALON Force would be needed next. The past few days, with separate missions to Iraq and the Balkans, was proof enough that there would always be dirty covert ops work on the global stage for this Technologically Augmented, Low-Observable, Networked Force.

Krauss found this more discouraging than encouraging. He turned from the Osprey and stood at the rail of the *Roosevelt,* to watch the dark, choppy sea.